I0570945

DRONE SWARM
A Techno-Thriller Comedy

By Jonathan Yeakey

Dedicated to Mom, Dad, Allison and Biggie

CONTENTS

INTRODUCTION

"The Killer Bees of Longville, MO"

In the early part of the 21st Century, there was an unfortunate incident in northern Missouri. An incident that left a family terrorized, a community shaken, and everyone else quite a bit confused. Not to mention all the dead people.

Lots and lots of dead people.

At the time, sightings of the swarm had almost become commonplace. Area farmers would trade stories, often in hushed tones, of seeing an ominous cloud over their fields at random times of the day. And then, just as abruptly, the swarm would disappear.

Similar accounts were given sporadically over the course of the year. That is, until the incident occurred. Then the sightings stopped altogether.

Details concerning the incident were vague, at best. Government files were classified. News reports were incomplete or just plain wrong. And the people involved were either unavailable for comment or dead.

Fortunately this missing information has gone public thanks to a series of internet leaks.

For the first time since the incident, a clearer picture has come to light of what actually happened that fateful week in February. Through a combination of leaked documents and anonymous testimony, the true story can now be told in its entirety. Warts and all.

The government continues to disavow all knowledge.

J.Y.

PROLOGUE: FLIGHT OF THE HONEYBEE

The curious little bee landed gently on the bright yellow sunflower. Adjusting its tiny antenna, the insect tilted its head and circled in place, surveying its new surroundings.

To an ordinary bee, this locale would appear to be a small patch of vibrant flowers on a bed of dark green grass. To a human, however, it appeared to be a flower-printed pillow resting on top of a messy bedspread.

The bee continued its detailed analysis, unconcerned with the possibility of being attacked by the resident humans nearby. Fortunately for the bee, these three young ladies didn't notice the bug in the room as they were engaged in a heated discussion.

"Shut up, you sexy, little brat!" said one of the females, towering over the bed.

The bee was immediately dwarfed by a well-manicured hand, literally snatching the ground from beneath it. Before even having a chance to react, the bee found itself being hurled headfirst towards the face of one of the giant females!

The pillow hit only the side of her head and the bee was flung violently into space, head over abdomen. Disoriented and panicky, it frantically beat its wings and regained its equilibrium just in time to avoid colliding into a wall. Unfortunately, the corner of another pillow struck the bee, sending it spiraling into a sudden explosion of feathers and fluff!

As chaos rained all around, the bee zipped through the air, dodging gigantic feathers at every turn. The second it spotted an opening, the bee shot through it as fast as it could, nearly flying into the gaping mouth of one of the laughing humans.

Expertly navigating away from danger, the bee flew to the other side of the room. Landing safely on a window sill. The bee took a moment to find its bearings before giving its wings a quick buzz and antenna a small tweak. Since nothing appeared to be damaged, the bee continued with its expedition.

Using its six tiny, claw-like feet, the bee proceeded to climb up the window curtain and nestled itself into one of the folds of fabric. Now completely hidden from view, the bee repositioned itself and studied the three human females who were now laughing uproariously on the bed.

The young ladies had a couple of things in common, the most prominent being that all three were quite beautiful; the woman sitting at the foot of the bed was a slender brunette with olive colored skin and eyes that looked like almonds but probably didn't taste like them. Sitting next to her was a small, curvaceous brunette who looked similar but not related; in addition to being tan, her brown eyes were also shaped like almonds but slightly bigger, like the fancy shelled kind you find in wooden barrels at some organic food stores. Seated next to them both was the one who first instigated the pillow fight, a tall, vivacious blonde with blue, walnut shaped eyes and skin the color of peach-flavored yogurt.

Besides looking like models, all three were dressed in sexy lingerie for some reason. This was curious because a) it wasn't particularly comfortable and b) none of them currently had romantic partners.

As their gay laughter dwindled to a bicurious giggle, the slender brunette in a purple negligee turned to her shorter friend and said, "I'm so glad you moved here, Fatima!"

"Me too!" exclaimed her dark haired friend in a turquoise babydoll nightie, "It'll be just like when we were kids!"

"School will be a lot more fun with you around."

The tall blonde in a hot pink corset and stockings smiled at her slender friend and shook her head in disbelief. "It's so weird to see you like this, Khadijah," she said gently stroking her friend's long, silky hair, adding, "You have such a great body, it's a shame you dress so modestly at school."

The slender young lady shrugged in response and the loose-fitting strap of her purple negligee casually slipped off her shoulder. "My father doesn't approve of skimpy outfits," she replied, matter-of-factly adjusting her wardrobe, "Besides, the only man I want to see this side of me is my future husband."

The tall blonde stole a glance at her friend's slim figure. Biting her lip, she gave a mischievous smirk and said, "Well, I hope you find a good one 'cause he's going to be one lucky man."

Looking down to her smooth legs, the slender

brunette smiled and felt an enticing warmth that made her blush.

"Are there a lot of cute boys in your classes?" the small brunette in turquoise asked with excitement.

"There's plenty," the busty blonde snickered, " but, unfortunately, they all act like boys."

"Not all of them," the slender brunette in purple politely retorted, "what about Jacob Shapiro?"

Glancing from one friend to the other, the shorter brunette asked, "Who is that?"

Just as the slender young lady in purple was about to answer, her blonde friend leaned over her lap and exclaimed, "Just this guy she totally has a crush on!"

"You should ask him out," the small brunette gleefully suggested.

"I can't do that, I've never even been on a date, have you?"

"A few."

"You ever kiss a guy?" the tall, curvaceous blonde asked the short, vivacious brunette.

"Yes," she said smiling as if she had gotten away with being especially naughty.

"You ever make out?"

She shifted nervously on the bed and giggled, "Once."

At this revelation, the taller brunette's eyes widened and she leaned forward. "What's it like?" she asked eagerly clutching her pillow.

Her dark haired friend nodded and sheepishly replied, "It was okay."

The leggy blonde raised an eyebrow and smirked provocatively. "Just okay?" she teased.

The short brunette in turquoise looked up and suddenly found herself getting lost in the blonde's vibrant, blue eyes. Feeling a little warm and light headed, she wet her lips and took a deep breath, "It was pretty good."

"Well…" the blonde in the pink bustier said, getting up from her place on the bed and squeezing in between the two gorgeous young ladies, "Sounds like you all could use some practice." She brushed her golden hair back with her fingers and placed her hand on the bedspread, close behind the brunette in the lacy, turquoise nightie. Tilting her head to the side, she took a moment to admire her alluring shape, "You ever kiss a girl before?"

And for the next hour and nine minutes, the bee remained completely motionless.

Watching….

CHAPTER 1

"Hey, Rosemary, how 'bout this one?"

The middle-aged man pranced across the frozen countryside toward yet another tree. He was far ahead of his twenty-something daughter who struggled to keep up. While there wasn't much snow on the ground, the fact that she was wearing boots was enough to slow her down. There was no way she was going to stop her father now. The land was starting to slope upwards, making it harder for her to run and her father was practically sprinting towards the barren hickory.

As soon as he reached the aging tree, he wrapped his arms and legs around the trunk and proceeded to climb it like a doped up bear looking for some Honey Krisp cereal. He shimmied up the tree until he reached the lower hanging branches. Pulling himself onto the nearest branch, he began to go out on a limb. Just as his daughter caught up to him gasping for air.

"Great," she said under her frosty breath, "Just great."

This wasn't the life Rosemary wanted.

Despite having just turned twenty-one, Rosemary

Combs-Dogwood was already a bitter old woman at heart. So much had happened in the last five years to embitter her past the point of no return.

First her mother dies, then her father goes crazy, meanwhile her sister runs off and becomes an overnight success, leaving only herself to take care of things at home. No, there was nothing for Rosemary to be bitter about. Nothing at all. What bright, young woman wants to go to college when instead, she can stay home and clean out her father's poop every time he takes a dump in the toaster?

"Would you please get down from there?" she said from the snowy ground below.

"Come on, precious..." her father said perched upon the frosted branch, "...where's your holiday spirit?"

Frustrated, Rosemary sighed and rubbed her temples, "Dad, it's the middle of February, we don't need a Christmas tree!"

"I know that, silly," he said inspecting the rickety hickory, "this is for Presidents Day!"

"Well, would you at least put some pants on?" Rosemary pleaded, holding up a pair of slacks she grabbed on her way out the door, "It's freezing!"

Unfazed, her father shifted his weight and gazed up at the topmost branches, "Nope," he said thoughtfully shaking his head, "this won't do at all....not nearly big enough."

A long creaking sound came from within the tree followed by an immediate snap as the man, and the branch he was sitting on, fell onto the soft, half-inch of snow below.

"Houston, Tranquility Base here. The Eagle has landed!"

These type of shenanigans were a daily routine for Rosemary.

At first, she was happy to help her father around the house but, as his condition worsened, Rosemary found herself resenting him more with each passing day. But nothing compared to the animosity she felt towards her long-absent sister, even if she did support them financially.

Rosemary stood silently above her father as he happily made snow angels.

Her sister was supposed to be the older, more responsible one. For most of their lives, Rosemary had been the reckless, free spirit. It was only after their mother died that their roles somehow got switched. Suddenly, Rosemary was forced into the role of caretaker. All while she was still in high school.

Now she was the one watching their father writhe on the ground, singing "I'm a Yankee Doodle Dandy." While Rosemary loved her father she hated his off-balance way of thinking. Often, it was much too frustrating to even try and have a normal conversation with him.

If she wanted to, she could just leave him outside the entire night. He certainly wouldn't mind. At this moment, though, she still generally cared about his well-being. No matter what kind of basket case he had turn into.

Her father noticed that she had been standing there, staring at him, the entire time. He froze in place and tilted his head towards her, "What's the matter, kitten?"

"Great," Rosemary said softly to herself, "now he thinks I'm a cat."

Her father slowly came to his feet and casually brushed a mix of dirt and snow off himself. Gazing warmly into Rosemary's pistachio-green eyes, he smiled. "Hey, now don't you worry," he said placing a reassuring hand on her shoulder, "we're going to find the perfect tree yet."

He then abruptly sprinted towards the next nearest tree, a medium-sized oak about thirty yards away. Rosemary looked down to where her father had attempted to make snow angels and sighed. It was no use trying to stop him, he was going to do what he was going to do until he wore himself out.

Rosemary had tried to live a life outside of being her father's caregiver but even that was a bust; her failed marriage was merely the cherry on top of her butt-fudge sundae.

She wed at such a young age because that's what you do when you decide to stay in your rural hometown; you get married to a guy who railed you in high school before he joins the military or pursues an exciting career in methamphetamines. She knew it was never going to work but she was lonely and needed the companionship. Once Danny got shipped off to Fort Matson thirty minutes away, it only added to their marital strife. Long story short, it didn't end well.

Her long, auburn hair wafted in the gentle breeze. The cold winter air was starting to bother Rosemary. In her rush out the door she left without putting on a coat and had only a forest green cable-knit sweater to keep her warm. Up to this point, her little jog up the hill had warmed her to the point of sweating but, now that she was at a standstill, she was beginning to feel chilly.

Any other time of year, the farmland and surrounding wilderness was beautiful. Floral whites and pinks in the spring, a cascade of greens in the summer, and a lush explosion of reds and golds in the fall. During the winter, however, it was just dead. Endless shades of brown earth and gray skies. Of course, it didn't help that it had been a particularly gloomy day to begin with.

"Hey, Rosemary," her father called out merrily, "you ought to see the view from up here!"

Crossing her arms tightly, she walked in his general direction. It was pointless for her to be in a hurry now, her father was already in the tree, waving like a loon.

That wasn't fair. It wasn't her poor father's fault that he was a special kind of an idiot, it was her sister's for leaving him when he needed her most.

If only Rosemary herself could get away and start anew, let her sister take care of things for a while.

Rosemary had done her time, it was her sister's turn to pick up the slacks and make sure their father wore pants. She was certainly in a better place financially to do so. She could even hire a professional to look after their father for a while. With how successful she's been recently, her sister could probably afford to just move him out to California.

"Oh....Hey, Rosemary, look over there! Computer generated bees!"

Then maybe she'd finally have a chance to go out and see the world herself. And why not? She was still young enough to throw caution into the wind and leave on an impulse.

So far she had lived her entire life in the same town where she was born. She was long overdue for an adventure. There were so many strange and exciting places for her to see! Places she's never been before, places she's only read about in books. Places like Des Moines or Omaha or, heck, maybe even Chicago.

"The computer generated bees! They're comin' this way! Rosemary!"

Maybe she'd even find herself in the process.

"Oh no...Rosemary, LOOK OUT!"

Glancing up to her father in the tree, she saw him frantically pointing to something behind her. That's when she heard it. A loud buzzing that was like a thousand tiny electric razors coming towards her. She turned around just in time to see a large swarm of bees engulfing her!

Letting out a surprised yelp, Rosemary shut her eyes and threw her arms in the air, swinging wildly at the bees with her father's slacks.

"Hey, careful," her father scolded, "you're going to get honey all over my pants!"

She could feel individual bees brush past her hair, face and hands; every now and again, one would angrily buzz directly in her ear. Each with a venomous stinger ready to strike! While she wasn't allergic to bee stings, she definitely didn't want to get stung. All of a sudden, she felt a sharp, painful prick at the nape of her neck. Swatting at her assailant, she felt a warm tingle from the sting. Instinctively, this only amplified her fight-or-flight response.

Clenching her teeth, Rosemary blindly broke through the swarm, her father cheering her on. After about a hundred feet, she paused to look back and get her bearings but the frenzied cloud of bees were still flying towards her.

"Keep going!" her father yelled, "Get out of here!"

Rosemary needed to find shelter fast! But she couldn't desert her father with all these bees flying around. Maybe she could draw them into the woods, come back for her father and make a run for the house. It wasn't much of a plan but, under the circumstances, it would have to do.

First, she would need to buy some time. The woods were a little over fifty yards away and the knee-high boots she was wearing weren't the best for running in. Wadding up her father's pants, Rosemary threw them into the center of the angry swarm and made a run for it.

As she predicted, her stylish brown boots slowed her down immensely. She tried to run the best she could but, in the slippery snow, it was more of a panic-stricken trot across the field. Running with cats clenched around her ankles would be easier.

She was already starting to feel fatigued, which was strange because she ran all the time in high school, she must have been really out of shape. Regardless, she pressed on.

Rosemary knew she had put some distance between herself and the bees but the ominous buzzing was gaining on her.

She didn't dare look back.

She ran.

The long line of trees ahead seemed to grow taller and taller until they closed around Rosemary and she found herself inside the dark sanctuary of the woods.

Almost immediately, Rosemary regretted her decision.

As soon as she stumbled into the scraggly forest, she was already slipping on wet leaves and tripping over fallen limbs. Rosemary didn't consider that the woods would be a hindrance against her. In any case, it was too late now. The bees were closing in, streaming past the outermost trees.

Looking over her shoulder as she staggered through the brush, Rosemary didn't notice the small ravine right in front of her. All of a sudden, she found herself tumbling down the hill like a frat boy trying to do a cartwheel down the stairs.

Rosemary tried to grab hold of something, anything, to slow her down but all she could see was a mixed up world of ground, trees and sky; violently spiraling out of control!

After, inadvertently, missing every tree on her way down, she finally reached the bottom of the valley; plowing through snow covered brush and rolling into the spiny undergrowth. Everything around her was still spinning.

Even when she closed her eyes everything was still spinning.

Breathing heavily, she rested her head in the prickly brush. All she needed was a moment to catch her breath. Just a moment for her nauseated senses to settle. Just a moment.

Of course, all the bees needed was a moment to catch up with her.

The dreadful buzzing snapped her back to reality and she opened her eyes to hundreds of little black dots silhouetted against the gray sky. Slowly increasing in size and urgency.

Struggling to untangle herself from the brambles, the wrathful swarm descended upon her.

'Great,' Rosemary thought to herself, 'Just great.'

Colonel George Armstrong Madder was having a most pleasant evening at home; he was spending his favorite day relaxing in his favorite chair while watching his favorite movie. Life didn't get much better than this and, if it did, he didn't want to know about it. This was all he needed to be truly content.

It also helped that he was slightly drunk on his favorite drink, a cocktail of his own invention that was equal parts sweet and unsweet iced tea, a shot of Ozark Moonshine and a twist of lemon. He called it the Missouri Compromise.

He casually swirled his glass; holding it up to the light, admiring the ice cubes floating in a sea of golden brown. The determined, slightly confused, face of Dwight D. Eisenhower smirking at him from his commemorative, Presidential Republicans glass, of which Madder had the entire set. He was most fond of this particular set because, unlike most collections, this set only contained Republicans; those that were president and those that *should* have been president. Lately, Colonel Madder had been drinking from his President John McCain glass but, seeing as it was Presidents' Day, he decided to bring out one that wasn't a loser. Ike was a solid choice.

Above a roaring fireplace and next to the Presidents' Day tree, hung the colonel's shiny, new flat screen TV. He was watching the controversial 1967 film, *Custer's Revenge*; in which, General Custer somehow survived the Battle of Little Bighorn and launches a counterattack against the remaining American Indians.

Even upon its theatrical release, the film was heavily criticized by Native American and Women's Rights groups for its brutal depictions of violence, but the colonel found it to be a good, old-fashioned, adventure story. In fact, it was one of the movies that inspired him to join the army.

Madder sat in his beloved and well-worn I-Dull-Boy

recliner which was leaned back to the optimal 120 degree angle; perfect for television viewing and snacking. While there was no spoken rule in the house, it was understood that the forest green chair was continuously reserved for the colonel. He didn't mind if other people sat in it but it was always a little awkward when a visitor unknowingly dethroned him.

On the opposite side of the living room sat his favorite spouse, curled up on a gray-blue loveseat, reading a magazine about how to be a better housewife. A strong, athletic woman who wasn't too strong for the colonel. She knew her role in their relationship and played it well.

In between him and his wife, sprawled out across the matching couch, was his second-favorite stepchild Jeremy. The awkward teenager was tall and gangly with greasy black hair. Mindlessly tapping away on his damned computer.

He had tried to connect with his geeky stepson on several occasions but every attempt ended in frustration or embarrassment. If only Jeremy was a little more like his ambitious older sister; she had already moved out and joined the military. Madder preferred the company of his step-daughter, which was really saying something considering she was gay, a woman, *and* in the Air Force!

Madder sighed, took another sip of his drink and continued to watch his movie.

On the TV, General Custer was mustering the troops with a big, inspiring speech that always brought a tear to Madder's eye. A tall and imposing General Custer sat atop his trusty steed, his adoring men hanging on to every word. Pulling out his cavalry sword, the battle-scarred general triumphantly shouted, "Saddle up and give 'em all you got, pilgrim!"

And then the phone rang because of course it would.

While Madder tried to ignore it and enjoy his movie, his mind couldn't help but run through a list of people who would call on his day off. It was probably work, he had a sinking feeling that it was. Best case scenario, it was one of his wife's silly relatives.

As Madder watched General Custer heroically set fire to a tepee, his wife calmly set her magazine down and got up to answer the phone in the kitchen. His stepson, too stupid or lazy to even care.

"Madder Residence," he heard his wife say from the other room.

The colonel concentrated on his movie and attempted to enjoy the melee of violence on screen. "Stop cryin' ya' damn savage," drawled the rugged actor portraying Custer.

"One moment, please," Madder's wife said.

Taking one last swig of his tasty beverage, Madder pushed himself out of the recliner and turned towards his wife who was already standing in the living room. He, rather reluctantly, took the call. Hopefully it wasn't anything major or else Madder was going to miss the rest of his movie.

"This is Colonel Madder," he said. Madder stood and listened carefully to the voice on the other end, occasionally responding with an affirmative-grunt before asking, "What do you mean gone rogue?"

CHAPTER 2

Inside her new designer purse, Hunnie Combs' cell phone buzzed for the third time in seven minutes. And for the third time in seven minutes, the call went unanswered. On any other night, she would have checked to see who had called. But not tonight.

Tonight she was busy.

Hunnie strutted across the red carpet like the superstar she was born to be....or, at least, that's how her manager told her to walk. She was still getting used to this whole fame and fortune thing. It helped that she was wearing a gorgeous dress she had picked out herself.

Felix, her manager, insisted that whatever she wore in public had to reflect her personal brand. This proved to be more difficult than Hunnie expected; she had to wear something that made her stand out without looking completely ridiculous. She thought she found a good balance in her current ensemble of a yellow cocktail dress, black pumps and a black stretch belt.

The bumblebee hair clip may have been a little much but Hunnie thought it was cute. She felt proud and she felt confident. Let the Hollywood fashion critics do their worst.

Finding her mark on the red carpet, she paused, smiled and held her body in the photogenic pose her manager taught her. One hand on her hip, the other casually at her side, shoulders back, chin up, one leg slightly bent. She felt like a star.

"Sorry, love, that one's garbage."

Her manager was seated across the room in a tacky pink zebra print accent chair his wife insisted on getting for the guest room.

"That's what you've said about all my picks," Hunnie said placing her hands on her hips. She caught a glance of her reflection in the bedroom mirror, "I like it."

"You can like whatever you like, my dear but I'm here to make you a star, not Ms. Iowa going to her first Root Beer Kegger."

Standing up, Felix walked over to the bed and rummaged for the next outfit from the pile. They had been trying on clothes all day and what started as a neat stack of dresses was now an unruly mess! Hunnie sighed and wondered how many more costume changes she would have to make before they agreed on something.

As he finished selecting pieces for the next outfit, Felix's cell phone began to buzz. Fishing the phone out of his pocket, he glanced at the incoming call and haphazardly handed off the clothes to Hunnie.

"Here," he said pushing her into the guest bathroom, "try those on, I've got to take this."

Hunnie meandered back into the bathroom and closed the door.

She could hear Felix enthusiastically answer the call, "Alejandro, you fabulous gay son of a Spaniard! What do you got for me?"

The man calling Felix was a mutual associate of theirs; a hair stylist by the name Alejandro Bonito Narciso. Whether that was his real name, was anybody's guess. It was certainly beyond Hunnie since most people she met on the coast were putting up a front of some kind.

"Jennifer Ganner?! Really?" Felix spouted in the next room, "Wow! Her career really must've tanked if she's coming to you....Alejandro, I'm kidding, you're the best!....Of course....So when's her appointment?...."

Hunnie began to quietly change, enjoying the secondhand banter between the two people who helped her become a celebrity.

It was through her hairstylist that she first met Felix. She had just made the drive to Los Angeles and was in desperate need of a new do, her new roommate recommended a salon on North Gower. It was within walking distance and wasn't too expensive (at least, for California). "Ask for Alejandro," she told her.

Alejandro was a swarthy man in his late thirties who had an air of superiority that was masked by a baby face.

"So what are we doing today?" he asked threading his fingers through Hunnie's dirty blonde hair.

"Just a trim and highlights."

"Okay, you know what shade you want?"

"I was thinking platinum."

"No offense, dear, but platinum's been done to death. May I suggest Santa Monica Blonde, it's a tone of my own invention, you'll love it!"

"Oh....okay."

"Don't you worry, by the time I get done with you, you'll look like you've always lived here!"

"That'd be great."

"You're new to the area, yes?

"How'd you know?'

"Sweetie, you live here long enough and you can spot a transplant from a mile away."

Alejandro began working his magic and a momentary silence fell between them. All of a sudden, the ambient sound of passing traffic became more prominent. Observing her face in the mirror, Alejandro was the one who picked the conversation up off the floor.

"You look very familiar, you an actress?"

"No."

"Model?"

Hunnie shook her head 'no'.

"Hold still. I definitely know you from someplace."

Hunnie took a breath, as if she was going to admit something, but then just shrugged and said, "I wouldn't know from what?"

"Drop the modesty, honey, the meek don't make it in this town." Suddenly Alejandro remembered, "Wait.... I know where I know you from! You have that internet video where everyone sees your goodies!"

Hunnie still wasn't used to being recognized by strangers. Since her video went viral, it would happen every now and again but not enough to be a common occurrence. Before she could respond, Felix walked through the front door of the salon. He was an artificially tan man in an overpriced suit and cheap shades, texting in one hand and holding a stack of business cards in the other.

"Felix!" shouted Alejandro, "Impeccable timing!"

Not looking away from his phone, Felix walked up to the front counter, "Alejandro, word on the street is that one of the Wahlberg's is a new client of yours, I need to know which one and is he worth my time."

"Donnie and he was barely worth my time."

Good, you just saved me a phone call," he said, setting the stack of business cards on the reception desk, "Leaving these here, I'm double parked."

"Before you go, come here, there's someone I want you to meet."

That was almost two years ago.

For Hunnie, becoming accustomed to Los Angeles was almost as difficult as becoming famous. She had never considered herself a "country girl" until she moved to the big, loud, filthy city. There was so much she took for granted growing up in the sticks; like parking.

Back home it was a parking paradise, she could park anywhere at anytime and there were parking lots as far as the eye could see, but in L.A. she could only park on the street and even then, she would have to move her car for street cleaning every Tuesday at 5:30 pm, Friday at 6:00 am, fourth Wednesday of odd numbered months at 7:00 pm and third Saturday of prime numbered months at 2:00 pm (assuming it wasn't a leap year).

She was so glad that she didn't have to deal with that anymore, not since getting her own driver. The only thing she had to worry about now was her music and her image. Which was a relief. For the first time since coming to Hollywood, Hunnie felt like she belonged....but this was mostly due to being rich and famous.

Her manager had been tireless in making sure she became a superstar.

Of course, there were certain aspects of stardom where they didn't see eye-to-eye.

Hunnie looked at herself in the bathroom mirror,

frowned, and stormed back into the bedroom. Her manager still sitting in the chair talking to Alejandro.

"....Well you tell her that if she wants to be back on top to give me a call, she's got too much talent to be in sappy movies made by greeting card companies!....yeah, sounds good...."

Hunnie began to angrily tap her foot; she really didn't like this outfit, she felt naked.

Probably because she practically *was* naked.

The only thing "covering" her was black and yellow striped leggings, a pair of yellow suspenders with bumblebee wings attached to the back and a pair of women's boy briefs with the word HUNNIE printed in gold on the butt. That was it! Nothing else. If it weren't for her crossed arms, her breasts would have been completely exposed.

The fact that Felix was ignoring her to finish his little chat only pissed her off more.

"....Listen, I've got a brand new client signed up, I'm sending her your way....she's a comedian....uh-huh....I don't know, just make her look funny....okay, bye."

Felix ended the call and finally acknowledged the half-naked woman shooting daggers at him, "Now THAT'S more like it!"

"I am NOT wearing this!" Hunnie said, keeping her arms securely crossed.

"Why not?" Felix shrugged, seeming genuinely baffled by the statement.

"Well, for starters, I've got nothing covering my tits!"

"What about the suspenders?"

"NO!" Hunnie turned around and grabbed the bathrobe hanging from the open bathroom door behind her. Furiously putting it on.

"They're wide enough to cover your nips, aren't they?"

Hunnie had wrapped the fluffy white bathrobe around her and was tying the belt around her waist, "That's not the problem," she said turning back towards him, "boobs don't work that way!"

Calmly, Feix stood up and walked towards the bed. "One sec," he said rummaging through the pile of clothes, "I forgot a very important accessory?"

"I'll say!'"

"Here we are," he pulled out the article of clothing and held it up for Hunnie to see.

It was a headband with a pair of springy bug antenna attached. Felix approached Hunnie and gingerly placed the headband atop her head. She could feel the fuzzy poms-poms at the end of each antenna bounce gently in the air conditioned breeze.

"This isn't what I had in mind?" she said completely deadpan.

Taking a step back, Felix studied the novelty antenna and shook his head.

"You're right," he said snatching the headband and tossing it aside, "way too gaudy, not enough naughty."

Hunnie sighed, slumped her shoulders and tossed her head back; she was tired and she was cranky.

"Felix, how about we call it a night?"

"One more, love, just one more, I promise." Before Hunnie had time to respond, he added, "I know I've said that a dozen times before but, remember, this is showbiz, baby!"

It's true, this was showbiz. And if Hunnie was going to be a star she had to get used to doing otherwise stupid things on a regular basis. "Okay, fine," she said.

For this outfit, Felix didn't go to the stack on the bed.

Instead, he reached over and grabbed a small paper sack that had been sitting on top of the dresser. He pulled out a medium sized jar of honey; it was in a plastic mason jar and had an old timey brown label on it, the kind that purposely looks like someone jarred it in their basement but really it was manufactured by some giant food conglomerate somewhere.

"Let's see how this one looks on you," Felix said holding up the jar of thick, golden honey.

"Well...." Hunnie said, looking for the appropriate, sarcastic response, "....it looks like a jar of honey."

"Yeah, try it on."

"Try what on?"

"The outfit, love, the outfit," Felix tried handing the jar to Hunnie but she didn't accept, "Slather it on you, head to toe."

"That is NOT an outfit."

"Sure it is! Now, listen," Felix said setting the jar down, "I had a feeling that you wouldn't like it, what with your simple midwestern values and all but you've got to realize that this is the PERFECT way to play up your brand as the next wild 'n sexy, Hollywood party girl! Just imagine...."

"I am..." Hunnie interrupted, "...and I'm naked and sticky at The Tween Choice Awards!"

Felix shook his hand dismissively, "The tabloids the next morning are going to go absolutely gaga for you!"

"I'm going to get honey everywhere!"

"You'll be the talk of the town for weeks on end."

"Yeah, because I ruined the seats in Shrine Auditorium."

Hunnie could hear her phone buzz. Lord knows how many messages would be waiting for her, she'd been ignoring it all afternoon. She was ready for a break and literally anything would be a welcome distraction.

"I appreciate your advice, but this is *my* image, okay?" she said to the night stand, "I'll be fine."

Picking up her purse, Hunnie pulled out the vibrating phone and answered it.

She would be on the first flight home that night.

CHAPTER 3

The man in a white lab coat pressed record on the camcorder and took note of the experiment start time, 13:03. Both the man and the camcorder were facing a glass terrarium. Inside, an ash-grey stick rested on top of a bed of brown coconut mulch. Perched on the thin, dry stick, stood a bright green praying mantis who was watching her human observer's every move.

Despite being named after the snowy flower blossom, Dr. Hawthorn White was tall, dark and handsome....but in an exceedingly caucasian kind of way. Thick, black hair, soulful, brown eyes and the fashion sense of a Sears catalogue. Underneath his lab coat, he wore a plaid dress shirt and solid navy tie, slacks, and a pair of black rimmed eyeglasses. The only thing missing was a pipe and the evening paper.

Picking up a white plastic baggie, Hawthorn took a pair of science tongs and extracted a single corn dog from the bag. Carefully, he lowered the golden corn dog into the terrarium and set it in front of the praying mantis. The mantis paid little attention to the giant piece of food in her tank. She was indifferent.

This reaction, or lack thereof, was to be expected.

Mantis religiosa wasn't known for eating junk food; it was a predator that only ate other insects, but Dr. White was a man of science and discovery, plus he had nothing better to do. In his mind, he may as well spend the afternoon in the lab experimenting.

After seven years at the Malsanto Corporation, Hawthorn wanted to work someplace a little different and a lot less evil. Fortunately he found his current position as a Research Entomologist at State Fair College. While it wasn't a big school by any means, he enjoyed it well enough and it allowed him a certain amount of freedom not found in private labs

At the college, Hawthorn was tasked to not only study how insects affect the Carnival industry but also what can be done to resolve the common problems they cause. For instance, nobody likes getting bitten by mosquitoes; it annoys the carnies and makes attendees want to go home. But what if these summertime pests were bred to only bite the *really* drunk patrons/personnel?

This was the kind of project that could, one day, win Hawthorn the Nobel Prize.

For now, however, he was busy trying to get a praying mantis to eat a corn dog.

This was what science was all about.

Hawthorn reached for a small, glass vial, the kind that's amber colored and comes with a rubber cap that doubles as an eyedropper. Unscrewing the top, he meticulously squeezed four drops across the length of the corn dog. The female mantis immediately showed a greater interest in the strange food and moved slowly towards it. Tilting her head to the side, the mantis playfully twirled her antennae with her front legs and gave the corn dog a seductive wink.

Pleased by this reaction, Hawthorn smiled and scribbled notes across the clipboard. So wrapped up in his work, he didn't notice a man with greying hair standing in the doorway. Looking important yet approachable, the man at the door was dressed in a charcoal-black suit and a blue, open collared dress shirt.

"Knock-knock," he announced, entering the all-but-empty lab.

Hawthorn glanced up from his clipboard and gave an obligatory smile to his boss, "Hi, Gibson," he said immediately returning his attention back to the experiment, "What's new?"

Gibson, the Biology Department Head, confidently meandered towards Hawthorn with a manila envelope in his hand. "Got a special project for ya'," he said slapping the brown envelope against his free hand, "you got a moment?"

"Yeah, give me one second."

Hawthorn hated being interrupted in the lab; he couldn't prove it, but it seemed like his boss only liked to bother him when he was in the middle of an experiment. Gibson would walk in like he owned the place, press him about some inconsequential office policy (like how the fridge in the faculty break room is not to be used for lab samples, despite the fact that the biology department had been in desperate need of a bigger refrigerator for well over a year), and then casually ask what the heck he was working on. As if he needed to justify the importance of his research.

True to form, Gibson gestured toward the terrarium, "So what are we researching today? The long-term effects of transfat on bugs?"

"Not quite," Hawthorn said as he peeked through the camcorder viewfinder and noted the progress, "Attempting to get insects to digest non-biodegradable substances."

"You mean like carnival food?" he said pointing at the corn dog.

"Yes."

"For what reason?"

"Imagine how much trash is tossed aside at your average county fair, now imagine if all that refuse was able to be broken down by your garden variety insects, think of how beneficial that would be to not only county and state fairs but also the World's Fair?"

"Hawthorn, that would be an amazing breakthrough," His boss said with building excitement, "Do you realize how much notoriety our school would get…." Gibson stole a glance back at the terrarium and then promptly lost his train of thought, "Good lord!" he exclaimed, "What's that praying mantis doing?!"

The once indifferent mantis was now vigorously rubbing her green body against the deep-fried corn dog.

For Hawthorn, these results were welcome.

"She's trying to mate with it," Hawthorn said jotting down additional notes with satisfaction, "I put a few drops of mantis pheromones on the test sample."

His boss was flabbergasted.

"Why in the world would you do that?"

"Simple," Hawthorn calmly explained, "I'm trying to get insects to eat garbage and, in the case of a female mantis, she mates before she kills."

Transfixed by the erotic display, Gibson crouched down and peered through the glass, "Wow, would you look at her go!"

While his boss wasn't getting in the way of his experiment, he was a distraction.

Hawthorn didn't think he was any better than his boss, just smarter. Generally, Hawthorn had a hard time connecting with people. To him, humans were a collection of irrational fears and personal quirks. That's why he preferred the company of bugs.

"Now, Gibson," Hawthorn said, hoping to move the conversation along so he could get back to work, "I know you didn't come all this way just to watch the mating habits of Mantids."

"Uh, yeah," said Gibson, trying to look more like a boss and less like the creepy neighborhood kid watching dogs do it in the backyard, "Got a special project for you."

Hawthorn didn't like the sound of that. Special projects meant that all other research would have to be put on hold. He just hoped his boss had something academic. Last time, he was asked if it was possible to get lightning bugs to spell out 'FORGIVE ME, JUDY' outside Gibson's house.

Gibson handed Hawthorn the manila envelope.

Hawthorn briefly examined the clean, brown envelope and held it up questioningly, "What's this?"

"Itinerary and ticket to Longville, Missouri."

"Longville?" Hawthorn had lived in Missouri nearly his entire life and had never heard of the place; it was no doubt one of the countless rural communities held together by a big-box superstore, "Where's that?"

"About halfway between Moberly and Kirksville."

That was in the central-northeast region of the state, a good distance from any major cities or points of interest, except, of course, for the Museum of Osteopathic Medicine thirty miles north.

"What's happening there that needs my attention?"

"According to the sheriff's office, there was a killer bee attack there yesterday evening."

Hawthorn shook his head, "Highly unlikely, killer bee season won't be for another couple of months. Even then, there hasn't been any recent reports of roaming swarms." If there had it would have been published in a reputable scientific journal like American Bee Journal or National Geographic Kids.

"Well, one woman was killed from the attack and they need an entomologist to help with the investigation."

"What about Dr. Bladdernut at Truman? He's up in that area, they should contact him."

"They've already tried. No one knows where he is, so someone at Truman recommended you."

Hawthorn had known Bladdernut for years and he found it odd that he would not only be unavailable but completely unaccounted for. The man wasn't famous for going on impromptu adventures or even leaving the safety of campus. He was a small, timid man who preferred staying in the lab over field research.

Yet Hawthorn was just the opposite. While he enjoyed lab research he would rather be out in the field. In Bladdernut's absence, it would make sense for the authorities to reach out to him.

"I doubt that I will find anything," said Hawthorn, "but I'll assist any way I can."

"Good," Gibson nodded, "I'll let them know you're on your way. Everything you need to know is in your packet, along with your bus ticket."

"Why did you get me a bus ticket? It's only two hours away, I could just drive there."

His boss never concerned himself with details and

was already walking towards the door, "Your bus leaves tomorrow at seven!" He exclaimed with a wave.

Hawthorn glanced down at the manila envelope and sighed, he then looked back at his experiment.

The praying mantis was now eating the corn dog.

CHAPTER 4

Eddie was in front of his coworker's computer wondering how a so-called "journalist" could be so negligent. He had told the newspaper staff multiple times to regularly backup their files and yet, here he was, sitting at his coworker's desk in a futile attempt to retrieve lost data from a crashed computer. After that he'd have to figure out why his boss' email wasn't working.

The thing is, this wasn't even his job, Eddie was hired as a webmaster.

When Eddie Hwa-Young Mallow graduated from college, he was thrilled to get a job at a professional news organization. Designing websites was his gift but journalism was his passion. He loved the idea of reporters going out and digging up the latest scoop. If he wasn't so good with computers, Eddie probably would have become a reporter - he already had the hat and everything.

After working with the old farts at the Daily Chronicle, it didn't look that hard.

Eddie bet he could do it. He wrote for his college newspaper and while nothing he reported on ever got published, he was confident he could still make it as a journalist. He was young, he was savvy, he had his entire life ahead of him.

At twenty-two years old, Eddie was the youngest person working at the Chronicle. Much like the paper's readership, most of the office was in their sixties or above. Compared to his more weathered coworkers, Eddie's fresh face looked like a very old baby. If not for his wispy attempt at a mustache, he could have easily been mistaken for a 168-month old. He even had the extremely thin body and bad posture of an angst-ridden teenage boy.

As Eddie quietly worked on fixing his coworker's computer, a silver haired man in a white dress shirt and navy tie approached the desk. The man was the Chronicle's editor-in-chief, Ben Boneset. An overall pleasant man with a confident but laid-back temperament, he was perfect for the country paper.

In his hand Ben held a small, yellow piece of notebook paper. Eddie couldn't understand why his boss preferred assigning tasks in person. Email was faster, easier and you didn't have to make uncomfortable small talk with coworkers with whom you share nothing in common, but this was the office culture and old habits stay alive long enough to become a burden on everyone else.

"Ed, how are you doing today?" Ben casually asked in a way that was more of a greeting rather than a question.

"Good," Ed replied flatly, keeping his focus on the project at hand.

"Get any new wax cylinders for the phonograph?"

Back when Eddie was interviewing for the job, the editor-in-chief asked what kind of hobbies he enjoyed. Eddie, in an effort to stay ahead of the trendiest of hipsters, had started listening to all of his music on the earliest audio format, phonograph cylinders. Since then, Ben made it a point to ask him about his collection. Every. Single. Time.

"No," Eddie lied, he actually found a rare recording of Thomas Edison reciting "There once was a man from Nantucket" online.

"You haven't seen Fran around, have you?"

"She's out covering Gun Safety Day at La Plata Elementary."

"I have an obituary for her to write up, could you make sure she gets this?" Ben set the note on the desk.

Scrawled across the top of the paper was the name Rosemary Combs-Dogwood. Underneath were various details scribbled out about the woman's life: where she was born, what schools she attended, what her favorite food was, etc. While this information didn't mean anything to Eddie, one sentence immediately caught his attention.

....*survived by her father Sean and her sister Hunnie Combs.*

"Wait," Eddie said picking up the note, "is this *the* Hunnie Combs?"

"The only one I'm aware of," the chief said. Raising an eyebrow, he asked, "Why? Who is she?"

Eddie knew his co-workers weren't the most up-to-date on pop culture but he expected them to have at least heard of the pop music sensation. "She's kind of the biggest thing right now."

"What is she known for?"

"Love Stings?"

No response.

"Queen B?"

No response.

"I Want UR Honey Dripper?"

The chief blinked twice and asked, "Are these songs?"

Eddie scooted to the other end of the desk where his work laptop was resting. He opened the browser and brought up a video titled: THIRSTY THURSDAY - HUNNIE COMBZ. He pressed play.

The music video that played featured a scantily clad Hunnie partying the night away at various bars and nightclubs.

At a glance, one could tell the video wasn't professionally made; the picture quality was low, the shots weren't framed very well, lighting was nonexistent, and there were several times the videographer dropped the camera.

The song itself was basically Hunnie singing about the drinks and various misadventures she has on a typical Thursday night. It was surprisingly catchy and had a good beat. There was a playful sexiness throughout that was very tongue-in-cheek, especially the part when she started licking people's cheeks.

While it wasn't the type of music the aging editor-in-chief would listen to, he had to admit, that it had a memorable hook and the tantalizing star of the video was very pleasant to look at.

As she sang, Hunnie appeared to get progressively drunker with each new verse until the song was nothing but a slurred mess. It was the type of video that the young people found hilarious and anyone over thirty found either confusing or just plain annoying.

It had over 166 million views.

"Is this what's popular nowadays?" Eddie's boss asked in a confused, slightly annoyed manner.

"Kind of," Eddie replied, "People mostly liked the video ironically but then she used it to become a legit pop singer."

"This is the first I've ever heard of her."

"I'm pretty sure we did a story about her last spring," Eddie looked at his boss for confirmation.

Embarrassed that he didn't know and couldn't remember, the editor-in-chief shook his head and shrugged.

Eddie hadn't actually been hired at the time, but he knew he had come across the article somewhere on their website.

He quickly brought it up.

"Yeah, here it is," he chimed, "A local teen posted a video asking her out to prom, it went viral, she said 'yes' and then never showed up."

The chief tapped his finger against the note still resting on the desk, "And you say she's the same woman mentioned in this obituary?"

"As far as I can tell, I know for a fact she's from the area," suddenly, Eddie had an idea; one that would get his journalistic foot in the news media door, "If you want, I can go over and investigate, you know, get a statement from the family, maybe get an interview."

The editor-in-chief solemnly shook his salty head, "Sorry, Ed, I appreciate your can-do attitude, but this is a simple, country paper not the big city tabloids. Our readers want to read about the local apple picking festival and how the high school FFA is going to the state championship."

"But chief don't you think that our readers would be interested in this?" Eddie pleaded, pointing to the obituary, "I mean, it's about a local woman who happens to be the hottest thing in music right now!"

The old man looked down at Eddie, shaking his head. "Son, I can almost guarantee that none of our loyal readers have ever even heard of this Honeycomb lady," the chief patted Eddie's shoulder, "Let me know when you've finished, I'm still having trouble accessing my emails."

The chief left and Eddie was once again stuck doing IT. He was sick of IT!

Even when he had spotted a breaking story, one that was developing before his very eyes, it was immediately rejected by his boss. And the worst part was, Eddie *knew* it was going to be a big story!

It was only a matter of time until one of the other news outlets caught wind of Hunnie's sister dying. Once that happened, there would be round-the-clock updates on all the entertainment websites.

Sure, Eddie could write up and post his own investigative report on the matter, but he'd much rather his story be published by an established news site.

Preferably one that would pay him well.

Setting all other work aside, Eddie opened a window on the computer and ran a search for 'celebrity gossip sites'.

CHAPTER 5

Hawthorn stepped off the bus and adjusted his glasses, taking in his new surroundings. He was immediately struck by how gray the town of Longville was, as if someone drained all the color out of every surface. It was hard to tell if the surrounding buildings were abandoned or just in serious need of maintenance. Paint peeling off of warped siding, crumbling bricks, cracked windows, and enough vacant lots to catch every form of Tetanus.

The so-called bus depot was nothing but a greasy spoon diner called EAT. Once a shining beacon to hungry truckers, now merely a grime-covered, rusted-out shack. Nonetheless, it did have the best tap water in town, which it proudly proclaimed with a custom-made, neon sign.

Parked in front of the diner were a couple of banged up pickup trucks and a newish looking cop car. Leaning against the squad car was an angry looking policeman in his late forties. Hawthorn gave a friendly wave and approached the man.

"Good morning, you must be Sheriff Gayfeather," said Hawthorn holding out his hand, "I'm Dr. Hawthorn

White."

Slowly, the stout sheriff looked Hawthorn up and down and began studying his face with his grayish-blue eyes. The man stared deep into his skin. Skeptically.

Hawthorn waited for a response; the bus idling in the background.

After what felt like twenty hours, Hawthorn cleared his throat and said, "So I understand you've been having problems with a swarm of killer bees?"

Twenty more hours of awkward silence.

In that time, Hawthorn looked down the street at the abandoned drive-in movie theater and gazed out over the cloudy horizon. Small black silhouettes of birds flew about erratically in the distance. Glancing back at the sheriff, he raised his eyebrows and said, "It's chilly today."

"Bet you think you know everything, don't you?" the sheriff snapped, throwing his shoulders back and taking a couple of steps forward.

While he was thrown off by the sheriff's abrupt hostility, Hawthorn stood his ground.

"Pardon?" he asked.

"You come from that fancy, big city college?"

"I...I wouldn't really call Sedalia a big city."

"You better not be one of those homosexual deviants looking for a good time...." Sheriff Gayfeather said in a threatening but not at all convincing manner, "....'cause you won't find it here!"

Being so close to the engorged sheriff made Hawthorn uncomfortable, not very many people got in his personal space, especially someone who was all hot and bothered.

A cool breeze blew between them. Gradually, the fire faded from the officer's eyes and the tension passed.

The sheriff took one last swig of his beer and tossed

the can aside, "Come on," he said motioning to the car, "I'm taking you to the coroner."

Confused by what just happened, Hawthorn took a moment to review his options before deciding to go with the sheriff anyway.

In spite of his gruff exterior, Sheriff Gayfeather was, at heart, a real piece of $#*%.

The sheriff had his reasons for being the way he was; mainly, he was sick of all the negative stereotypes about police officers being nothing but patient, respectful, open-minded pansies. If there was one thing he hated more than that, it was Muslims. "Not in *my* town!" the sheriff had once said to no one in particular about nothing specifically.

He also didn't much care for the federal government despite being violently patriotic.

Hawthorn sat quietly in the passenger seat as Sheriff Gayfeather drove them to the mortuary. Frozen farmland drifted by on either side of the police car. The morgue was a fifteen minute drive but, being a master conversationalist, the sheriff was able to fill any uncomfortable silence with uncomfortable mouth noise.

"You one of those Hebrew Nationals, aren't you?"

"Excuse me?"

"Or some kind of Spanish/Italian mix? It's alright, if you are," the sheriff said with a not-so-reassuring wave of the hand, "You have no control over that, just so long as you're not queer!"

"Now see here!"

"I'm just letting you know 'cause that thing might fly in *Sedalia* and the rest of the country but not here; city council voted against it so you just watch yourself."

"Sheriff, I'm only here to help." Hawthorn said calmly,

"The sooner I figure out what caused this killer bee attack, the better."

"Okay, then, as long as you're not pushing your libtard agenda on us!" the sheriff sneered, he then nodded towards the passing countryside, "This is a simple community with simple folks. We believe in two things: God and America. We still call french fries; *freedom fries* and french toast; *freedom toast.*"

Half-jokingly, Hawthorn asked, "What do you call the French New Wave?"

"Pretentious. Any other questions, smart guy?"

"Actually, yes," Hawthorn said, seeing an opportunity to talk about the case at hand, "Has the area had any history of bee attacks before? Specifically from any species that may have been Africanized?"

Keeping his eyes on the road, the sheriff shook his head, "No, we ran them all out of town, in fact, my old deputy was let go 'cause he shot one jaywalking...."

Dumbfounded, Hawthorn tried to explain, "Sheriff, you misunderstand me, what I meant is...."

"It's a shame...." the sheriff continued, lost in thought, "He was the best deputy I ever had. I hated to see him go, he was a real good guy."

Hawthorn wasn't positive, but he thought he caught a glimmer of a tear forming in the sheriff's eye.

With a snort, the sheriff cleared his throat and asked, "So, uh, where you staying tonight?"

And once again, Hawthorn felt extremely uncomfortable. He wasn't the best judge of character but there was just something about the sheriff that rubbed him the wrong way. Hawthorn silently stared out the passenger window.

"I only ask 'cause, you know, the wife is out of town at

a Bible retreat and my house is technically outside the city limits...."

At that moment, Hawthorn saw a small, brick building with a wooden 'Office of Medical Examiner' sign out front. He let out a sigh of relief and muttered, 'Thank goodness."

There was never a man happier to see a morgue.

The sheriff parked the squad car out front and he and Hawthorn entered the square building.

It was cold inside.

The morgue's reception area was small and looked like the waiting room at a dentist's office. Every piece of furniture looked as if it were pulled from a dumpster outside a Salvation Army store. Even the magazines looked like they were secondhand from other waiting rooms.

Hawthorn could hear romantic music playing.

The sheriff strolled up to the waiting room window and knocked on the frosted window pane. The music suddenly stopped and Hawthorn heard a frantic shuffling of clothing coming from the other side of the glass. A disheveled man in a lab coat slid open the window; he had wild, unkempt hair, a scraggly five o'clock shadow and, what appeared to be, hot pink lipstick smeared across his crusty mouth.

"Oh, hi, Sheriff," the man said, "forgot you were coming by today."

"Jim, this is the professor from Sedalia," the sheriff said pointing to Hawthorn, he then motioned back at the man in the window, "College boy, this is Dr. Bolander."

Hawthorn and the coroner nodded at one another.

"Mind if we come on back," the sheriff said opening the door to the autopsy room.

The coroner, caught off guard by the sheriff's barging in, could only stutter out, "Oh, uh, okay, sure."

Hawthorn followed him into the next room.

The autopsy room was small and from what Hawthorn could tell, relatively clean. It was hard to tell considering it was only lit by candlelight. Along the back wall sat three large freezer chests. In the center of the room was a silver autopsy table and lying on top, next to a bottle of merlot, was a cadaver in a cocktail dress.

Pointing towards the lifeless body, Hawthorn asked, "Is that her?"

"No, that's just old man Johnson," he replied wiping the lipstick from his mouth, "I was just finishing up."

"I bet you were," said the sheriff, "don't worry, we won't be long."

The coroner retrieved the pale body of a young woman on a gurney and wheeled her in.

On the bus Hawthorn had read about the young woman who was killed in the attack. Rosemary Combs-Dogwood: age, twenty-one; blood type, AB; favorite soda, ginger ale. By all accounts, she was perfectly healthy and had no prior history of allergic reaction to bee stings.

While Hawthorn had been to funerals before, this was the first time he had seen a cadaver professionally. He was struck by how pretty she was, even in death. Long red hair, trim figure, a pretty freckled face.

Along her neck, Hawthorn noticed tiny puncture marks.

"May, I take a closer look?" Hawthorn asked, approaching the gurney.

He still couldn't see much in the candlelit room.

"Can we get some more light in here?" said Hawthorn.

The coroner grabbed a gooseneck lamp and turned the

light on towards the body.

Upon closer examination, the puncture marks on her arms, face and neck didn't look anything like bee stings, more like pin pricks. As if she had gone in for a discount acupuncture.

"That's strange," Hawthorn remarked, examining the body and adjusting the lamp as needed, "No swelling, no rashes or hives.... Were any stingers left behind?"

"Just one," said the coroner.

"May I see it?"

The coroner grabbed a plastic sandwich baggie off his desk and handed it over to Hawthorn.

Peering inside the transparent bag, Hawthorn spotted something that was similar to a bee's stinger, but different. It was small and pointy, like the stinger of a honeybee, but had no trace of abdomen attached to it. The tip of the stinger was slanted and hollow, like that of a syringe. It even looked metallic.

"Where was she attacked?" he asked thoughtfully.

"Everywhere," the Coroner said, pulling back the sheet and pointing, "See?"

"No, doctor, the *geographic* location of the attack," Hawthorn clarified, "where did this happen?"

CHAPTER 6

The sheriff drove Hawthorn to the Combs residence, dropping him off. According to the sheriff, he had more important things to do than drive Hawthorn's "candy-ass" all over the county.

"Give my deputy a call if you need a ride," he said, handing him a slip of paper with two phone numbers written on it, "And call *me* if you need a warm bed tonight."

Hawthorn shrugged off the invitation, grabbed his bag, and walked down the long, gravel driveway towards the house.

From what he could tell, the Combs family seemed to have a nice place. It was out in the country, so it was quiet and the house itself was well maintained. The split-level ranch-style home had ample space and dark, wooden plank siding that was popular in the late eighties.

Stepping onto the porch, Hawthorn gave the front door a couple of knocks.

When the door opened, Hawthorn was greeted by a gorgeous blonde woman in blue jeans and a black long-sleeve t-shirt. She was clearly related to the corpse he had seen earlier. She had a similar face but with bright blue eyes and a stronger chin. Short, stacked, and noticeably stressed, the woman held the door in one hand and the door frame in the other.

"Yes?" she sighed, trying her best to look welcoming.

"Hi, I'm Dr. Hawthorn White, may I speak to a Mr. Sean Combs?"

"I'm his daughter, Hunnie. May I ask why you need to see him?"

"I'm here to investigate the bee attack."

"Oh, yeah?" the woman said looking past Hawthorn, "Anyone else with you?"

"No, the sheriff was kind enough to give me a ride but he had-"

"Hunnie!" a man's voice called out from inside, "Who's at the door?"

Behind the young woman, a middle aged man in a bathrobe approached the doorway. He was tall with a friendly face and gray hair. He smiled at Hawthorn.

"Well, hello there, are you here to fix the tractor?"

Hawthorn found the question odd, but not unreasonable and began to answer 'No' before being interrupted by Hunnie.

"Dad, we don't have a tractor."

Laughingly, the father responded, "Sure we do," and motioned for Hawthorn to enter, "Come on in, I'm Sean but friends call me Mr. Combs."

Though Mr. Combs was indeed the owner of the house, Hawthorn got the feeling he should look to Hunnie for the go-ahead. She nodded and opened the door a bit more for Hawthorn.

As Hawthorn walked through the front door, Mr. Combs pleasantly said, "Hunnie, be a dear and take this gentleman's coat, we can talk in the kitchen."

Mr. Combs then left the breezeway, disappearing into another room of the house.

Helping Hawthorn take off his black peacoat and scarf, Hunnie leaned in and murmured, "Don't mind him, he's....he's been better."

The Combs house was spacious yet cozy. The dark wooden floors, walls and ceiling made it feel like a ski-lodge, it was even decorated like one. The walls were adorned with snowy landscape paintings, vintage mountain trail signs, and even a pair of skis stolen from Rainbow Basin Ski Resort.

Hawthorn followed Hunnie into the kitchen were Mr. Combs was standing next to the kitchen island. The Combs' appeared to be pretty well-off as all the appliances appeared to be brand new. Picture windows provided the kitchen with plenty of natural light and a picturesque view where Hawthorn spotted deer frolicking through the woods.

"You certainly have a lovely home. Thank you for your hospitality," said Hawthorn, approaching the table, "As I was just telling your daughter, my name is Dr. Hawthorn White and I'm an entomologist sent to-

"Have a seat," Mr. Combs said, pulling a bar stool up to the countertop, "can I offer you some toast?"

"No. Thank you," said Hawthorn, briefly confused by the offer, "I was sent to find the swarm of bees that-"

"How about a nice, hot mug of cola?"

"I'm....good, thank you," he looked towards Hunnie, to gauge her response, but she was unfazed. He continued, "As I was saying, I'm here to locate the bees that have been swarming in-"

"Here we are," Mr. Combs said, taking a steaming cup

of cola out of the microwave and setting it down in front of his bewildered guest, "Now, tell me how did you kids meet?"

"Well, you must understand, Mr. Combs, we-"

"Please, Mr. Combs was my father, call me *Reverend* Combs."

"Oh, I beg your pardon, are you a minister?"

"No," Mr. Combs said, taking a sip of hot cola.

Hawthorn was now taken aback for two reasons; the first was from Mr. Combs response and the second was that he was drinking from the mug that *he had just given to Hawthorn.* Granted, Hawthorn didn't want the warm soda to begin with but it was the principle of the thing!

"Hey Dad," Hunnie said, reaching over and placing a hand on her father's shoulder, "I think I hear the toys coming to life, again. You might want to go upstairs and check it out."

Mr. Combs face lit up and he patted his daughter's hand, "Good idea," standing up, he turned to Hawthorn and said, "Excuse me, I've got toys in the attic."

Mr. Combs hurried out of the kitchen softly saying to himself, "I'm going to catch those bastards if it's the last thing I do!"

It was hard enough for Hawthorn to know how to properly react to the sheriff, but now he was really thrown for a loop! None of the books on etiquette dealt with how to politely converse with the mentally unstable.

Hunnie gave a half-shrug and smiled apologetically, "Sorry."

"He seems to be taking it pretty hard."

"No, he's always like that," Hunnie would have explained further but there were more pressing matters at hand, "So you're wanting to find the bees that killed my sister?"

"Yes, it's of vital importance that we locate this swarm before they cause any more harm."

"How do you plan on doing that?"

"Well, surveying the area where she was attacked is a good start."

"Let me grab my coat, I'll take you there."

The Combs family had a good ten acres of rolling hills and forest behind their rustic home. Even in the dead of winter, there was a natural beauty in the starkness, unlike the rest of town, which reminded Hawthorn of a post-apocalyptic wasteland.

Hunnie led Hawthorn across their property, climbing up another frosted mini hill. It was still overcast and the air was getting noticeably colder but being something of an outdoorsman, Hawthorn enjoyed the hike.

"This is lovely land you've got here," he said walking beside Hunnie, the frozen grass crunching beneath their feet.

"Thanks, it was a failed vineyard before my parents bought it."

"What do your folks do for a living?"

"My dad's a retired radar operator at the Air Base and my mom was a music teacher before she died."

"How long ago was her passing?"

"Going on six years now."

"I'm sorry for your loss."

"It's okay, it was especially hard on my dad, that's why he is the way he is. I don't know how losing Rosemary will affect him in the long run. Guess I'll just have to wait and see."

"If it's any consolation, I once lost a colony of termites

I had become quite fond of."

"Oh?,"

"I was on my way to an entomology conference and the airline lost my luggage, never saw them again."

At the top of the hill was a plateau surrounded by forest, a number of trees dotted the field. Hunnie pointed towards an old hickory tree and then towards an oak.

"That's where my sister was attacked," her finger waving between the two trees, "or, at least, according to my father."

They walked to the spot where Hunnie was pointing, a whole mess of footprints scattered in the dusty snow. The panicky footprints then zigzagged away from the chaos and went into the woods.

Hawthorn kneeled down and examined the tracks, hoping to find some evidence of the attack. Unfortunately, bees don't usually leave footprints behind, especially while inflight. He stuck his finger in the snow, brought it up to his mouth and tasted it. Not a single trace of honey.

He held his finger up to the air, gauging the wind. It wasn't very strong, but a chilly breeze was coming from the northwest.

"Any idea which direction the swarm flew in?" Hawthorn asked.

"No, Dad only said they came from behind."

"Hmmm," Hawthorn stared thoughtfully at the ground, the soft breeze sweeping past his ears, "I've got an idea."

Hawthorn stood up and pulled out his little whistle.

Intrigued, Hunnie asked, "What is that?"

Hawthorn held up the yellow piece of plastic, "A device of my own invention."

"What does it do?"

"It's a whistle designed to produce a low-frequency buzzing only bees can discern. Since we can't find the bees ourselves, maybe we can get the bees to find us."

Hawthorn brought the whistle to his lips and began to blow. The only sound Hunnie could hear was Hawthorn's breath passing through the empty plastic chamber.

"Well I hope you have a plan in case they do."

Momentarily taking the whistle out of his mouth, Hawthorn replied, "Don't worry, I know how to handle them," adding, "I hope you are wearing good hiking boots."

Hunnie almost never had appropriate footwear.

Her feet were either overdressed, underdressed or not dressed at all. One moment she's going to a friend's wedding barefoot and the next she's running a charity 5K in her most expensive pair of pumps. Being uncomfortable never stopped Hunnie from being stylish.

Today, however, her red leather cowboy booties were as practical as they were cute.

Following frozen footprints, Hunnie and Hawthorn entered the barren woods and descended the steep hill where her sister had fallen. Taking hold of every nearby tree and branch, the two carefully made their way down, Hawthorn intermittently blowing his whistle with each cautious step.

"Does that thing really work?"

Taking another step down, Hawthorn took the whistle out of his mouth and looked behind him at Hunnie.

"In theory, yes," he responded, "but then, this is the first time it's ever been field tested."

"How often are you out in the field?" Hunnie reached

out to balance herself and Hawthorn took her by the hand, "Thanks."

"Not very often; typically I'm in the lab and, since the buildings on campus are infested with a wide variety of insects, I don't have to go far to find a good specimen."

As the two of them cautiously approached the bottom of the ravine, Hawthorn spotted the place where Hunnie's sister was killed. Bright yellow police tape was stretched out across three trees forming a kind of triangle. Scalene, if Hawthorn was correct. Within this triangle lay brush and leaves but, unlike the rest of the forest floor, the topsoil had been disturbed.

Hawthorn heard Hunnie sniffling behind him. He turned around and saw tears streaming down her cheeks.

Putting away his whistle, Hawthorn reached into his other pocket, brought out a handkerchief and handed it to her.

Wiping away her tears, Hunnie cleared her throat, "Sorry," she said.

"It's okay," Hawthorn softly replied, "You're not bothering me."

Ducking underneath the police tape, Hawthorn once again crouched down to examine the cold ground.

The thin layer of snow and leaves had been tossed about, leaving an almost perfect imprint of the young woman in the dirt. It was as if a silhouette of her body had been sprawled out across the forest floor. As far as death poses go, it was a beaut!

Practically pressing his face against the ground, Hawthorn slowly scanned the area for clues. He had read once that bees die after they use their stinger. If he could find one of those dead bees, he could take it back to the lab and run some tests. Unfortunately, the only thing he could find were more leaves and twigs.

Standing upright, Hawthorn shook his head.

"This is all so strange," he said surveying the woods, "Bees usually fly south for the winter." Hawthorn looked back at Hunnie and asked, "Are you sure that's what your father saw? A swarm of killer bees?"

"It's hard to say *what* he saw; he has a very active imagination and can't tell the difference between what's real and what isn't.... He once had a dream where he was flying and now he's convinced that he actually can!"

Contemplatively, Hawthorn frowned.

This could be a problem. If he couldn't trust the eyewitness testimony of a crazy person, what could he trust?

Science, that's what.

Generally, Hawthorn found people to be well-meaning but stupid. Especially when it comes to solving complex problems. Most people tend to go with the simplest answer that involves the least amount of critical thinking, then proceed to stick their head in the sand. The scientific method, however, is unbiased and adaptable to changing variables.

He had a stinger to analyze, but that didn't necessarily mean it was bees that killed Rosemary Combs.

Hawthorn took off his glasses and began to thoughtfully clean them with his spare handkerchief.

"Well, your father may not be the most reliable of sources, but I still have a few tricks up the sleeve of my labcoat."

"You're not wearing a labcoat."

"I know," replied Hawthorn, putting his glasses back on, "it's a little expression us scientists use."

CHAPTER 7

The trick Hawthorn had up the sleeve (of his labcoat) was another scientific instrument of his own design. This device was a pocket-sized bee trap that could be fastened to any tree, branch or shrub. Hunnie took Hawthorn back to where her sister was first attacked and Hawthorn attached the trap to the nearest tree.

The cylindrical trap was small and made of clear plastic; one end had an opening for the insect to enter and the other had a tiny, metal antenna. He explained that he would receive an alert the moment a foreign body entered the trap. Because killer bees were not common this time of year, it was likely any bee captured would be from the same swarm.

He then went on to talk, in length, about the intricacies of particular insects.

Hunnie didn't quite understand all the science behind it, but he was nice to look at and she found him genuinely interesting. Having spent so much time in Hollywood, Hunnie wasn't used to talking to someone with a brain.

As they made their way back to the house, Hawthorn

shared facts about his favorite thysanura, "....and what most people don't understand about silverfish is that they're not actually fish."

"That's odd...."

"I know, you would think that it's common knowledge, but it's not, in fact, I once had to explain this to a local sushi restaurant."

"No, I meant in the drive," Hunnie interrupted, pointing towards the house, "whose vehicle is that?"

Parked outside the house was a brightly colored Italian scooter.

"You don't know anyone who drives a plaid moped?"

"Not outside California," Hunnie responded.

When they reached the house, Hunnie led Hawthorn in through the backdoor. Coming in through the kitchen, they found Mr. Combs talking to a sharp-dressed young man at the counter.

The man appeared to be in his twenties but had the mustache of a 14-year-old boy (or 80-year-old woman). He had on a wool vest and tie and on his head wore a gray fedora with a PRESS pass sticking out of the band. Hawthorn thought, if not for the skinny jeans and bowling shoes, he'd look like an old-timey reporter.

Hunnie thought he looked like a prick.

Seeing they were no longer alone, the stranger stood up from the bar stool and nodded at Hunnie.

"Hello," he said.

Hunnie already didn't like this guy.

Her father excitedly pointed to the man and exclaimed, "Hunnie, a man from the paper's here, he wants to talk to me about the time I met Elvis," turning to the newspaper man, Mr. Combs softly added, "I know it wasn't really Elvis. It was Bigfoot in disguise."

Staring at Hunnie, the man smiled and replied, "Naturally."

"I'm going to get the autographed picture," Mr. Combs said, crossing to the other side of the living room, "I'll be right back, make yourself at home!"

As Mr. Combs left the room, the stranger's gaze remained fixed on Hunnie. Once it was clear that Mr. Combs was no longer within earshot, the young man folded his arms and spoke.

"So we meet again for the first time, I guess better late than never."

"What?" Hunnie snapped, "Who are you? What are you doing talking to my father?"

Taking out his smartphone, he pointed the camera at Hunnie and pressed record.

"Who is this?" he gestured towards Hawthorn, "New boyfriend?"

"He's here to investigate my sister's death, you jerk!"

"I see," he said, holding the phone up in her face, "and how exactly did she die?"

Hawthorn couldn't stand to see Hunnie being badgered and decided to step in.

"Excuse me," he said, putting himself between Hunnie and the pressman, "before the lady answers any more questions, I believe you owe her an explanation."

"Of course," the young man responded, lowering his phone, "I'm Eddie Mallow of the Daily Chronicle, your father was kind enough to let me in."

Hunnie was still irked at the so-called journalist and retorted, "My father is a sick man and would have let anyone in."

"Nevertheless, here we are," Eddie said calmly, raising his phone back in front of his face, "Now, how will your sister dying affect you being on tour?"

"Well, frankly, I don't really feel like talking about that right now.... and, another thing, how the hell did you get my home address?"

Lowering his phone, Eddie scoffed, "Are you kidding? It's not that hard," he then picked up a stack of envelopes off the kitchen counter, "Judging from your fan mail, I'm not the only one who knows your permanent address."

Flipping through her mail, Eddie paused, "Looks like one guy's *really* obsessed with you!"

"Okay," Hunnie snatched the stack of envelopes, "I want you the hell out of here!"

"I'm back!" Mr. Combs announced, parading in with a framed picture, "Here it is, my good man, photographic proof of Bigfoot."

Mr. Combs handed Eddie the picture, it was a signed photo of a big, blue monster truck.

Eddie read the autograph aloud, "Sean, Thanks for coming out and showing your support! Signed, Team BIGFOOT."

Giving Hawthorn a playful nudge, Mr. Combs said, "See? What'd I tell ya'? Most people think I'm full of baloney when I tell them I met Bigfoot." Suddenly struck by inspiration, he then exclaimed, "Hey, who wants toast?"

Grabbing a loaf of bread out of the pantry, Mr. Combs went about frantically shoving slices into his collection of toasters.

Beaming, Eddie chuckled and said, "This is great stuff, sir, I had no idea *the* father of Hunnie Combs was so....certifiable."

"And now you need to leave!" Hunnie spat, shoving the young reporter to the other side of the kitchen.

"Hunnie!" Mr. Combs scolded, "That's no way to talk to your friend."

"He is NOT my friend!"

Eddie adjusted his tie and straightened his hat. "It's alright, Mr. Combs," he said, "I'm not surprised she doesn't remember me, we were only in college."

"So? It was a public university, a lot of people went there."

"Yeah, but I'm the only one who tried to interview you for the school paper."

"I never did an interview with you in college."

"That's right, you didn't. You blew me off just like the fan you promised to go to homecoming with."

Hawthorn calmly stepped in and pulled Eddie aside, "Excuse me, Mr. Mallow, perhaps this interview can be postponed for a later date...."

"I don't want to be interviewed!" Hunnie called out, "Especially not by him!"

"....as you can see, Ms. Combs is going through a lot at the moment..."

The toast popped up and Mr. Combs enthusiastically yelled, "Toast is done!"

"....and today just doesn't seem to be the right time...."

Quickly stacking the toast on a plate, Mr. Combs took it and rushed out of the kitchen.

"....or place."

Eddie shook his head and pointed at Hunnie, "She owes me an interview!"

"I don't owe you anything, you creep!"

Hawthorn began leading Eddie out of the kitchen and down the hall, "How about you get in contact with her publicist and then I'm sure you'll be able to work something out."

The two men had reached the front door, Eddie stopped, "Look, Mr. Whoever-you-are, I wouldn't be the journalist I am today, if I had just played by the rules."

"I'm not entirely sure you are," remarked Hawthorn, opening the door.

Cold evening air rushed in and Eddie was faced with the approaching darkness outside. He glanced at Hawthorn, who stood firmly, awaiting his departure. Hunnie stepped out into the hall, glaring.

Eddie regretfully grabbed his vintage tweed jacket off the coat rack and turned to walk through the open door. Just as he had taken a step outside, Mr. Combs called out.

"Wait!"

Mr. Combs came running down the hall with the plate of toast, "Before you go, at least have a slice for the road."

"Thank you, for *your* hospitality, Mr. Combs," Eddie said picking up the topmost slice, which appeared to have some sort of Chocolate-hazelnut spread smeared across it, "Wish everyone here were as thoughtful."

Taking a big bite of the toast, Eddie walked out the door and started down the steps. Halfway through, he stopped dead in his tracks and glanced back at Mr. Combs with a quizzical/disgusted look on his bread-filled face.

Hawthorn shut the front door. "I should probably get going myself," he said, not noticing the sound of a young reporter throwing up outside, "it's getting late and I need the sheriff to come pick me up."

Mr. Combs turned to Hawthorn, "Say, Mr. Doctor, where are you spending the night?"

"I believe it's called the Cloud 7 Hotel."

"That dump! I'd rather spend the night in the 7th Circle of Hell, don't stay there, stay with us.

"Oh, I couldn't impose."

"Nonsense, you can sleep with Hunnie."

"*DAD!*" Hunnie cried in disbelief.

"What?!" said Mr. Combs, honestly confused by his daughter's response.

Hunnie pulled her father aside, "If you must have him over, why don't you give him Rosemary's room instead?"

Dismissing the suggestion with a wave of his hand, Mr. Combs said, "You know how she feels about strangers sleeping in her bed, she was never quite as open-minded as you."

Hawthorn was touched by the offer but etiquette dictated that he politely decline, "Mr. Combs, you really don't have to…."

Mr. Combs, still holding the plate of toast, approached Hawthorn and placed a hand on his shoulder, "I know we don't have a fancy ice machine or exotic stains on the walls but I think you'll find it more comfortable than a night in the Iron Maiden, trust me," he gave his shoulder a fatherly squeeze and smiled, "Now, let's all sit down and have some toast."

As Mr. Combs led his reluctant guest back into the kitchen, a single bee hovered in the darkness outside. Silently watching through the window above the sink. The two men sat at the counter talking, neither suspecting a thing. The conversation was muted but it didn't matter to the impassive insect. Its only concern was to maintain its position in the ever-changing breeze.

Soon, the lone bee was joined by another; this one taking the window closest to the refrigerator. When Hunnie entered the kitchen, another bee joined the other two. While Hawthorn, Hunnie, and Mr. Combs continued their conversation, the bees quietly formed a perimeter around the house.

CHAPTER 8

In spite of his better judgment, Hawthorn decided to spend the night at the Combs' house.

He called the sheriff's office for an update and was told he'd have a lab to work out of in the morning. This was good. With any luck, the lab would have all the necessary equipment to run his scientific tests.

Once he got off the phone, Mr. Combs asked if anyone was hungry and, much to Hawthorn's relief, Hunnie ordered a pizza from the local gas station. At first Hawthorn thought she was joking. Although, he had to admit, the gas station pizza was pretty much exactly what he expected it to be; technically food. Of course, it was still preferable to anything Mr. Combs might have prepared.

After dinner they moved into the living room where Hunnie strummed on her guitar and Mr. Combs showed off his toenail collection. They would go on to play a game of *A Clockwork Orange-Opoly* until Mr. Combs ate all the pieces.

It was an odd, but quiet, evening.

The next morning, the sheriff's deputy stopped by to drive Hawthorn to the science lab. Riding with Probationary Deputy Vance proved to be a much more pleasant experience than going anywhere with Sheriff Gayfeather. Vance was younger and a bit on the soft-spoken side.

Hawthorn got the impression that he was an overall nice guy.

They pulled up to a long brick building.

"Why are we stopping here?" Hawthorn asked gazing out the squad car window.

The deputy gestured towards the building, "This is it."

"This is what?" he said looking directly ahead, "It's a public school."

"Yup, Longville R-I."

To the left of the main entrance, attached to red brick, were the words LONGVILLE R-I SECONDARY SCHOOL.

Sensing Hawthorn was distressed, the deputy reassured him, "Don't worry it's a good school, I went here."

The deputy took Hawthorn inside the high school and introduced him to the principal, who seemed more than annoyed that his daily routine was being disrupted by some big-shot scientist from out-of-town.

"Come along," he said, "I'll show you to the biolab."

They walked down the long empty halls, silently passing by crowded classes already in session. Each time they passed an open door, Hawthorn could feel the curious, heavy-laden eyes of high schoolers watching them from their desks. They reached room number 150 and the principal opened the thick, wooden door.

The classroom didn't look much different from any

other high school biolab. Wooden cabinets aligned the walls, heavy lab benches were attached to the floor, and next to the blackboard hung an embarrassingly outdated periodic table.

The good news was that the classroom had the basic equipment he needed: test tubes, Bunsen burners, paper, et cetera. He also had enough foresight to bring his more specialized tools with him. Just in case.

It wasn't what Hawthorn was accustomed to, but he would use the available resources to the best of his ability.

"The first hour class dismissed a few minutes ago," said the principal, "We'll need you out at one o'clock for Mrs. Clover's fifth hour biolab, perhaps you can take a lunch or something."

He didn't usually have feelings of attachment, but, at that moment, Dr. Hawthorn White missed his lab at the college.

Hunnie was too young to have to deal with this.

"I... I don't understand, why can't you sell me the one?"

She didn't even know how to balance a checkbook let alone plan a funeral, yet here she was, pacing the kitchen, arguing with the cemetery sexton over the phone.

"That's the stupidest policy I've ever heard of!"

Back when her mother died, her dad was still well enough to take care of all the arrangements. She just had to show up and let the painful moments pass.

"I don't need six plots...."

Now she had to take on that responsibility.

"....I just need one for my sister!"

Hunnie never thought she'd live longer than

Rosemary. After their mother's death, Hunnie's plan was to live fast and die young. Living like a rock star seemed to be the best way to achieve her dream.

But her little sister had to be a brat and ruin it all.

"My father didn't have to when we buried my mom...."

This nonsense is probably what drove her father crazy in the first place.

"....well, it must be brand new, what the hell am I going to do with five other burial plots?!"

Everyone was so caught up in grief, they didn't notice their father's deteriorating mental health.

"Are they at least all together?.... Unbelievable...."

Until he was completely off his rocker!

As Hunnie continued her argument, Mr. Combs snuck past the kitchen and escaped out the front door.

Usually he wasn't allowed outdoors unsupervised; the last time he went out by himself, Mr. Combs thought he was a werewolf and started chasing cars. He would have gotten himself killed if animal control hadn't come by and picked him up.

Prowling the length of the house, he crept underneath the kitchen windows until he reached a small bush. It had been a while since the evergreen shrub had been trimmed. The branches of tiny leaves went every which way. Mr. Combs stretched himself out, directly into the bush.

Lying face down in the soil, he took out a set of keys, moved his pocket knife keychain out of the way, and began sawing into the bush with his house key.

He could hear the faint mumble of his eldest daughter

arguing with someone on the phone.

Poor girl.

If today's expedition was a success, she wouldn't have to worry about anything for the rest of her life.

Finally, Mr. Combs sawed through the main stem of the bush. Forcing as much of his body into the spiny shrub as possible, he sat up and lifted the entire mass off the ground. It was a little cumbersome but he would only need camouflage for a bit.

Carrying the shrub by its stalk, Mr. Combs tippy-toed across the yard towards the shed. If Hunnie looked out the window at that moment, she would have seen a walking bush wearing pajama bottoms and rain boots. But she was too busy cursing out a funeral director to care.

Mr. Combs reached the barn-style storage shed and threw off his bushy facade.

He open the double-doors and entered the dark and cluttered shed. Grabbing a wooden box from the nearest shelf, he carelessly dumped its contents on the floor and began filling up the box with the items he needed.

A baseball bat, a butterfly net, and a burlap sack full of bear traps.

Setting his stuff on top of the riding lawn mower, Mr. Combs stared inside the box, contemplating.

There was something he was forgetting.

When he remembered, he immediately walked straight to the house, went inside, grabbed the missing item from the kitchen, and then walked back to the shed. It took less than a minute and, still preoccupied, Hunnie barely noticed or cared.

Gathering his things, Mr. Combs left the shed and made for the woods.

◆ ◆ ◆

The item Mr. Combs went back to the house for was a box of Marshmallow Shamrocks; a breakfast cereal that featured a cartoon leprechaun on the package. Mr. Combs hated that Irish bastard! In the commercials, children would be happily eating a big bowl of Marshmallow Shamrocks on the playground or in class and that greedy, animated punk would show up and steal them away!

If that wasn't bad enough, the little bastard was apparently stealing cereal from the Combs' own house!

Ever since Hunnie came into town, more and more of Mr. Combs favorite cereal was missing.

So now, Mr. Combs was in the forest setting traps.

Bending down to the forest floor, Mr. Combs opened the cold, metal jaws of the bear trap and carefully poured a handful of brightly colored cereal onto the steel pan. He attached the chain to a nearby stick and then went about setting the spring.

Satisfied with his work, Mr. Combs grabbed his box of supplies and stood.

"There," he said to no one in particular, except maybe the trees if they were listening, "That'll take care of the little bugger!"

Venturing deeper into the woods, Mr. Combs searched for another good spot to set-up Leprechaun traps. Ideally, he'd prefer to place the traps near a pot of gold or at the end of a rainbow but the forest by his house should do the trick.

It was a foggy morning and while it was warmer than the day before, there was still a brisk chill in the air.

Enveloping him were tall, barren trees and a grayness

that seemingly stretched forever. Even though he could hear Route PP in the distance, there was an eerie silence that made the woods seem all the more isolated and remote.

Or, at least, it would have been eerie if Mr. Combs wasn't happily whistling "When Irish Eyes Are Smiling."

Mr. Combs paused and set his box down. Surveying the wet ground, he kicked around globs of brown, deteriorating leaves. He was on the lookout for a nice little crevice to hide his next trap.

Finding a good spot, Mr. Combs crouched down and began to set things up..

Merrily whistling to himself, he didn't notice an electronic buzz in the air. From out of the fog, one tiny, black dot materialized; flying sporadically but with purpose. Then two more appeared. Then eight. Then seventeen more appeared. All swarming towards their next target.

By the time Mr. Combs noticed, the deadly bees were all around him.

"YIKES!" he examined, jumping up at least three feet, "Not you guys again!"

Frantically waving his arms around like a spaz, Mr. Combs accidentally stepped into the bear trap he had just set.

The steel metal jaws snapped down on his shin and a searing pain shot through his body.

He screamed out, "SON OF A B!" and fell to the ground.

Luckily, for Mr. Combs, he had bought the cheap generic bear traps made of aluminum and wasn't too terribly hurt. For the time being.

The bees came down upon him, ready to strike. Desperate for protection of any kind, Mr. Combs grabbed the first thing he could get his hands on and started swinging; in this case, it was the box of Marshmallow Shamrocks cereal.

As he madly swung the box, cascades of green marshmallows and brown oat pieces splayed out into the air. Most of them missed, but some didn't, bouncing off a random bee here or there. While the bits of cereal didn't kill any of the insects, it was enough to deter them for a second or two.

Crawling through the leaves, to the closest tree, Mr. Combs pulled himself up and limped as fast as he could. Making his way towards the highway.

Route PP wasn't *that* far away. But it wasn't close either. Time and distance are all relative anyway.

The road was a heck of a lot closer than the Copacabana, which is where Mr. Combs really wanted to be at the moment. If he could get to the highway and flag down a passing motorist, he could get a ride to the airport and fly to Manhattan. There, he would assume the identity of Lola La Mar, a young dancer who dreams of making it in show business. Through a lot of hard work, and a little bit of luck, he'd get his big break as a showgirl at the hottest club in New York City.

The bees would *never* think to find him there!

In the meantime, however, the swarm was hot on his tail.

Hunnie folded her arms and rested her head on the kitchen counter. She was exhausted, both emotionally and physically. Lying awake in bed, softly crying to herself, did not prepare her for a full day of haggling.

She had just gotten off the phone with the funeral director who insisted that, any casket buried at the town cemetery, had to be lined in an airtight burial vault, which was completely ridiculous! Rosemary would have wanted the most ecological, earth-friendly form of burial.

'Ashes to ashes, dust to dust' and all that crap.

While it was morbid to think about decomposing bodies being feasted on by worms and things, Hunnie preferred it over the idea of her factory-sealed sister stewing in her own juices for all eternity.

On the counter next to her, Hunnie's phone began to buzz.

She lifted her head and glanced at the number. The incoming call was from an unfamiliar number and while she didn't normally answer unsolicited calls from strangers, she decided to answer it anyway. After all, it was a local number and she had been making calls all over town.

"Hello?"

The voice on the other end was deep and masculine, "Hunnie, it's Dr. Hawthorn White," he said in a warm but professional manner, "I just wanted to call and give you an update about your sister, do you have a moment?"

Hunnie sat up, eagerly, "Yeah, of course." She was glad to hear his voice but it sounded like he was in a room full of other people.

"I ran some tests on your sister's blood sample and can confirm that she was not stung by any ordinary species of bee. In fact, I'm hesitant to even call them insects."

"Wait, what?!" she exclaimed, standing. Then taking a few steps to the window she asked, "How is that possible?"

"I should clarify," said Hawthorn, "your sister was stung by something, however, the toxins that caused her death seem to be a mixture of bee, wasp and, what appears to be, jellyfish venom. Also, within this mix is a powerful neurotoxin not found in nature." Hunnie could hear Hawthorn turn his face away from the phone and ask, "Jamie, can you hand me my notes? Thank you."

"What do you mean, not found in nature."

"Venomous invertebrates do not typically produce pancuronium bromide."

Bewildered, Hunnie stared out the window looking for a response and settled with "Guess I'll have to take your word on that one."

"Once I obtain a proper lab, I can perform a series of follow-up tests to make certain." The sound of other people had steadily become more loud and obnoxious.

"Where are you calling from, anyway? Sounds like you're in a high school cafeteria."

Not surprisingly, Hawthorn said, "Longville R-I, fifth hour biolab."

"Whose class?"

"Mrs. Clover."

"Oh yeah, I had her, she's tough."

In the background, Hunnie heard a familiar woman's voice shriek, "Dr. White, I have already confiscated one cellular phone today, do I need to take yours as well?"

Undeterred, Hawthorn continued, "I'd like to speak with your dad again, if I may, see if I can get some more clues from his description of the swarm."

"Sure," she said with a shrug, "I mean, I don't know how reliable he'll be; there's no telling if he actually saw bees or if he was just imagining them."

Somewhere in the woods, Mr. Combs was hopping around on one leg, like a diabetic easter bunny who just lost his foot due to one too many Cadbury Eggs. Despite his injury, Mr. Combs was able to stay one jump ahead of the pursuing bees. The aluminum bear trap still clasped to his ankle.

But after nearly a mile and a half, Mr. Combs was running out of steam.

He reached for the closest tree and paused to catch his breath. The road in sight, hiding behind a couple of hundred yards of scraggy forrest. Unfortunately, he wasn't out of the woods yet.

The constant buzzing had caught up to him and he had to get going.

His empty box of cereal proved to be an effective weapon against the bees. Every time the swarm got too close for comfort, he'd swing the box like a crazy person. They'd scatter and then regroup.

Mr. Combs looked at the cereal box, glanced back at the encroaching swarm and said, "Why didn't I bring Honey-O's?"

Throwing the box at the bees, he hopped as fast as he could towards Route PP. The swarm continued on.

Bouncing through the leaves and over sticks and fallen trees, Mr. Combs did his best not to fall. As luck would have it, this part of the woods gently sloped down, making it easier for him to make his escape.

He emerged out of the forest onto the strip of grass that ran parallel to the rural highway.

The roadside slanted upwards sharply, and as Mr. Combs attempted to hop up it, he instead fell forward to the ground. The brown grass was cold and soaked with melted snow. Mr. Combs could feel mud seep through the knees of his pajama bottoms.

"Aw, man!" he exclaimed, "my favorite pants!"

Behind him, the buzzing intensified. He looked over his shoulder and saw the swarm filter out of the shadowy forest. Clawing at the wet ground, he scrambled up the hill. The vicious buzz screaming in his ears. The bees now hovering on top of him.

As soon as his fingertips reached the gravelly edge of road, he pulled himself up and ran out onto the blacktop.

Then he was struck by the irony truck.

CHAPTER 9

Frank Blumen was on his way home from work. He mainly worked in Longville but his house was out in the country, off Route PP. It was a short but winding drive through hilly wilderness. Lots of twists and turns that made it feel almost like a roller coaster if one drove fast enough, which Frank was.

Winter was usually a slow time of year for Shudder-Bug Pest Control and Frank decided to take off a little early. He'd make up for it in the summer. By then, the bugs would be back in full force and he'd be working seven days a week.

In the meantime, he had a comfy couch with his name on it. Literally. His smart aleck son thought it'd be funny to print out a label and stick it to the sofa.

Frank absentmindedly drove down the country road, wondering how best to remove adhesive from the couch, when he turned the next sharp corner.

Suddenly, he spotted a man in the middle of the road! The man was in pajamas and he appeared to be swatting at bees. At least, they looked like bees, he didn't have time to examine them.

Frank slammed on his brakes with both feet, gripped hold of the steering wheel for dear life, and closed his eyes as hard as he could. The tires screeched, followed by a loud thud as the work truck came to a stop. Engine idling.

Frank reluctantly opened his eyes to find the man splayed out on the asphalt, twenty-yards in front of his bumper.

Bees nowhere to be found.

Putting the truck into park, Frank took a deep breath and sighed.

"Welp, there goes my evening."

The school day had ended and Hawthorn now had the entire biolab to himself. All the students and teachers had gone home for the evening. He could quietly work in peace and wouldn't feel obligated to help students with their schoolwork. Somewhere in the school, a lonely janitor vacuumed.

Despite Mrs. Clover's best efforts, it had been a productive day for Hawthorn. As he was conducting research he kept being scolded for not paying attention during class. Surprisingly, he was able to make good use of their lab equipment, even with the limitations of a poorly funded public school.

Today, he ruled out bee venom as the cause of death.

Tonight, he would do a detailed analysis on the alleged stinger.

Or, at least, he would have if he didn't receive an urgent call from Hunnie.

"There's been an accident." she said, frantically, "Can you meet me at the hospital? Dad was attacked by #@$

%ing bees!"

Hawthorn called the sheriff's office to inform them of the situation and arranged for a ride.

He had hoped that Probationary Deputy Vance would be the one to pick him up from school. Unfortunately, this would not be the case. Fifteen minutes later, when Sheriff Gayfeather pulled up to the building, Hawthorn was tempted to stay inside and call a taxi.

But he didn't have time for that.

Hunnie needed his help and he couldn't let the sheriff's nonsense get in the way of his work.

So Hawthorn sat and listened to the sheriff talk about how "illegal Mexicans" were talking all the "best jobs" from "real" Americans until they arrived at the hospital.

Knowing his way around the clinic, the sheriff took Hawthorn upstairs to where Mr. Combs was being kept. In the darkened bedroom, lit only by the light of the hallway, they found Mr. Combs sleeping in a tiny, uncomfortable-looking hospital bed. He was hooked up to a monitor and IV but was breathing on his own. Hunnie was sitting next to him in an equally uncomfortable-looking armchair.

Taking notice of Hawthorn and Sheriff Gayfeather standing in the doorway, Hunnie mouthed a 'hey' and rose to meet them. She led them into the hall and said, "Thanks for coming."

"How's he doing?" Hawthorn softly asked.

"Hold on there, sonny," said the sheriff, frowning, "I'm the sheriff here, better let me do the talking." The sheriff poked his head into the room, looked around, leaned back in the hall and asked "How's he doing?"

Hunnie decided to answer Hawthorn's question first, "He's doing okay; the doctors said he's got a few broken bones and some lacerations," she glanced at her father through the doorway, adding, "they think he may have gotten a concussion but, with my dad, it's hard to tell."

The sheriff shook his head, "These so-called doctors don't know what they're talking about, you'll be lucky if he makes it out of here alive."

Ignoring the sheriff, Hawthorn asked, "How did this happen?"

"According to the man who hit him, he ran out in the middle of the road swatting at a swarm of bees. The driver slammed on the brakes but still hit dad with his truck. He ran outside, loaded dad in the truck, and came here."

"If I were you, I'd lawyer up and sue the crap out of that guy!" the sheriff said.

Once again, Hunnie and Hawthorn pretended not to hear the sheriff.

"Was he stung anywhere?"

"No and he's allergic to bee stings."

"Has he been unconscious the entire time?" Hawthorn asked.

"He was awake when I first arrived but the medication has pretty much knocked him out for the night."

"Did he mention anything about the attack?"

"Not really, just kept repeating 'bees, bees' over and over again."

Faintly, from inside the shadowy room, a low, scratchy voice moaned.

"Dad?" Hunnie said, entering the bedroom. Hawthorn and the sheriff close behind. By the green glow of the bedside monitor, Mr. Combs was weakly writhing in his sleep. He reminded Hawthorn of a panicky moth caught in a spiders web. Hunnie knelt beside her father.

"Bees..." he softly said, "...bees..." he repeated,

"...computer generated bees!"

"Shhhh..." Hunnie whispered, soothingly petting his forehead, "I know, dad, I know. Dr. White is here to help."

Hawthorn took a step next to Hunnie and spoke up, "Mr. Combs, as long as I'm in town, I'll do everything I can to find out what's causing this."

"Yeah," said the sheriff, "and I've got my top man patrolling the streets for any strange bee activity."

"Dad, is there anything else we can do for you," Hunnie said, tenderly, "Can I get you anything?"

Mr. Combs raised a shaky hand into the air, "Revenge... revenge.... " he gasped and then added, *"Revenge of the Nerds 2: Nerds in Paradise."*

Having used the last of his energy, he fell back to sleep.

"What's he talking about?" the sheriff asked.

"His favorite movie," said Hunnie, she returned to her father, "I'll bring it in tomorrow, dad."

"In the meantime," the sheriff announced, hitching up his pants, "we've got to get you to a safe house."

"Why do I need a safe house?"

Hawthorn injected, "Sheriff, don't you think that's a little excessive."

"Listen, honey, in the last couple of days, *two* of your family members have gotten themselves attacked by killer bees. Now I don't know what you all did to piss 'em off; maybe your Pa stuck a M-80 in a hornets nest, I don't know, but they are clearly going after you and your family."

Hunnie shook her head, "Sheriff, that's possibly the stupidest thing I've ever heard you say....and you were my *D.A.R.E.* officer!"

"All the same, I think you should find someplace to stay for the night; Dr. Hawthorn has a room at the Cloud

7, so you stay there and he can stay with me."

"I'm pretty sure they have other rooms at that hotel," Hunnie said, holding back as much sarcasm as humanly possible. She turned to her sleeping father, gave his hand a squeeze and kissed his forehead, "Dad, I'm leaving now but I'll be back tomorrow, you take it easy and don't get into any mischief while I'm away."

She stood and walked out into the bright hallway with Hawthorn and the sheriff following.

"I'm still waiting on that phone call from your publicist," a smug voice said.

Leaning up against the wall of her father's room, Eddie Mallow stood typing on his phone.

Hunnie almost couldn't believe it.

"You!" she snarled.

Cooly, he pushed himself off the wall and stepped out to the center of the hallway. Never lifting his eyes from his phone. "So what did your crazy dad do now?"

"#@$% off! This isn't the time."

"Easy there, kitten, I'm just a humble newsman looking for a story."

"Don't you have something more important to report on? Politics or world affairs or something?"

Eddie chuckled, looking up from his phone, "Nobody really cares about that stuff, they say they do but they'd rather hear about celebrities in extraordinary circumstances."

Hawthorn calmly put himself between Hunnie and the reporter, she looked like she might spring on him at any moment.

"Ms. Combs deserves some privacy at the moment," said Hawthorn, "How did you find out about her father anyway?"

Holding up his phone, Eddie gave a big, fish-eating grin and said, "Police scanner app."

Hunnie had little patience for anyone at the moment, especially not some geek from college.

She rubbed her eyes, saying, "Sheriff Gayfeather, could you make yourself useful for once and see this man out?"

"My pleasure, come along now, how about we take a little walk and you can show me your green card," said the sheriff, grabbing Eddie by the arm and pulling him down the hallway.

"Green Card?" Eddie protested, "I'm a third generation American citizen!"

Annoyed, Hunnie looked to Hawthorn and remarked, "Can you believe that guy?"

"Which one?"

"Take your pick."

Hawthorn snickered, slightly; which, to him, was the equivalent of a loud, boisterous laugh. Upon seeing his reaction, Hunnie smirked.

"Hey," she said in a much lighter tone, "thanks for coming, I really appreciate you being here for my dad and all."

"Of course, Ms. Combs, that's what I'm here for."

"Please, call me Hunnie."

Hawthorn would have preferred not to but reluctantly said, "Alright….Hunnie."

"So, I have to ask, do you think bees are responsible for all this?"

It was a blunt yet fair question, like when an arsonist asks if something is flammable. Hawthorn wasn't quite sure how to answer. He took a moment to gather his thoughts and responded.

"At this point, I can't say one way or another; according

to your father, and the man who hit him, it was an angry swarm of bees, however, the blood test from your sister proves it was something else."

"Why are these attacks only happening to people in my family?"

"If what we're dealing with is indeed a killer swarm, then their hive is most likely close to your house."

"Do you think I should find someplace to spend the night?"

Hawthorn hated to suggest it, especially since there were so many unknown variables, but he felt a certain responsibility to her safety and decided to err on the side of caution.

"Until we have an idea of what we're dealing with, it would probably be a good idea."

"Great," said Hunnie under her breath. Now, on top of everything else, she had to find a room for the night. She didn't have any other family nearby and she certainly wasn't going to call any old friends from high school. Not now. Not after what happened. She had enough to deal with already.

With only one option left, Hunnie shrugged, "Well, guess I'll be staying at the Cloud 7 as well. You need a ride?"

CHAPTER 10

The city of Longville's only hotel went through several name changes since it was built in the 1950s. Originally The Heavenly Cloud 9 Motel was a roadside oasis for travelers until it hit hard times in the eighties and fell into disrepair. By then, it had changed ownership and was downgraded to The *Super* Cloud 8, which eventually became The Cloud 7 Hotel.

Hawthorn could almost guess the hotel's entire history just by looking at at it.

First of all, the big neon sign only *partially* worked; with only enough letters lit-up to spell 'The loud Ho'. The sign also proudly announced each room included the latest amenities such as COLOR TV, AIR-CONDITIONED, and PHONE. Near the bottom of the sign was a marquee with VVELCUM SHRIN3R5 C0NVO 97 in a mismatched array of cheap plastic letters.

Second, the two brick structures that made up the motel were obviously in terrible shape. Even in the dark, Hawthorn could tell they hadn't been maintained in decades. Each room featured either a cracked window or busted up screen door. Above every door, was a rusted aluminum awning. On the roof of the single-story building, shingles weren't so much attached as they were resting in place.

In short, it was a real dump.

The two long buildings formed an L-shape with the front office closest to the highway. Hunnie pulled her sister's pickup truck into the gravel lot and noticed an unusual number of motorcycles parked all along the front. Outside of each room, barrel-chested bikers were hanging about. Laughing and drinking as they passed from one room to the next. The gruff, chunky sound of Canada's second greatest rock band thundered in the night.

Hunnie parked the truck and accompanied Hawthorn inside the cramped, tollbooth-sized office.

At the desk stood a haggard woman with glasses and a cigarette hanging out of her mouth. She had a pleasant yet weathered face that made her look much older than she really was. On the counter, sat a partially completed jigsaw puzzle that the woman was quietly piecing together.

"What can I do for you folks?" the woman asked, not looking up from the puzzle.

"My name is Hawthorn White, I have a reservation, and we would also like a room for the lady."

The woman took out a large, black notebook and gently set it next to her puzzle. As she started flipping through the pages, Hawthorn noticed that the puzzle she was working on was a picture of an actual jigsaw power tool.

"Let's see here," she said, reaching the page she was looking for, "White.... Room 22, here we are."

She reached for the pegboard on the wall and grabbed

the only remaining set of keys.

"Unfortunately, all of our other rooms are taken," she handed the keys to Hawthorn and turned to Hunnie, a thin stream of smoke rising from her cigarette, "Hope you don't mind bunking with him tonight."

"All the rooms are taken?!" Hunnie exclaimed

"Yep."

"Who else would stay in this $#*%hole?"

"Hecks Canucks"

"What's that?"

"Canadian motorcyclists," said the hotel manager. Noticing the confused expression on her guests face, she added, "Now I know what you're thinking, and don't worry, they're actually very nice, young men."

Hawthorn wasn't so much concerned with his fellow hotel patrons as he was the sleeping arrangements.

"If we are going to be sharing a room, would it be possible for us to get a cot and some spare blankets?"

"That's okay," Hunnie said with a careless wave of her hand, "there's enough bikers here, I won't have any problem finding a bed for the night."

"Alright, whatever you say," said the manager, handing over the room key to Hawthorn, "You can find your room on the far end of the building, between twenty-one and twenty-three." She then went back to her puzzle.

Hunnie moved the vehicle to a space in front of their room and Hawthorn grabbed their luggage; one black overnight bag and a plastic sack of toiletries and clothing Hunnie picked up at the 24-hour pharmacy. Outside every room was a small porch area, which was basically a slab of concrete fenced in by decorative metal railing. Crappy metal lawn chairs were placed sporadically on some of the porches.

On either side of Room 22, leather-clad bikers sat out on their porches, talking. The bikers themselves ranged from gruff to gruesome; some had scars, most had tattoos and all but one had varying lengths of facial hair. The only one without a scruffy beard or five o'clock shadow was a leggy woman in fishnets.

She took notice of Hawthorn the moment she saw him.

As Hawthorn and Hunnie walked up to their room, the tall biker chick watched lustfully from her lawn chair on the neighboring porch. She had her legs crossed, propped up on the banister facing them.

"Hey there, handsome," she said with a sly smile.

"Evening," Hawthorn replied, unlocking the door.

"If you and your lady are looking for a good time, me and my boys can oblige."

It had been a long day. While he was open to socializing, he certainly was tired and could only assume Hunnie felt the same way. Plus, he wasn't quite sure what kind of 'good time' the woman and her companions were offering.

Hawthorn was about to politely decline but Hunnie jumped in, saying, "Thanks, we just might take you up on that!"

Hunnie, on the other hand, felt she needed a night to let loose. After all, it had been almost three days since her last bender. These Canadian Bikers looked like a wild bunch and some of them were pretty hot.

Hawthorn open the door for Hunnie and they both went inside.

As soon as Hunnie flipped on the light switch, Hawthorn was ready to leave.

The entire room had an amber tinge to it, like looking through a pair of ugly, but stylish, yellow-tinted sunglasses. All the furniture looked like it had been stolen from the dumpster of other, nicer hotels, except the mattress, which looked like it came from the side of the road. The walls, ceiling, and floor featured a wide variety of stains, chief among them was a giant inky patch above the bed that, Hawthorn could only assume, was black mold. In the air was the musty smell of beer, cigarettes and vomit.

The room reminded Hawthorn of a gas station bathroom.

"Your father certainly wasn't kidding about this place."

It reminded Hunnie of her first apartment.

"I've been in worse."

Hawthorn set their luggage on top of the particleboard desk. Just to be safe. While he was eager to see the room's entomological ecosystem, he didn't necessarily want it in their things.

"Depending on how many different species we find, I could probably write an entire dissertation on this room alone," Hawthorn joked.

"If these walls could talk..." Hunnie said, admiring the peeling, yellow wallpaper, "...they'd need some serious therapy."

Hawthorn went about inspecting the room. Opening drawers, examining bed sheets, flipping over seat cushions. All the while, wondering if sleeping in the car was a better option.

"And this is the only hotel in town?" he asked, already knowing the answer but hoping for a different response.

Unflinching, Hunnie sat on the bed, "I'm afraid so."

"Uh... I still wouldn't sit there."

Hunnie stood and swept any unseen parasites off her backside, "I don't know about you, but I could go for a drink right about now. Do you drink?"

"I've been known to have a scotch and water on occasion."

"Well, I've been known to have a lot more than that on more than one occasion."

"I suppose we could go out to a tavern, if you like."

"Naw," she abruptly said with a dismissive wave, "There's only one bar in town and, you don't want to go there, it's a real dump!"

Taking a moment to look at their current surroundings, Hawthorn said, "Worse than this?"

He had a point but Hunnie couldn't go there; the regular patrons would recognize her. It was nice to be with someone who didn't take notice of her stardom. These days, most of the people she was surrounded by were only there to help their career or get free tickets to the Grammys. But here, in this crappy motel, in this crappy town, she could hang out with some people who had never heard of her or her poppy brand of music.

The muffled sound of the party next door rumbled through the walls.

"What'd you say we meet the neighbors?" Hunnie said with a smirk.

On the other side of the wall, beer-soaked bikers were having the time of their lives. Those who weren't drinking, were dancing. Those who weren't dancing, were telling biker stories. Those who weren't doing any of those things, were going around giving people high fives.

Hunnie and Hawthorn stood in the open doorway and

were immediately greeted by the one high-five guy.

"Give me five, brother!"

Hesitatingly, Hawthorn raised his hand. The biker enthusiastically slapped his open palm, laughed like it was the funniest thing in the world, then galloped to the next group of people to do the exact same thing.

As he ran away, Hunnie caught a glimpse of the giant patch on the back of his vest. At the top, in big bold letters, were the words, HECKS CANUCKS. Underneath that, inside a big flaming-red maple leaf, was a devil dressed as a lumberjack, holding a flaming pitchfork/hockey stick. Scrolled across the bottom were the words VANCOUVER, BC.

From the other side of the room, the tall leggy woman who had invited them waved and called out, "Hey! Come on in, Yanks!"

Hunnie and Hawthorn made their way through the crowded room to greet their hostess who was drinking with two other guys in the corner. Hawthorn wasn't used to being around so many people; he was very careful not to bump into anyone and made sure to say 'pardon me' as often as possible. Hunnie didn't really care how many people she unintentionally groped; she wedged through the crowd like an icebreaker ship cutting through frozen waters.

Once they had reached the biker chick, she shouted over the rowdy music, "Glad you made it!"

"Thanks for the invite!" Hunnie shouted back.

"Let's get you some beers," she turned her attention to a big, bald guy standing next to the dresser, "Yo, Jack," she yelled, "Grab us a couple of Mooseheads, will ya?"

The man aped a salute and reached into the cooler atop the chest of drawers.

Returning to Hunnie and Hawthorn, the motorcycle madame introduced herself, "I'm Slayer…." she gestured to a stocky man next to her and a mustachioed man next to him, "….this is Axel, that's Maurice….."

The shorter man named Axel simply nodded while Maurice stroked his horseshoe mustache and said, "*Bonsoir*," giving Hunnie a wink.

Behind Hunnie and Hawthorn, the giant bald man by the cooler appeared with beers in hand. Hunnie immediately grabbed hers and popped it open, Hawthorn carefully took his and held it awkwardly.

"And this guy here," Slayer said, pointing to the large bald man, "we call Gassy Jack."

Hawthorn began to ask Gassy Jack, "How did you get that name?" but found himself being interrupted by an ear-deafening belch that rattled the windows, shook the walls, and smelled like fermented meat. The belch was so loud that everyone in the room fell momentarily quiet, only to raise their beers and cheer after he had finished.

"That…" said Hunnie, searching for the right words, "….was disgusting."

"Thanks," Gassy Jack said proudly.

The man known as Maurice shook his head, "*Tu me dégoûtes.*"

"He can also belch all one hundred fourteen elements of the periodic table," Slayer bragged.

"Actually…" interjected Hawthorn, "…there are one hundred eighteen now; Tennessine, Nihonium, Moscovium, and Oganesson."

Slayer raised her brow and nodded, "Sounds like you're pretty smart."

"He better be," said Hunnie, "he's a scientist."

"Oh yeah? What kind of science do you do?"

"Entomology.... I study insects."

"No way, I love insects!" Slayer said, turning her back to the group and lowering her jacket, "Check it out." Moving the shoulder strap of her tank top out of the way, she showed off the coolest tattoo Hunnie had ever seen.

On her left shoulder, a praying mantis was making a totally sick jump on a skateboard. It was wearing sunglasses and a backwards baseball cap. Around its neck, swinging in mid-air, was a gold chain with a big, diamond-encrusted cross at the end. In one arm, the mantis held a pair of nunchucks and, in the other, an electric guitar. The entire thing was engulfed in flames.

Hunnie already had three tattoos of her own but seeing the lady biker's made her want to get another one. Maybe a rose on her ankle.

Hawthorn leaned in for a closer examination. Despite the many scientific inaccuracies, he was impressed by the artistry of the tattoo.

"Looks to be the species of *mantis religiosa*," he said, "I've been conducting a research study with them in the lab."

Slayer spun around, her curly, black hair brushing against Hawthorn's face, and winked. "If you like that, you should see the cockroach I have on my inner thigh!"

Hawthorn wasn't positive but he was pretty sure he was being flirted with.

Some of the other bikers heard talk of Hawthorn's profession and joined the group.

"Hey, Bugman," said one of the bikers, "can you tell me what bit me last night?" Shoving his hairy, beefy arm in front of Hawthorn's face.

"Yeah, and what kind of critters do I have living in my beard?" another biker said, pushing his way forward.

"There's a wasp nest in my tailpipe," said one, scratching himself, "Also, I slept with this lady trucker and now I got ants in my pants."

"Those probably aren't ants," Hawthorn replied.

"Hey, fellas, give Bugman some space, huh?" Slayer interjected, putting herself between Hawthorn and her compadres, "He's here to party, not solve all your gross hygiene problems."

"Yeah, he ain't even had a drink yet!" stocky Axel said, pointing at his beer.

"Come on, Bugman, join the party!" Hunnie yelled from the back.

Hawthorn wasn't the biggest fan of cheap domestic beer. He'd much rather have a Dirty Martini or Hot Toddy, but he knew that wouldn't be an option with this particular crowd. They were a rough and rowdy bunch and, at this point, they were all chanting 'Bugman' over and over again. Hawthorn had taken enough cultural anthropology courses to know the social significance of this particular moment. These people were initiating him into their tribe, it would be rude of him to decline.

With a half-hearted shrug, Hawthorn opened the can of beer and took a small sip. The room exploded.

Amongst the cheers, Hunnie was getting better acquainted with Maurice. Or at least as well acquainted as the circumstances allowed. Having already downed her first drink, Hunnie was escorted to the cooler by Maurice who handed her another beer.

"Thanks!"

Hunnie pointed to Maurices bare, hairy chest where a grimy necklace was proudly on display, "I like your Iron Cross."

"*J'aime tesgros seins,*"

Slightly bewildered, she nodded, "Oh, okay."

There was something about the biker that Hunnie found alluring. Maybe it was the way the oil glistened on his face, or maybe it was that he apparently didn't speak English, but Hunnie found him different from all the other guys she'd dated recently. Her last boyfriend was a fussy backup dancer and her boyfriend before that was a washed up rock star who believed in aliens.

She had been out in Hollywood for so long, she almost forgot what a real bad boy looked like.

"*Je bande pour toi*," the French-Canadian said, taking her by the hand.

"I have *no* idea what you just said but it sounded beautiful."

Guiding Hunnie, they made their way to the front door, brushing past every bulky, sweaty body.

Over the noise of the crowd, Maurice stated, "*Allons quelque part moins bruyant.*"

"Whatever," snickered Hunnie as they exited through the front door. With everything that had happened in the last few days, Hunnie could use a good time.

Outside, right next to the half-lit Cloud 7 Motel sign, an intrepid, young "reporter" lurked in the bushes. Having followed Hunnie to the seedy motel, Eddie Mallow was patiently lying in wait for something to happen. Preferably something borderline scandalous he could sell.

He had seen Hunnie check in with the handsome, young doctor but couldn't figure out the low-light settings on his camera in time. Briefly, Eddie considered snooping up to their window but noticed all the rowdy bikers wandering about and decided against it. So for the last forty minutes, he had been crouched down on his hindquarters, silently watching.

All was quiet. Except for the loud, obnoxious party inside. From the parking lot Eddie could only see silhouettes passing in front of brightly lit windows with the occasional biker stumbling outside to puke or take a leak. It was a cold, dark, chilly night but Eddie's determination kept him warm (that and his favorite studded denim jacket he found at a thrift store).

The hotel room door opened and Eddie spotted Hunnie walk out in the company of a haggard biker. They were holding hands.

Scrambling for his camera, Eddie briefly lost his balance, falling headlong into the bushes. Cursing under his breath, he pulled himself upright and aimed his camera towards Hunnie on the front porch. Switching the camera to video mode, he pressed record. By the yellow glow of the porch light, the man took a seat on a patio chair with Hunnie taking a seat on his lap.

Then they started making out like teenagers at the type of parties Eddie never got invited to.

Excitedly, Eddie zoomed in on the couple as tight as he could. They were all over each other. Kissing, groping, hugging. It was disgusting but impossible to look away, like watching a naked conga line. Eddie was so mesmerized by their alcohol-fueled embrace that he didn't notice the dark figure headed towards him.

In the parking lot, one of the drunk bikers stumbled his way to the bushes. He was a heavyset gentleman with a bottle of Canadian whiskey in one hand and a bottle of pure maple syrup in the other. Both nearly empty. As he shuffled through the gravel, he softly sang to himself, pausing only to take a swig from one bottle and then the other.

While Eddie was determined to keep filming Hunnie and her male companion, he suddenly found his shot blocked by an enormous, hairy potbelly. Eddie froze, daring not to breathe. If the biker looked down, he would have seen a frightened little man crouching in the bushes. But, luckily for Eddie, the biker seemed distracted by the stars in the evening sky.

Unfortunately for Eddie, he'd have to stay in the bushes until after the man left.

The man towered over Eddie, swaying back and forth in the breeze, looking as if he could topple at any moment. He took a deep breath and swallowed back vomit. His arms listlessly holding a bottle on either side.

Letting the empty bottles clink to the ground, the biker proceeded to unbutton his pants right in front of the terrified paparazzo. Eddie closed his eyes tightly and wished he could be literally anywhere else at the moment.

Eddie then felt a hot stream of unpleasantness shower over his face, neck and vintage jacket.

CHAPTER 11

Hawthorn woke up feeling like he had spent the night nuzzled between a wet dog and a sick hobo.

Blinded by sunlight streaming across his face, Hawthorn rolled over and felt nauseous. The pillow underneath his head didn't feel like his own; his was soft and fluffy, this one felt like insulation wrapped in plastic. He then noticed that the entire bed didn't feel like his own; the mattress was way too springy and the covers were way too crunchy. Hawthorn wasn't in his comfortable bed at home. He was at cheap motel in Longville, Missouri.

He was thirsty. Incredibly thirsty. Hawthorn figured he must have slept with his mouth open. That would explain the dry mouth, but he didn't feel much like getting up. The room was a little swirly, like he was on a raft, floating in the middle of a hurricane.

Hawthorn couldn't remember the last time he had gotten so drunk. Maybe at Science Mardi Gras. That was in grad school, of course. The last thing he remembered about last night was being held upside down by his ankles, bikers cheering him on to guzzle beer out of a plastic funnel.

Why had he done that?

He remembered the biker woman asking him if he was acrobatic in the bedroom and then one of the guys asked him if he could do a headstand. Next thing he knew, a dirty automotive funnel was being shoved in his mouth and a tidal wave of beer came rushing down his gullet.

Things got a little foggy after that.

As he lay there, trying to remember what else happened, he noticed the soft breathing of someone else in the room. Someone lying right beside him. He slowly turned his head to find a naked woman sleeping in the shadows; a tattoo of a praying mantis surfing was displayed on the woman's bare shoulder.

Hawthorn certainly didn't have any recollection of *this* happening.

While Hawthorn had undeniably had his share of "intimate relations" with the fairer sex, they were few and far between. Usually, he was too busy in the lab to have time for a relationship. He never engaged in one night stands and especially not with wild, biker women he had just met that night.

He again thought back to the party, Slayer *had* been rather flirty with him. Hawthorn had commented that he thought Slayer was traditionally a boy's name to which, she responded, "It's short for Slaying Mantis." Seductively adding, "Because I mate, then I kill!"

Hawthorn then went into a detailed, slightly slurred, description of how various insects mate.

"Come here," she interrupted, pulling him aside by the collar, "I want to show you the rest of my tattoos." She then dragged him by the arm outside. He remembered passing Hunnie on the porch, who was busy making out with two other guys. Slayer lead him to his room and practically kicked the door down, leading him in.

Before he knew it, he was pinned against the bed, being sloppily kissed by the increasingly attractive biker. Her smoky tongue slithering over his. Her long legs, wrapped tightly around his waist. Her skintight, leather pants rubbing up against the crotch of his classic fit, polyester/cotton blend khakis.

And then she screwed his brains out. It had been so long since his last time with a woman, he had almost forgotten what it felt like. It felt good.

However, he was in no way ready for a committed relationship. He had too much work to do in life. Plus, he was in the middle of an important case: find the alleged bees that have been terrorizing the community.

Faintly, Hawthorn looked at his watch. It was already 2:45. He and Slayer must have *really* humped the night away!

He had little recollection of it happening, just brief flashes of tattoos on various body parts; a monarch butterfly boxing a bee on her lower back, an imperial moth knitting across her chest, and an upside down cockroach smoking a joint on her inner thigh (to name a few).

In any case, it happened and Hawthorn had to get up, find Hunnie, and get back to work. He slowly pushed himself up onto his elbows, being careful not to wake Slayer or puke all over the sheets. Hawthorn noticed that he was completely naked. Looking to the floor, he saw an intermingled pile of his and Slayer's clothes.

Reaching down from the edge of the bed, the naked scientist nearly fell to the floor. He balanced himself with his hands and began digging through the untidy mound. Slacks. Panties. Shirt. Pants. Socks. Tank top. Another Sock. Leather jacket. Shoes.

No boxers.

Where was his underwear?

Hawthorn took a moment to sit back and scan over the dark corners of the room. Then, he spotted them. A pair of plaid boxer shorts hanging from the bedside lamp next to Slayer. At first, he was hesitant to grab them, in fear that he would wake her up. But then he thought of Hunnie and her father in the hospital and found his resolve.

As slowly and carefully as he could move, Hawthorn scooted across the bed until he was almost touching Slayer. Gradually distributing all his weight into the arm closest to her, Hawthorn pushed himself up, hand sinking into the mattress, and arched his naked body over the sleeping woman. Stretching his arm out as far as he could until his fingertips were touching the waistband. Fortunately, years of practicing yoga had given Hawthorn great flexibility and control over his body.

Having taken hold of his underwear, he lifted it off the lampshade and smoothly lowered himself back to his side of the bed. Hawthorn let out a silent sigh of relief and took a moment to rest. Changing his position, he let his legs slide off the mattress and stood up.

His head was swimming and he could feel his pulse throb through his brain, but he was able to keep his equilibrium. Holding on to the nightstand for support, he fumbled with his boxers until he was able to pull them up around his ankles. Only realizing they were on backwards after he had already put them on.

"Morning, babe," a sultry voice said behind him, "I can

see your pooper."

Clenching up the fly of his boxers, Hawthorn spun around, nearly losing his balance. Slayer, who looked well rested and satisfied, lay stretched out across the bed, propping her head up with her hand.

"Looks like you could use some breakfast," she said with a smirk.

Just the thought of food made Hawthorn want to throw up.

He swallowed and said, "I think it's a little late for that."

"What time is it?"

"A quarter to three."

"Fine." Slayer said, getting up and letting the sheet fall to the floor, "We can grab an early lunch."

Even though he had already seen every inch of Slayer's naked body, Hawthorn felt compelled to avert his eyes.

"I think I'll hold off on eating, for now," he said, rubbing his temples.

"Aww, you not feeling good?" she said, walking round the bed and tenderly holding her toned body against his, "I'll tell you what, you stay here and rest and I'll bring you back a beer and some of Gassy Jack's homemade moose jerky."

Hawthorn's stomach churned at the thought, "I don't believe that'll cure my hangover."

"Sure it will! Bite of the dog that bit ya'!"

"Isn't it hair of the dog?"

"Whatever it is, it'll do you some good, but we can't stay for long. We gotta hit the road soon," Slayer said, bending over and collecting her clothes.

Once again, Hawthorn got a whole eyeful of Slayer. He looked away, but not because he didn't like what he saw.

Instead, he chose to stare at something that wouldn't get him aroused.

"Where were you planning on going after this?" he asked a crooked painting of a clown.

Slayer had started putting on clothes, setting Hawthorn's on the bed. "Wherever the open road takes us," she said, adding, "This is our summer, don't cha know?"

In turn, Hawthorn began putting on his clothes, wondering what he had gotten himself into. While he wasn't well-versed in their social mores, he had seen a documentary once on Cinemax about marital relations between bikers. Personally, it didn't seem like his cup of Earl Grey.

"Listen, Slayer," he said, trying to think of how to let her down easy, "I had a good time last night and you seem like a very.... stout-hearted woman but I don't think I could be your "old lady," or whatever the male equivalent to that is."

Slayer had put on her pants and tank top and had begun tying the laces on her boots when she had to take a moment and chuckle at Hawthorn's suggestion.

"Bugman, you're a funny guy and I love ya' but you're a little square for my tastes. Don't get me wrong, you're a freak in the sheets, but I've got a career and can't afford to get tied down."

Hawthorn felt a sense of relief. While there was a part of him that was curious about the vagabond life of a biker, he was glad he didn't have to make that decision. Before he could figure out a proper response, there was a knock at the door.

Opening the door, Hawthorn was temporarily blinded by the bright afternoon sun. Hunnie stood before him in the same clothes from last night; blue jean jacket, maroon v-neck t-shirt and black pants. She looked disheveled but pretty, like Miss America after riding a broken roller coaster.

"Hey, can I watch your TV?"

Remorsefully, Hawthorn glanced at Slayer, "Actually, can you give us a…."

"Thanks!" Hunnie barged in, "Axle broke the one next door."

"Well, hey there, girly!" Slayer excitingly said, "I was hoping you'd come by."

Hunnie went straight for the remote resting on the nightstand and turned on the ancient television set. Sitting down on the bed, she started flipping through channels.

Slayer approached Hawthorn at the door and said, "I'm going to grab us some grub." Looking back at Hunnie, she added, "But when I come back you and I can talk about doing a Hot Banana Split with this lucky bastard."

As soon as Slayer had left the room, Hawthorn asked, "What's a Hot Banana Split?"

"I can take a guess," Hunnie said, frantically changing channels.

Just as Hawthorn was about to ask what program she was looking for, Hunnie settled on a brightly colored screen, with the letters FSR flashing across in big, loud text.

The video then cut to, what looked like, a newsroom full of the most casually dressed reporters Hawthorn had ever seen. Everyone in the office was young and wearing shorts or jeans. In front of them all was a tiny, leathery-faced, muscular guy holding a comically large travel mug. Leaning over a cubicle wall, he asked the room, "What's the buzz on Hunnie Combs?"

Hawthorn was surprised to hear her name on television. He glanced at Hunnie, who was sitting on the edge of the bed. Transfixed.

The video cut to a man with a goatee and newsboy cap, leaning back in an office chair, "So Hunnie Combs has been spending the week in her home state of Missouri because of a "family emergency" but the thing is, last night, she was spotted partying it up at a hotel with some bikers."

The room pretended to act shocked, some gasped and one person exclaimed 'WHAT?!'

Up front, the tiny muscular man said, "Wait, so what was the family emergency?"

"Her sister died."

People in the office responded with overly-judgmental disgust.

"And she's already out partying with a bunch of bikers?" said the man sitting in front.

Jarringly, the video cut to shaky, low-res footage of Hunnie out on the hotel porch, passionately kissing the mustachioed biker from last night. On top of this video, the most annoying voiceover in the world loudly announced, "Losing family is tough, at least Hunnie's found a *bee*-reavement support group!"

Cutting to the office, the man in the newsboy cap declared, "That's not all, she was seen making out with one of the biker dudes and then started sucking face with anyone who stopped by!"

The screen then flashed back to the hotel footage; while Hunnie was busy kissing one biker, another walked up and said something. The video then cut to her kissing the other biker while the first one watched. Once again, another biker showed up, said something, and Hunnie jumped into his beefy arms.

"Hunnie bunches of gross!" said one of the people in the office.

"Un-bee-lievable!" said another.

The guy in the newsboy cap continued, "So after about ten minutes of making out, Hunnie went inside with the guys and had an all night orgy."

As the television cut to footage of Hunnie leading the bikers inside, Hunnie looked to Hawthorn and exclaimed, "It wasn't an orgy, I only made out with, like six guys!"

It didn't matter to Hawthorn, he didn't think any less of her one way or the other. Hawthorn found human sexual preferences to be as wild and diverse as those in the animal kingdom. If a gamma male stag beetle can assume the female role and mate with both sexes, then Hunnie could certainly sleep with six bikers if she so desired.

Back on the tv, the entire office was braying like jackasses at a state fair.

Someone scoffed, "Talk about Easy Rider."

Another sneered, "More like Sleazy Rider!'

Over a still photo of Hunnie, the annoying voiceover said, "Let's just hope she's keeping her Hunnie Pot clean!"

Angrily, Hunnie flipped off the tv and then turned it off.

Taking a moment to let her frustrations pass, Hunnie sighed, "At least this will be good for my public image."

"How?" Hawthorn asked, taking a seat on the bed furthest from her, "I don't know much about Hollywood, but I would think this type of negative press would be bad for your image."

Hunnie chuckled and shook her head, "Publicity is

weird like that."

"I didn't realize you were even a celebrity."

"Yeah, it's kind of my claim to fame."

Ignoring the perplexing statement, Hawthorn asked, "How long have you been famous?

"About as long as I've been sharing my music online."

"Do you like it, being famous?"

"It's okay. I'm doing what I love and it beats working for a living," Hunnie said, staring contemplatively at her reflection in the black television screen, "Being a celebrity is kind of a performance art that's hard to turn off."

Hawthorn found himself fascinated by this new side of Hunnie. He had never known anyone famous. The closest Hawthorn had come to meeting a celebrity was when Dr. Michael Engel gave a dissertation on the giant fleas of Mesozoic era China.

Placing her hands on her knees, Hunnie hoisted herself off the bed.

"I don't know about you, but I feel dirty," she said ruffling her frizzy hair, "Think I'll take a shower."

Hunnie grabbed her makeshift overnight bag and began to take a shower.

The bathroom was gross; fossilized grime between every tile, stray strands of stranger's hair clustered in the corners, and a permanent poop ring round the toilet and bathtub. But it was still better than the rest of the room.

Upon turning on the water, the shower head started shaking violently before shooting out spurts of reddish brown water. Eventually, a steady stream of clear water flowed from the rusty shower head and Hunnie deemed it clean enough for use. She disrobed and step in.

The water wasn't nearly as scaldingly hot as Hunnie

preferred but it was still a few degrees warmer than room temp. Hunnie had decided not to wash her hair today and had put it in a ponytail. Even though it could use a rinse, it still looked hella good and she wanted to save washing it for someplace cleaner than a scuzzy motel bathroom.

Nevertheless, it felt good to wash her face and body. Refreshing. As long as she didn't think too much about the brown ring around the tub. She closed her eyes and just let the lukewarm water flow over her.

Over the rushing water, she could faintly hear Hawthorn talking in the bedroom. He had said that he needed to call work and see what the next step would be; whether he should stay in town and continue his fieldwork or go back to the college and run tests on the recovered stinger.

Hunnie hoped he didn't have to go.

Taking the bottle of shower gel, Hunnie squeezed some of the mango flavored body wash into her hand and began rubbing it all over her supple skin and boobs. Absentmindedly, she started humming a song from the *13 Going on 30* movie soundtrack. Unaware that she was not alone.

Up on the ceiling, a single bumblebee was cramming its body through the aluminum grille of the ventilation fan. Its small legs struggled getting traction across the rusted metal surface. Once it popped its fat abdomen out, the bee began erratically circling above.

Soon, another tiny head popped out of the vent. And another. And another. Some struggling to fit through the slits, others walking straight through. All of them leaping out into the foggy bathroom. Wings a'buzzin'.

Distracted by the noise of rushing water and deep in her own shower thoughts, Hunnie didn't notice the little black silhouettes flying on the other side of the plastic curtain. The room quickly filled up as bees trickled out of the vent overhead. A couple of the bees ventured over the shower curtain, flying as close to the ceiling as humanly possible. Gradually, they were joined by a couple dozen more. Collectively swarming directly above the young, sexy, naked woman's head.

Finally sensing that something was amiss, Hunnie cast her eyes to the ceiling.

"OH, $#*%!"

CHAPTER 12

While Hunnie was in the shower, Hawthorn had made a call to his boss at State Fair College. According to Tom, the school needed Hawthorn to come back immediately. Still feeling a bit woozy, Hawthorn sat on the bed, phone in hand.

"Tom, I can't leave now. I've barely scratched the surface of what's causing these attacks."

He paused and let the department head respond.

"I'm not even sure they are bees," Hawthorn said, looking at his reflection in the hotel mirror, "That's why I need more time out in the field."

Hawthorn examined himself in the mirror, politely waiting for his boss' reply. He looked rough; his hair was a mess, his face was shrouded with stubble, and his dress shirt was wrinkled and untucked. From the bathroom, he could hear Hunnie singing in the shower. She did have a lovely voice. Hawthorn could understand why she was a professional vocalist.

Hawthorn responded, "Tell me, what's so urgent that you need me back so soon?"

He listened to his boss' answer and said,

"Theoretically, yes, a stink bug can be genetically engineered to smell like your wife's favorite perfume but I fail to see why I this should take top priority."

His boss' reason wasn't the most honorable but at least it was honest.

"Well, perhaps it's time to stop cheating on Judy," Hawthorn suggested.

All of a sudden, Hawthorn heard Hunnie screaming in the bathroom.

"I've got to go.'"

Hanging up the phone, Hawthorn sprang into action but was quickly slowed down by his hangover. He felt like he had been hit by a drunk fish. Reaching out for balance, he steadied himself against the wall and staggered towards the bathroom as fast as he could. Knocking down wall paintings as he went.

Over the sound of rushing water, Hawthorn could hear an electric buzzing from inside the bathroom.

"Is everything alright in there?" he said, resting his body against the doorframe.

"Oh.... I'm just dandy," she said with a pause, " would you come in here, please!"

From the tone in her voice, Hawthorn could tell something was wrong. Slowly, he opened the door and was astonished to find the bathroom full of bees! Hundreds and hundreds of bees! Hawthorn was struck by how many different species were swarming together in one place. Carpenter bees, sweat bees, honey bees, he even spotted some hornets and yellow jackets in there. Hawthorn had never seen anything like it before. Typically, insects didn't set aside their differences for a common goal; especially not mortal enemies like wasps and bees.

Hunnie was crouched down in the bathtub, trying to cover herself with the shower curtain. The swarm seemed to be staying away from the water shooting out of the shower head. Which was good, since Hunnie was staying directly under the jetting water. While she certainly looked frightened, more than anything else, Hunnie appeared to be annoyed.

"Well? Any suggestions?"

Hawthorn was at a loss. Fortunately, the bees either hadn't taken notice of him or didn't care. He searched the room for resources, saw the overhead vent and flipped the switch to the bathroom fan; this would at least keep anything else from coming in. The bathroom fan roared to life and effectively did nothing.

Undaunted, the bees continued to swarm.

"Okay, good," Hunnie remarked, "anymore ideas?"

Much to her surprise, Hawthorn rushed out of the bathroom, slamming the door behind him.

She sat awkwardly, crouched in the tub. The bees gradually descending, ever closer. Hunnie Combs could already picture the headlines of her somewhat ironic death: DIRTY GIRL KILLED IN BATHTUB.

Swiftly, Hawthorn burst through the door. Holding a comforter over his head and waving around a loaded hairdryer, Hunnie could tell he meant business....what business exactly, she couldn't say.

"I already don't like this plan," Hunnie commented.

Bending low to the floor, Hawthorn sidestepped towards the shower. Holding the hairdryer up, Hawthorn turned it on full blast and blew away any bees that came close. In a loud, clear voice he said, "When I say so, join me under the cover and we'll make a run for it."

The bees were buzzing more fiercely now; swarming

near Hawthorn and bouncing off his bedspread. He felt like he was in one of those plexiglass money blowing machines, where someone had replaced the swirling cash with deadly bees! Through the chaos, Hawthorn and Hunnie made eye contact and shared a breath.

"Now!"

Leaping out of the shower, Hunnie slid across the bathroom floor before being caught by Hawthorn. He took the naked popstar under the cover and hustled her out of the bathroom. Using the screaming hairdryer to drive a path through the bees. As soon as their feet touched the bedroom carpeting, they ran for the front door, only to be yanked back by the hair dryer cord. Falling backwards, Hawthorn and Hunnie hit the floor, hard. The comforter settled on top of them, covering them from head to toe.

It was dark underneath the thick comforter and Hawthorn and Hunnie could already hear the bees hovering above. Tiny stingers began poking through the bedspread. Hawthorn adjusted his position; lying on his back and tucking his legs in, so that only the soles of his shoes were holding up the comforter. Hunnie curled up into a ball so that no part of her stark naked body was touching the bedspread. Unfortunately, it wouldn't take long for the bees to find their way underneath.

If Hunnie and Hawthorn weren't hiding in terror, they would have seen Slayer walk in with Maurice and Gassy Jack.

"Here it is, y'all," Slayer announced, holding up a bag of moose jerky and a six-pack of beer, "the breakfast of.... " she stopped at the sight of angry bees attacking her one-time lover and acquaintance.

"Bugman!" yelled Slayer.

"*Mi amor!*" cried Maurice.

"BrUUUUUAAAAAHHH!" belched Gassy Jack in terror.

The three bikers rushed to their friends aide. Gassy Jack grabbed the nearest object he could find, in this case a cheap hotel lamp, and began to swing wildly at the bees. Maurice, taking out his trusty switchblade, started slashing vigorously at the swarm. Meanwhile, Slayer helped the blanketed mass of Hawthorn and Hunnie to their feet and led them out the door.

"We gotta get you out of here!" said Slayer, shoving them out onto the front porch. The air was cold, even underneath the encrusted comforter, but the bright sunshine made it feel a bit warmer. Slayer tossed the blanket off of Hawthorn and examined his face, neck and arms. Hunnie took the remaining bedspread and wrapped it around her nakedness. "Are you guys okay?" Slayer asked, completing her examination of Hawthorn and turning her attention towards Hunnie. Peeking under the comforter, Slayer got an eyeful of Hunnie's exquisite breasts and glanced back at Hawthorn, "Wow, you didn't waste any time!"

The brief moment of levity was interrupted by a blood-curdling burp from inside the room. Slayer, who was already facing the scene, said, "*Chit.*" Hawthorn and Hunnie turned around to see the horror within.

Splayed out across the floor, Maurice lay covered head-to-toe with vengeful bees. Every inch of his body was crawling with a multitude of black and yellow striped dots. Stinging him without mercy. While he desperately tried to swat them away, the giant Gassy Jack was stumbling about in a thick haze of flying insects. Gassy Jack shrieked as the bees entered his mouth and stabbed his gums like a bunch of miniaturized dentists with jet packs.

"Damnit, I hate it when this happens!" said Slayer, referring to the time Gassy Jack got his head stuck in a bee hive.

Gassy Jack fell to the floor, writhing in pain next to Maurice. All that Hawthorn, Hunnie, and Slayer could do was watch in horror. Hawthorn's mind was racing, trying to think of ways to deal with the vicious swarm but nothing was coming up. He was transfixed by the grisly scene in front of him; it was like watching a couple breakup in public, tragic but impossible to look away.

As the two insect shrouded bikers began to lose strength, a number of bees started taking flight; swarming just above the injured men. At first it was only a few dozen but soon almost half the swarm was airborne. The ever expanding cloud of bees slowly set in motion towards the wide open door.

Slayer lunged for the door and slammed it shut. Just in time, too. If she had waited a second longer the bees would have gone through the doorway. "Well, what now?" she asked.

Turning to Hawthorn, Hunnie said, "You're the scientist, do something!"

Gathering his thoughts, Hawthorn calmly replied, "First, we've got to get those men to a hospital, then I need to see the sheriff at once."

"How are we going to them out of there?"

"One sec.," Slayer said, hopping over the waist-high metal railing to the neighboring porch. She swung open the front door and yelled, "Get your asses out here, Maurice and Jack are in trouble!"

Moments later, a half dozen Hecks Canucks came running out of the room. Following Slayer's lead, they all jumped over the metal divider, joining Hunnie and Hawthorn on the front porch. All followed Slayer except Axel, who ran down the length of the motel, banging on doors, yelling, "Rumble!"

Everywhere, bikers leapt out of their rooms, ready to fight. Soon the entire gang was gathered round Slayer.

"Okay, dudes, we got a situation on our hands," said Slayer, addressing the crowd, "Some punk-ass bees attacked our friends here and now two of our own are hurt. We need to go in there, grab Maurice and Jack and teach those little flying pricks not to mess with Hecks Canucks! Am I right?"

Among the cheering bikers, Hawthorn and Hunnie could barely be heard, saying, "No," and "That's a terrible idea!"

Grabbing hold of the door handle, Slayer shouted, "Now let's go kick some ass!" and opened the door.

The revved up bikers gave a yell and flooded into the room, nearly knocking over Slayer who was waving them in; for some, she slapped on the back, for others, she slapped on the butt. Hawthorn and Hunnie stood safely out of the way, they could already hear the angry buzz of a thousand bees clashing with the drunken battle cry of Canadian bikers. As soon as the last remaining biker passed Slayer, she turned to them and said, "Don't worry, this won't take long,"

"Slayer, wait!" Hunnie cried, "Could you grab my car keys while you're in there?"

With a smirk and a nod, Slayer said, "You got it," and closed the door behind her.

The sound of chaos erupted from inside the room; yelling followed by the occasional crashing of broken furniture. In the background, the sound of relentless buzzing. On the porch, Hawthorn and Hunnie stood awkwardly in waiting. Hunnie felt like Hawthorn was staring and silently judging her.

"What?" she said.

"I didn't say anything."

"We need my car to get to the sheriff, right?"

"We do."

"And it's not like you have a car we can take."

"Correct."

"So don't look at me like that."

"I wasn't but I understand."

"Okay, then."

Abruptly, the front door open just wide enough for Slayer to peek her head out. Behind her, the brawl between bikers and bees raged on. "Where are they?"

"Oh, um, they should be on the nightstand."

"Already checked."

"And they weren't on the table?"

"Nope," she said, casually swatting away a killer bee by her face.

"Okay, uh, they might be on the chair, maybe sunk in between the cushions."

"Okay," Slayer said slamming the door.

A few more moments passed. All Hawthorn and Hunnie could hear were screams and the terrible hum of irate insects. Through the window, the curtain was being thrashed about by the unseen violence inside.

The front door open again and an out-of-breath Slayer poked her head through the crack, "Not there either." Her hair was frazzled, her clothes were torn and she appeared to have pinpricks across her face and neck.

"Did you look underneath the furniture?" Hunnie asked, "They may have gotten kicked under something."

"Already checked."

"You know, they're probably in my purse if you just want to bring me that."

"You got it."

Again the door was shut and a little while became an eternity; like when a commercial against animal cruelty comes on and no matter how many times you change the channel, it's still on when you turn it back. The racket inside seemed to die down; only a few were left screaming and it didn't sound like there was as much movement within. Still, the omnipresent buzz continued. Now more pronounced.

The front door slowly open and a weak, shaky arm held out Hunnie's black leather handbag. Slayer was in rough shape; all the color from her face was drained, save for the tiny red pinpricks all over, her skin was deathly white, and her eyes were half open and lifeless.

"Here....you....go...." she said, weakly handing Hunnie the purse before collapsing in the middle of the doorway. Face down on the ground, she cast her eyes skyward and croaked out, "Go!" For a second, her entire body tensed up; eyes tightly shut, teeth clenched, shoulders raised. Then with a long, labored breath, her body relaxed and she was gone.

Even though it wasn't his fault, Hawthorn couldn't help but feel responsible. If he had only kept his wits about him, he could have thought of better way to deal with the invading swarm. Instead he froze up and let a woman he had been intimate with die. Fortunately, he was carrying a little memento of their romantic encounter and would be reminded of her every time it itched.

Hunnie also couldn't help but feel somewhat

responsible. After all, it was her car keys that Slayer died looking for. Hunnie had never seen someone die before her eyes, it looked painful. She didn't like it. Slayer was a good person, she didn't deserve to die this way. None of the bikers did.

Yet, here they were. A hotel room full of dead or dying bikers, many of which Hunnie had made out with the night before. Littered across the floor like a bunch of jocks after a wild night of studying. And everywhere above the horrific scene, bees flew in a chaotic frenzy.

Recognizing that a path outside was now open, the bees regrouped into a single, massive cloud and made for the door. Cursing, Hunnie tried to slam the door shut but Slayer's body was in the way. Hawthorn grabbed Hunnie by the waist and thrust her into the parking lot, just as the swarm reached the open door.

Hawthorn expected to see the Combs' maroon truck still parked out front but in place of the four-door pickup was just another motorcycle. "Where's the truck?" he asked.

Hunnie, trying her best to run in nothing but a comforter, said, "This way!"

Hawthorn saw the direction she was headed and spotted the car, which was now parked on the far side of the motel, next to the main office. He made a run for it, passing by Hunnie who was taking small, tentative steps. The jagged gravel underneath her bare feet had slowed her down to a crawl.

Wincing with each step, Hunnie could hear the approaching bees and cursed under her breath.

"Don't wait for me or anything," she called out to Hawthorn who was less than a ten yards from the truck.

Hawthorn stopped in his tracks and looked back, he

was about equidistant from Hunnie as he was from the car. The bees, however, were out in the open and closing in on Hunnie fast!

Kicking up gravel and dust, Hawthorn sprinted to Hunnie. It was going to be close. The cloud of bees was becoming larger and individual drones were becoming more well-defined. As soon as he reached Hunnie, he swept her off her bare feet and hurriedly carried her away. She was light as a feather but the bedspread she was wrapped in was bulky and awkward.

With the deafening sound of bees buzzing in his ears and the car a good fifteen yards away, Hawthorn had to ask, "Why did you move it?"

"Late night taco run," Hunnie yelled over the noise, "Axel took my spot."

Hawthorn hiked up Hunnie and pushed forward. They would need time to actually get in the pickup once they got there. Having taken this into account, Hunnie had grabbed the key fob out of her purse and was already unlocking the doors with the push of a button.

They were almost there, only a couple more yards to go. Feeling like he had put some space between him and the bees, Hawthorn made the mistake of looking back; not noticing that part of Hunnie's bedspread was fluttering at his feet. Stepping on the comforter, Hawthorn tripped, falling forward. Whatever time was bought had been lost the moment they both went tumbling.

Once he came to a stop, Hawthorn found himself facing skyward. The blue, cloudless sky filled with the swirling swarm of little black dots. To his left, he heard a frantic rustling of gravel followed by the slamming of a truck door. He turned his head to see that Hunnie had made it to her sister's pickup and was sitting in the passenger side seat. Desperately waving at him to get in.

Without thinking about the logistics of it all, Hawthorn rolled towards the truck and crawled underneath. It was a tight fit; the gravel scraped his arms and face and the truck tore at his shirt and pants, but he was able to force his way to the other side.

Pulling himself out from under the truck, Hawthorn rose to his knees and open the door, slipping into the driver's side. By the time he closed the door and was safely inside, the swarm had completely encircled the vehicle. Amid the constant buzzing came the rat-a-tat-tat of individual bees hitting the car windows like an ice storm.

"Keys, please," he calmly said, holding out his hand.

Hunnie reached out and handed over the key fob. Once again she was nude; holding her breasts in with one arm and using her other hand to strategically place her purse atop her lap. Hawthorn caught a glimpse of a goldfish tattoo on her shoulder.

"Good lord!" exclaimed Hawthorn, "What happen to your-"

"Yeah, I lost it when you dropped me," she said, a little annoyed by the whole situation. Hunnie jerked her head at the killer bees outside, "Can we get out of here?"

Hawthorn started up the pickup and peeled out of the parking lot like a bat out of the Cloud 7 ice machine.

Leaving the bees in the dust.

Or so they thought....

CHAPTER 13

On their way to pick up some clothes, Hunnie made an emergency call to the sheriff's office and told him about the carnage at the Cloud 7 Hotel. Informing him of the killer bees attacking anyone who got in their way. Warning him that the swarm was still outside the hotel. Urging him to send as many paramedics as possible, even though, in her heart, she knew it was too late. The friendly bikers they had partied with last night were dead. All of them. They had given their lives in a misguided attempt to rescue her and defend their honor.

They were partying with the angels now.

Hawthorn pulled the truck into the parking lot of Golden Rural Farm & Home; a farm supply store that mostly sold feed, seed and guns but also had a small selection of hardware and home goods. Having grown up with the store, Hunnie knew that they would at least have some basic clothing options. She gave Hawthorn a list of what size clothes she wore and sent him into the store.

Instead of going in herself, Hunnie thought it best to wait out in the parking lot and try to keep a low profile.

No one seemed to notice except for one old timer who walked by, did a double take at the naked young woman, and shambled back to his vehicle clutching his chest. Instead of going to the hospital, this old man would go to Work and ignore this serious health condition.

Before long, Hawthorn came back with several sacks full of clothes.

"I hope this is alright," he said, handing over the sacks, "They didn't have much to choose from."

As Hawthorn pulled the truck out of the parking lot, Hunnie went through her new wardrobe; a red and black flannel shirt, blue jeans, a black pair of work boots and a heavy, brown coat.

"Don't suppose you got me any underwear or anything?" Hunnie asked, searching through the plastic bags.

Hawthorn kept his eyes on the road, shifted uncomfortably in his seat and finally admitted, "Those items seemed a little too, uh, personal for an acquaintance like me to purchase."

"Figures," said Hunnie.

Hiding her frustration, Hunnie shimmied into her new pair of pants. It wasn't the first time she had to dress in the car. Back in high school, she often changed on her way to a choir concert or music festival. Of course, there was also the time she lost her virginity in the VFW parking lot and had to quickly dress before her shift as a waitress.

The Sheriff's Department was located in "Historic Downtown Longville", which was little more than a city block of dilapidated brick buildings. If it weren't for a barbershop and Rusty's Ice Cream & Tattoo Parlor, Main Street would've been nothing but empty storefronts.

Hawthorn drove past window after window of purple and white Fliess Real Estate signs until he came upon Longville's only stop light. A sad, four-sided traffic signal hung over the intersection Hunnie pointed to the corner across the street and said, "Right there."

If Hawthorn didn't have someone telling him where to go, he would have driven right past the police station; mistaking the boxy structure for a bank branch. While it was a more recent addition to the area, it still looked like a product of its time. Small, square and made of brown brick and tall, tinted windows, the building was *at least* three decades old. Attached to one side was a large overhang originally designed for drive-thru banking. Out front, the squad car, signage, and communications tower helped make it look more like a police station, but it was still unmistakably a bank; to the point that some residents would still drive their cars up to the service window and try to make a deposit.

A now fully clothed Hunnie marched into the police station with Hawthorn close behind. The inside looked as much like a bank as the outside; an open, well-lit room with a couple desks, a long counter and a bank vault that had been converted into a holding cell. Sheriff Gayfeather was hunched over the front counter, in the middle of a phone call.

".... Listen, Jim, I don't care what you do with 'em...."

Hunnie stood directly in front of the sheriff but he refused to acknowledge her. When Hawthorn joined her at the counter, the sheriff gave him the briefest of nods and returned to his call.

"....Put 'em in a meat locker for all I care, I don't know....just keep 'em on ice for now and don't go foolin' around with 'em until after the investigation, you got that?.... *After*.... okay, bye."

The sheriff set the phone back on to its receiver and turned to Hunnie, sticking out a dry, cracked finger.

"Just so you know, you're making my life a living hell right now."

Hunnie was almost too disgusted to speak but spat out, "Excuse me?!"

The sheriff grabbed a pen and began scribbling through some official-looking forms. "Twenty-seven Canadian bikers dead! Do you have any idea what kind of paperwork I have to fill out? 'Cause I don't. My secretary took the day off."

"Dude, seriously," said Hunnie, with as much restraint as she could muster, "what is your problem?"

"I'm going to be filing paperwork out of my ass like it was a damned ticker-tape parade."

Calmly, Hawthorn said, "Again, I'm afraid I don't quite follow."

"Of course not, you're not a cop. You've never had to deal with the everyday problems of your local police department."

Behind the sheriff, a car pulled up to the service window and began honking its horn.

Spinning around, the sheriff motioned for the car to drive through, shouting, "Go ahead, drive through, we're not a bank anymore! This is the sheriff's office!!"

The elderly driver appeared angry and shouted something back.

"What?" said the sheriff, "WE'RE NOT A BANK! GO AWAY!"

With a flip of his middle finger, the elderly driver drove off.

"Damn fool," said the sheriff, returning to his

paperwork.

From the corner office, a voice yelled, "Do you guys mind keeping it down, some of us are trying to sleep!"

Hunnie glanced over her shoulder and saw a sickly-looking man in blue jeans and a white t-shirt standing behind the barred door of his jail cell/bank vault. The man was in ripped blue jeans and a stained, white t-shirt. In addition to having a mouthful of rotten teeth, his chalky face was covered in sores.

"Who's that?" Hunnie asked bluntly.

"Don't worry about it," the sheriff responded, keeping his eyes on his work.

"I'm Otis," the man in the jail cell said, "The lovable town meth head!"

"Shut up over there!"

It was clear the sheriff was in over his head. At most, he would normally be dealing with drunk drivers and wife beaters. Not a motel full of dead out-of-towners. Hawthorn felt a little guilty that he couldn't have done move to prevent it from happening.

"Sheriff, I'm here to help, what do you need from me?" Hawthorn asked.

Setting down his pen, the sheriff looked up from the form he was working on, "You say you're some kind of expert on bugs, huh?"

"Yes, sir, I am."

"What kind of bug spray do we need to kill them?"

"I suppose any insecticide would do," Hawthorn said with a tinge of regret, adding, "But I can't recommend we use it."

Outraged, the sheriff spouted, "You've got to be kidding me! Why the hell not?"

"Well, for one, we have yet to fully understand what

we're dealing with."

"Bees!" shouted the sheriff, "We're dealing with gawd damn killer bees!"

Unfazed, Hawthorn responded, "Yes, but what species is it; when we were attacked it wasn't just one genus but a large, organized, multifarious swarm of different species working in tandem."

"Listen, egghead, I don't give a damn about diversity among whatever, I just want to take care of this problem before someone important gets hurt."

"Uh…." Hunnie said with a raise of her hand, "my sister #@$%ing died and my dad is in the hospital, not to mention a hotel room full innocent people."

"Irregardless, this is my town, *mine*, and I will protect it by any means necessary."

"You guys having trouble with bees?" a shaky voice from the jail cell tittered, "I-I sometimes get bugs crawling all over my skins, s-so I-I itch and itch and itch but them little buggers don't ever go away."

"Stay outta this, Otis, this doesn't concern you!" the sheriff barked, "If we want to know how to cook meth, we'll let you know but, in the meantime, put a sock in it!"

Otis shamefully turned away from the others and shuffled back to his cot like a dog who had been scolded for saying something stupid. Hunnie shook her head at the whole situation and looked to the only sane man in town.

"Are you sure we just can't spray 'em with bug spray?"

"No," the sheriff responded, "Otis is the mayor's brother and he'd be all over my ass."

"The bees, Sheriff," said Hunnie, sternly, "I was talking about the bees."

Hawthorn folded his arms and plainly stated, "The

question isn't whether we can or not, it's whether insecticide will have any effect on the swarm. This is no ordinary swarm of killer bees; these are highly aggressive and more cooperative than any insect I've ever seen. At this point, I can only theorize about their genetics but it is entirely within the realm of plausibility that they are resistant to pesticides."

Sheriff Gayfeather slinked around his desk and approached Hawthorn, "Well, I guess there's only one way for us to find out then, isn't there?"

"Sheriff, we don't even know the location of the hive-"

"So?" the increasingly frustrated sheriff interrupted, "Used to be when trucks would drive up and down, spraying DDT all over town, and we never had any problems with bees or any other bugs for that matter, until nerds like you said it was bad for the environment or some nonsense."

"Sir, you can't in good conscience suggest we spray the community with dichlorodiphenyltrichloroethane."

"As a keeper of the peace, I say whatever it takes."

"Just for the record," Hunnie chimed in, "I'm all for killing all the bees at this point but we should probably listen to the scientist."

Meanwhile, unnoticed by anyone inside, a single bee flew past the teller window.

Having spotted the red pickup in the parking lot, the bee flew in for a closer look. It briefly hovered in front of the vehicle's license plate before flying to the rear drivers side tire. Perching on top of the tire valve cap, it was soon joined by two more drones; both landing on opposite sides of the black valve cap. Each bee positioned its tiny legs so that their feet were placed firmly in between the caps plastic grooves.

With a sudden burst of fluttering wings, the valve cap budged a bit. The bees persisted until the cap was free-spinning and eventually fell off. One of the drones placed itself back on top of the tire stem. Using its stiff legs, the bee pushed in on the tiny, metal valve; releasing a stream of air from the tire. As the single drone went about deflating the rear tire, the two remaining bees moved on to the next, unscrewing the front tire cap.

They would continue this process until every tire was flat.

"Sheriff, are there any local beekeepers I can get in contact with?" Hawthorn asked.

"There's Carson Flowers out on Highway V," said the sheriff, who was now seated behind his own desk, "She sells fresh honey but you picked a hell of a time to want some."

Hunnie, slouched in a chair across the desk, sighed audibly and rolled her eyes.

Pensively, Hawthorn crossed his arms and paced the sad little alcove sheriff called 'his office', "I would like to consult with her about any strange behavior she may have seen in the last six months."

"Just as long as we don't have to pay a consulting fee," said the sheriff, retrieving a set of keys from his desk drawer, "I swear, the only good thing to come out of all this is we get to keep the motorcycles; we might even come out ahead if we're able to sell 'em at police auction."

Hawthorn shook his head. "It appears that you are perhaps focused on the wrong thing right now."

"You act like you're surprised," Hunnie said under her breath. The sheriff got up from his desk and approached some filing cabinets that were up against the wall.

Passing by the file cabinets he stopped in front of a tall storage locker.

"Yeah, well, all I know is this whole ordeal is going to cost the department plenty before we're through," said the sheriff unlocking a grey, metal door, "Gonna have to pay for it somehow."

From the storage cabinet, Sheriff Gayfeather pulled out a military grade assault rifle and a black, metal case, about the size of a small cooler. Setting the items on his desk, he snapped open the metal case, pulled out a magazine and jammed it into the rifle. He lifted the black tactical rifle and began examining it like it was a fine antique at a rummage sale; holding it up and looking down the length of the barrel, palming the buttstock and rubbing it with his fingertips, occasionally sniffing the handguard.

By Hawthorn's estimation, the firearm looked to be an M16 of some kind, possibly a AR-15. He had read about local law enforcement stocking up on automatic weapons and armored vehicles from army surplus. Sheriff Gayfeather having access to that kind of firepower didn't give him much, if any, reassurance.

"Are you sure that's necessary?" Hawthorn asked.

"It'll have to be 'till the tank gets back from the shop."

"Jesus," said Hunnie.

"Do not take the Lord's name in vain, Gawd dammit," the sheriff snapped, "He watches over and protects us."

"V-Vance's back!" Otis called out from his cell/vault.

"Well, it's about time," said the sheriff, setting the assault rifle on his desk.

A moment later, Probationary Deputy Vance walked through the glass double-doors. He looked perplexed.

"Hey chief, I don't know if it's related to what's been

going on or nothin' but there's a bunch of bees outside."

Hawthorn and Hunnie both looked at each other with concern.

"What?! Where?" said the sheriff.

Pointing to the entrance, the deputy responded, "They're buzzing around the parking lot."

"Gawd dammit!"

Sheriff Gayfeather grabbed his rifle and bolted for the door. In his haste, knocking over half the items on the desk; including, but not limited to, his cup of coffee, computer monitor and keys. Which all came crashing down to the floor spectacularly.

Hawthorn and Hunnie walked across the room and joined the sheriff and deputy at the double-doors; getting close enough to see out into the parking lot but giving themselves enough distance in case something went wrong. Both Sheriff Gayfeather and Vance practically had their faces pressed up against the glass, searching for the aforementioned bees. From Hawthorn's position, a few feet back, all he could see were a couple of parked cop cars and Hunnie's vehicle, but no sign of the swarm.

It was uncomfortably quiet, like the moment after someone farts in an elevator.

"They were just there," said the deputy with a tinge of disappointment.

The sheriff slowly lowered his gun but kept a vigilant eye on the parking lot.

"There they are!" Hunnie called out, from the opposite side of the room.

Hawthorn was so intently watching the parking lot that he hadn't noticed that Hunnie had left his side. She was now standing at the counter, looking out the large service window where, minutes prior, an elderly driver had confused the police station for a bank. Hunnie pointed outside.

The sheriff and deputy nearly knocked Hawthorn down as they rushed to the other end of office. Careening past the counter, the police officers pressed themselves up against the service window like children looking for Santa Claus. Hawthorn quietly joined the others and looked out.

In the drive-thru, the bees were swarming just outside the shadow of the overhang. The late afternoon sun glistening off their little black and gold bodies. They didn't appear to be moving in any one direction, just hovering in one large mass in front of a rectangular metal box that used to be an ATM.

"What are they doing?"asked the sheriff.

"Trying to make a withdrawal?" the deputy wryly suggested.

From the jail vault, a shaky voice said, "I-I-I wanna see!"

"Nothing to see," Vance said matter-of-factly, "They're just hanging about."

Hunnie leaned over to Hawthorne, "I don't like this."

"Nor do I."

"Jezz-us H. Criminy!" exclaimed the sheriff, turning his back to the window, "You all sound like a couple of scaredy-cat crybabies. Afraid of some gay-ass bees outside. They're not getting in here, you don't got nothing to worry about."

"Hey, chief, somethin's happening."

The sheriff turned to the window and looked to where Deputy Vance was pointing. Hunnie and Hawthorn leaned over the counter, straining to see what was going on.

While the bees were still swarming, they weren't as spread out as before, they were more condensed. Hovering around the ATM like Costco members waiting for a fresh batch of pizza bagel samples. The large grey cloud of bees had become a small black cloud that continued to shrink until it was completely obstructed by grey, metal ATM.

"What are they doing?" Vance asked no one in particular.

A silence fell over the room as everyone anxiously stared out the window. The bees were no longer anywhere to be seen. It was as if they had never been there in the first place.

"I *really* don't like this," remarked Hunnie.

The sheriff turned towards the others, "What in the hell would a bunch of bees want out of a rusty, old ATM machine?"

"They're not wanting something out of the machine," said Hunnie, firmly, "they're looking for a way to get inside."

Hawthorn was struck by a terrifying thought, "Is there a pneumatic tube connecting the ATM to this building?"

"What's that?" Deputy Vance asked.

"Damnit, Vance!" snapped the sheriff, "It's that capsule-pipe-thing that'd let you make deposits from the car."

"Oh yeah, we got one right here," said the deputy, pointing to a metal box next to the service window; on the front of the box was a hatch door, jutting from the top was a large plastic tube connecting it to the ceiling, "Wanna see how it works?"

Before Hunnie could finish saying the words 'NO' and 'DON'T', the deputy had already open the hatch door, releasing a cyclone of trapped bees inside. The bees erupted out of the pipe, flooding the station like a broken toilet at a truck stop.

Instinctively, Hawthorn grabbed Hunnie and hit the floor. Bees raging above. Rifle in hand, the sheriff tumbled over the counter and scrambled to the opposite end of the room. Unfortunately, Probationary Deputy Vance took the brunt of the attacking swarm. Hundreds of bees fiercely swirled around the poor deputy, sending him into a category one panic-attack! Besides screaming at the top of his lungs, the deputy's only defense was frantically flapping his hands, which the bees stung on contact. On the floor, Hunnie grabbed hold of Hawthorn's arm and closed her eyes tightly.

Above the deafening roar of the swarm and the panicked screaming of both the deputy and the incarcerated meth head, Sheriff Gayfeather could be heard yelling, "Stop, drop, and roll, dummy!"

Still screaming, the deputy took his boss' advice under careful consideration and began spinning in circles. Which did absolutely nothing.

"No, not like that!" the sheriff hollered. Taking up arms, the sheriff gave the rifle a final check and took aim. Setting his sights in the deputy's general direction. "Dammit, Vance, I got to do everything around here."

"Sheriff, what are you doing?!" Hawthorn screamed from the floor.

"Vance, stand still, I'm going to pick them off one-by-one!"

Somehow, in spite of the loud buzzing and painful stings, the deputy had heard the idiotic plan; stopped mid-spin, lowered his hands and asked, "What?"

But it was too late. The sheriff pulled the trigger

and had already lost control of his gun/bladder. A thunderous, booming rat-a-tat-tat had replaced the buzzing as the most headache inducing sound in the police station. The recoil of the semi-automatic in the hands of the inexperienced sheriff had sent a barrage of bullets to hit everything but its intended target. Unfortunately, this included not only the wall, ceiling and floor, but also the front desk, a brand new computer, several filing cabinets, and Deputy Vance.

Just as quickly as it had started, the gunfire stopped; now replaced by the sound of the swarm buzzing and sheriff cussing. Overcome by the vengeful swarm; the sheriff's hands and rifle were engulfed by bees. The sheriff continued pulling the trigger but the bees had jammed his firearm. As soon as he realized this, he tried shaking them off.

Hunnie and Hawthorn could only watch in slack-jawed horror.

While the majority of the swarm had landed on the sheriff's hands and gun, a much smaller group was buzzing around his face. The sheriff desperately thrashed his head to-and-fro but it wasn't enough to keep the dozens of bees from landing on his face. Falling to the ground, the sheriff screamed a perfectly reasonable string of profanities as the bees began stabbing their needle-like stingers deep into the soft part of his eyeballs.

Turning away from the unpleasantness, Hawthorn spotted an unobstructed path to the main entrance. "We should probably go," he suggested.

"Oh, you think?" said Hunnie sarcastically. She too had looked away from the carnage but, instead, had come face-to-face with the bullet-ridden body of the deputy dangling over the front counter.

Seizing their opportunity, Hunnie and Hawthorn took each other's hand and sprinted for the door.

CHAPTER 13½

"**H**-HEY! W-WHAT ABOUT ME?"
Hunnie and Hawthorn, halfway out the door, turned back to see the town meth head trapped in his cell, reaching out for help. Sheriff Gayfeather a mere ten feet away, covered head-to-toe in bees, listlessly rocking side-to-side.

"Oh, #@$%!" exclaimed Hunnie, "What about that Otis guy?"

Holding the station door open, Hawthorn could feel the cool afternoon air waft across his face. He glanced towards Otis and sighed through his nose.

"You go ahead, I'll meet you outside."

"No way," Hunnie protested, "you'll be killed."

Hawthorn bit his lip. There was no time to argue.

"Alright, but stay here."

Trying his best not to draw attention to himself, Hawthorn hop-ran from the station entrance to the holding cell, making sure to give the bees a wide enough breath. Otis had a toothless toothy grin of relief. Hawthorn gave the cell door a firm tug, which did nothing but rattle the lock with a loud *clang*. The bees didn't seem to notice.

"Y-You got the keys, gee-genius?"

Hawthorn looked around his immediate area, then realized how silly an idea that was; as if the keys would be just lying around on the floor.

"Hey, Hawthorn," Hunnie whisper-shouted, "They're over there!"

Hunnie pointed to the area in front of the sheriff's desk, only a few feet from where the sheriff himself was frailly flailing on the floor. Hawthorn directed his gaze past the sheriff and, sure enough, the keys were on the ground, lying next to a shattered coffee cup and a broken computer monitor.

This would be tricky. So far the bees were too busy attacking the sheriff to care about much else. In a way, it was the perfect diversion. But all that could change in a moments notice. The keys were on the opposite side of the dying sheriff. Just feet away from the mound of alleged bees. In Hawthorn's mind, there was no doubt the swarm would notice someone trying to sneak by.

And yet, that's exactly what Hunnie was about to do.

Sensing Hawthorn's dilemma and not wanting him to take any more risks, Hunnie decided to retrieve the keys herself.

"Stay there, I'll get 'em," she mouthed.

Before Hawthorn had a chance to object, Hunnie was already making her way towards the keys. Crouched to the ground, she crawled across the floor like a spider trying to dine and dash. The closer she got to the keys the louder the bees buzzed. While the bees were crawling all over the sheriff's body, the sheriff himself was no longer moving. He was dead.

Putting this out of her mind, Hunnie creeped onward

until she was within reach of the keys. She stretched herself out across the imitation marble floor. The very tip of her middle finger had reached the key ring when she noticed a change in the air. The bees were starting to take off and make their advance!

"$#*%," she said, rather plainly for someone who had bees flying within inches of her nose.

Falling flat on her back, Hunnie used her feet to propel herself across the smooth surface of the floor. While it didn't push her very far, it did give enough time to hurriedly get to her feet and make a run for the door. The bees had collectively left the pin-pricked body of the sheriff behind and were coming towards her in a dark, angry cloud. On the opposite side of the cloud, she could make out the figure of Hawthorn standing petrified by the jail cell.

Giving him a broad wave, Hunnie tossed the keys over the swarm.

"Meet me outside," she called, slipping through the door at the last possible moment.

Having caught the keys, Hawthorn was now having a hard time finding the right key to the holding cell. Of the twelve keys total, he had already tried three with no luck.

"C-come on, m-man!" Otis pleaded.

Hawthorn wasn't panicking. Not yet. He was too focused on trying to unlock the cell door. Seven keys left.

"W-we don't have much t-time!"

He only had five more keys to go. Then he'd have a bigger problem to solve. Getting out unscathed.

"T-they're c-coming for us, m-man!"

Judging from the increased buzzing, the swarm was right behind him. Three keys left.

"D-d-d-d-"

The cell door unlocked with a loud click on the second to last key. Hawthorn swung it open and yanked Otis out by the collar. With the swarm directly in front of them, Hawthorn made a hard left towards the front counter, dragging the spastic meth head along as swiftly as possible.

"W-w-where w-we going?"

Hawthorn jumped the counter, struggling to pull Otis over with him. The roaring bees were right on top of them. There was no hope in reaching the exit now. They were cornered. So Hawthorn made for he only other way out; the shattered drive-thru window the sheriff had shot up.

"This way!"

Luckily it didn't take much convincing to get Otis to follow Hawthorn as they both jumped out the large teller window. Crash landing on the pavement outside, Hawthorn pulled himself off the ground and gave a brief glance over his shoulder. The swarm was beginning to filter out through the drive-thru window. Hawthorn hoisted his new acquaintance to his feet and hobbled round the side of the building. Running smack dab into Hunnie.

"Jesus! There you are!"

Hawthorn spun Hunnie around and pushed her along, "Keep moving, they followed us out," he said, hurrying them out into the parking lot.

"Well, I hope you're not wanting to take my car," said Hunnie.

As they approached the red pickup, Hawthorn saw what Hunnie was referring to. All four tires were completely flat.

This could be a problem.

Stopping just short of the vehicle, Hawthorn gathered his thoughts; the average bee files at about fifteen miles per hour and while the truck was still capable of going much faster than that, the damage to the tires would be irreparable. They could run but these were no average bees they were dealing with.

"So you going to do something or are we just going to stand around waiting for them to get us?"

She was right. There was no more time to think about their next move. They had to go. The buzzing sound of the swarm was clearly outside and it was getting closer.

"Yes." Hawthorn began, "I think we should-"

A loud *woop* of a police siren sounded off two cars over and waving from the deputy's SUV was Otis, sitting behind the wheel with a big, goofy grin.

"N-need a r-ride?"

Hunnie and Hawthorn ran for the police cruiser and jumped in the back, slamming the door behind them.

"Dude," said Hunnie to Otis, "you might want to roll up your window."

"O-oh, y-yeah, Otis flipped a switch and the windshield wipers turned on.

Looking out through the rear window, Hawthorn could see the bees swarming in the parking lot behind them. Apparently they hadn't seen them get in the police car. If they could only keep a low profile, perhaps the swarm would pass them by and they could get a clean break.

Still looking for a way to roll up his window, Otis accidentally hit the siren.

The long, loud wail of the police siren filled the air; blue, white and red lights flashed all over the vehicle, announcing their presence to the world.

As Otis figured out how to close the windows, the cloud of bees descended on to the car. Bees tapped against the glass from every direction.

"Any chance we can get out of here?" Hunnie asked, "Like today?"

Otis shifted the car into reverse and pressed on the accelerator. Nothing. Just revving of the engine.

"I think the parking brake is on," Hawthorn suggested.

Flipping switches at random, Otis eventually found the parking lever after cycling through the left and right blinkers, turning off the police siren and changing the radio station to Real Polka 1700. As soon as he released the parking brake, the vehicle shot backwards and slammed into the brick wall of the police station.

While the damage to the cruiser wasn't horrible, it was enough to smash the bumper and knock open the rear passenger side door. In the parking spot they had just been, the bees swarmed in place, assessing the situation.

"Good job," said Hunnie, picking herself up off the floor.

Shaken from the crash, Hawthorn found himself hanging out of the open car door. The cloud of bees moving back towards the vehicle. Spotting the bees in front of them, Hawthorn tried slamming the door but it refused to shut; limply springing open instead of latching into place. After a few failed attempts, he decided to hold the door closed.

"Now would be an appropriate time for us to leave," said Hawthorn.

"W-what?"

"Make. Car. Go. Vroom," Hunnie said pantomiming each word individually.

"O-oh, okay."

Obediently, Otis shifted gears and pressed his foot down on the accelerator. The car engine roared and, much to everyone's surprise, the car began to slowly roll forward. Directly into the massive swarm of bees.

Over the continuous hum of the accelerator and the steady tapping of a thousand insects on the windows, Hunnie asked, "Why aren't we leaving these #@$%ers in the dust?"

"He has the vehicle in neutral."

"B-buckle u-up!"

Otis put the pedal to the metal and steered the incredibly slow-moving police cruiser out of the parking lot. While the bees continued swarming all around, it appeared to Hawthorn that they were concentrating their attention on the front of the vehicle. Logically, if they were going to outrun the bees they would have to be going faster than a snail's pace.

"You need to put it into drive," said Hawthorn, pointing to the gear shift.

Caught up in his own little world and meth-ed out of his gourd, Otis didn't hear anything beyond the buzzing of bees, which were now gathering on the grill and front windshield. The car gradually rolled towards the four-way stop light just as it was turning red.

"H-hold on to your h-hat!"

Moving at just under five miles per hour, the police cruiser didn't so much run the red light as crawl through it. Luckily, there weren't any other vehicles on the road. Even if there were, no one inside the cop car would have seen them as the bees had now completely covered the windshield. A fluid wall of hairy bees were wriggling over the glass surface, blocking out the view ahead.

"W-whoa!" said Otis in amazement, "I-is anyone else s-seeing this?"

Hawthorn tightened his grip, holding his door shut with all his might. The bees were looking for an entry point and he didn't dare give them an inch with his wonky door. He looked at Hunnie with concern but she was transfixed by the solid swarm on the windshield.

"If you're not going to get us out of here could you turn on the windshield wipers or something?"

Upon hearing this idea, the meth-head went back to his strategy of hitting console buttons at random. Unaware that the car was on a slow, but reckless, collision course with a corner mailbox.

From the back, Hawthorn watched helplessly as Otis flipped on the AC and was hit by a full blast of bees shooting out of the driver side air vent. The bees had found a way inside! Without hesitation, Hawthorn grabbed hold of Hunnie's hand and dragged her out of the car. Both falling out of the busted door and hitting the concrete.

The police cruiser leisurely left Hunnie and Hawthorn behind, shrieks of terror escaping from its open door. Reaching the street corner, the bee-consumed car jumped the curb and ran into the mailbox. Exploding on contact.

"Holy $#*%!" Hunnie yelled over the thundering explosion, "what was in that mailbox?!"

Normally, Hawthorn would be asking himself the very same questions but he knew that this was only a fleeting moment to escape. The explosion had no doubt taken out a large portion of the swarm but high above the flaming cruiser, tiny specks swarmed chaotically, like a crowd of shoppers on Black Friday. Once the bees regrouped, they would be after them. After her.

"We should go," he said brushing off the burnt pieces

of metal and Otis.

"Yeah," said Hunnie, pulling a charred human molar from her hair,

The two got up and stole away into the late-afternoon. Initially, Hawthorn led them stealthily along the various closed businesses and unkempt houses of Longville, but soon Hunnie took the lead. Using a network of residential alleyways, Hunnie guided them across town. Every now and then they would pass by a house with a barking dog but, overall, they were able to keep a low profile.

Once they were some distance away, Hunnie asked, "You think we lost them?"

Hawthorn looked over his shoulder; above the rooftops he could see thick, black smoke billowing from the accident two blocks away. If he positioned himself, at the right angle, he could still see the flaming wreckage. Little black specks flying chaotically around it.

"I think it best we keep moving."

With that, Hunnie led them between another pair of houses and across someone's backyard. Hunnie could hear the siren of a fire engine wailing in the distance.

"Somebody must've called the fire department," said Hunnie, pressing on, "Hope they'll be okay."

While Hunnie was confidently cutting through other people's private property, Hawthorn had no clue where she was leading them. Finally, he asked, "Where exactly are you taking us?"

"Don't worry, we'll be safe once we get to Work."

Ten minutes later, Hunnie had taken them to the edge of Longville proper. Houses had become more sporadic, separated by bigger swaths of flat countryside. Across the street from a ramshackle baseball field, stood a ramshackle bar the locals called Work.

For years, the only bar in town was Chuck's Bullpen. Back in those days, Longville was the largest manufacturer of typewriter bells in the country. Unfortunately, with the advent of the electric typewriter, digital bells replaced the old fashioned, metal ones. Thus, Longvilles biggest employer went out of business. With over half the town unemployed, people needed an excuse to start drinking at eight o'clock in the morning. So the Bullpen was renamed the Work Tavern and the phrase 'going to work' was given a whole new, sadder meaning.

Hunnie opened the solid metal door and led Hawthorn into the dingy bar. It would take Hawthorn several minutes for his eyes to adjust. The entire joint was lit by handful of light bulbs and a couple of neon beer signs with the only natural light streaming in through one small, square window.

The sole customer was an old timer at the bar who happened to be the same guy that saw Hunnie naked in the Golden Rural parking lot. Upon seeing her, he turned bright red, fumbled for his wallet and tossed a couple of bills down, promptly leaving through the back.

Behind the bar stood a mountain of a woman; she was tall and solidly-built, with a pair of majestic peaks. The first thing Hawthorn noticed about the bartender (other than the plunging neckline of her purple, 'Who Sharted?' t-shirt) was how remarkably similar her hairstyle was to Hunnie's: same length and shape with only a slightly different shade of blonde. She appeared to be the same age as Hunnie. Maybe a year or two older. Like the old timer, the young lady recognized Hunnie but instead of shock and embarrassment she had a look of utter contempt.

"Well, #@$% me," the woman said, slinging a bar towel over her shoulder, "Look what the overpriced designer cat dragged in."

Hunnie approached the bar, "Hey, Hun," she said.

"Decided to come down from the Hollywood Hills and grace us with your presence."

"It's a little more complicated than that."

"I'll say. What brings you out here? Run out of Canadian bikers to sleep with?"

"Something's after me and I need a safe place to hide."

"What do you mean 'something?'" the bartender scoffed.

Hunnie took a breath.

"Bees."

"Bees???"

"Killer bees."

"Are you joking?"

"Does it look like I'm #@$%ing joking?" Hunnie snapped.

"No," the bartender eased back just a bit, "but it sure as hell sounds like it."

"They attacked my dad and killed Rosemary," said Hunnie choking back tears.

Grief fell across the bartenders face. She looked to the floor and then briefly back at Hunnie before turning her attention toward Hawthorn.

"What about you?" she said, "What's your story?"

Taking a step forward, Hawthorn solemnly introduced himself.

"Dr. Hawthorn White, State Fair College. I'm here to investigate the attacks and, let me assure you, this is a very serious situation we're dealing with, Miss....?"

"Bunn. Honey Bunn."

CHAPTER 14

"You both are named Hunnie?" Hawthorn asked, glancing between the woman who he only knew as Hunnie and the barmaid who was claiming to be one.

Hunnie Combs was about to answer but the towering bartender beat her to the punch with a dismissive wave.

"Nah, there's only one Honey in here and it ain't her."

Hawthorn looked to "Hunnie" for an explanation, it was hard to see in the dank bar but it looked like she was blushing.

"Hunnie is my stage name," she said, softly, "my real name is Primrose," abruptly throwing in, "But, to be fair, my dad called me honey way before we ever met."

"Yeah, well, my name's not the only thing you stole from me," Honey Bunn leaned on the bar and glanced at Hawthorn, "Before I moved here, she was just a mousy little choir girl who didn't know how to have fun."

"I knew how to have fun!" Hunnie Combs protested.

"If it weren't for me you would've spent every Friday night at home, singing show tunes to your goldfish. Instead I took you under my wing and made you one of the most popular girls in school."

"Who cares?" Hunnie Combs spat, "That was high school, that was #@$%ing years ago!"

"Don't act like this isn't a big deal, Primmy, you know damn well why I'm upset!"

Hunnie Combs crossed her arms and stood firm, "Indulge me."

"Look at you!" Honey B shouted, throwing her arms out in a 'ta-da' like fashion, "You stole everything about me! My look, my personality, my own #@$%ing name and then you used it to launch your music career and, worst of all, what really pisses me off is that you cut me out of your life completely! Dammit! You were like a sister to me! Closer than family."

"So, what do you want me to do?" Hunnie Combs exclaimed, "Apologize for my success?"

"Yes."

Hawthorn was no expert on women, or human interaction in general, but he could tell this little reunion wasn't going well. He leaned in towards Hunnie Combs, "We should probably go."

Hunnie Combs stared deeply into her old friends green eyes. Both women on the verge of tears. She was furious but could tell that her friend was hurting.

"Okay, fine, I'm sorry I kinda copied your whole image-thing but you gotta know I only based it off of you because you're the baddest bish I know."

With a heavy breath, the bartender nodded in agreement. She was touched. Hunnie Combs continued.

"And I'm sorry I never stayed in contact with you. I guess I was in such a hurry to put this place behind me that I forgot the people who made it somewhat bearable."

"Oh, Primmy, that's so #@$%ing corny, come here!"

With that, Honey B reached over the bar and hugged her best friend.

"I'm sorry, Hun," a muffled Hunnie Combs said, her face buried in her friends broad shoulder.

Feeling a bit out of place, Hawthorn attempted to take a step back and give the ladies some privacy until a large hand yanked him by the collar.

"And you, come here too, you knucklehead," the bartender said pulling him to her massive bosom.

It was an emotional reconciliation for all except Hawthorn. For him the group hug lasted about thirty seconds longer than he would have liked. Eventually Honey Bunn loosened her grip and he was able to gradually free himself of the warm embrace. Hunnie Combs also let go of her friend, wiping away a few tears in the process.

"Hun, I know it's asking a lot, but is it cool if we hang out here for a bit, until we figure out what our next move is?"

"Dude, don't be stupid, you guys are coming home with me."

"Thank you, that'd be great!"

"I get off in about an hour, so, hey, take a seat and let's do some shots, man!"

Hawthorn didn't like where this was going. Hunnie C and Honey B may have resolved the tension between them but he was still on high alert...keeping a close eye on the bars only window.

"Actually," Hawthorn began, "Miss Bunn, we are still in a great deal of danger and need to keep a low profile. Do you have a back room, preferably some place with no windows?"

Without saying a word, the Honeys gave each other a

knowing look. A look Hawthorn was quite familiar with to mean: 'Can you believe this cat? He is an absolute squareville!'

An hour later, Honey Bunn's shift ended.

An hour and twenty minutes after that, Hawthorn White and Hunnie Combs stumbled out of the bar and into the night. Honey B led them with a steady arm wrapped around each of their waists. She had become accustomed to helping her customers get safely to their vehicles so they could drive dangerously home.

"The ants go marching two by two, hurrah hurrah," Hawthorn sang, The ants go marching two by two, hurrah hurrah!"

"Bye, everybody," Hunnie Combs called out behind them, "Sorry we can't stick around for karaoke!"

The once deserted bar was now a hub of activity with the regular weeknight alcoholics. Pickup trucks of every make and color were spread across the small gravel parking lot. A single yellow street light was just starting to flicker to life in the darkening of nightfall. From the building, classic rock music blared out of the open back door but Hawthorn continued with his childhood song.

"The ants go marching two by two, they all use mandibles to chew. And they all go marching down, to the ground...."

Hunnie Combs took a moment to admire the evening sky. The pink and purple of twilight was awash in the glow of the pale moonlight. She had to admit that while her hometown was a dump full of bad memories, there was beauty to be found in even the ugliest of places.

That and ten shots of apple cinnamon whiskey could make anything tolerable.

"Oh, it eases the pain," she proclaimed.

"Just for the record," Hawthorn stated, "I still think this was a bad idea."

"Yeah, well, you should have said something before all those shots," said Honey B.

"I did."

"You'll feel better after we get some greasy food in ya'."

"Let's go to Pancake Pappy's!" Hunnie Combs enthusiastically suggested.

"You mean Pancake Crappy's?" snorted Honey B.

"Yeah."

"Can't, it closed down."

"Why?"

"Health inspector found mouse turds in the pancake batter."

"$#*%! I liked that place!"

"That's what happens when you leave town forever," Honey B paused, held up her phone and took a quick picture of her and her best friend, "Selfie!"

Putting her phone away, Honey B wrapped her arm back around Hawthorn's waist and led them to her car. A yellow Saturn Ion she had owned since high school. Opening the rear, passenger side door, she tenderly set Hunnie Combs down and did the same for Hawthorn on the drivers side. Honey B took her seat upfront, started the car and said, "I got a bottle of water back there if it isn't frozen solid."

"I definitely could use it," Hunnie Combs said, picking it up from the floor board and taking a swig, "Hawthorn, you want some?"

Hawthorn's head was swimming, he decided to lean back and rest his eyes for a bit. He wouldn't remember much about the car ride; only that he couldn't keep his head from lolling from side-to-side at every turn and the radio was playing an annoying catchy song about how much love stings.

"Ugh, turn it off," Hunnie Combs said, "I'm so sick of this song."

"Yeah?" the other Honey responded, "Now you know how the rest of us feel."

After a short drive, Hawthorn awoke to find the car pulling into a driveway off of a well-worn, outer road. It had gotten much darker since they left the bar but the luminous moon gave enough light for him to see his surroundings. The house at the end of the drive was small and made of brick. Yellow light emanated from square windows. In the yard were several barren trees, a couple of children's bicycles and a rusted out Dodge Charger.

"Isn't this your grandma's place?" Hunnie Combs asked.

"Not anymore, the old bat passed away and left it to me."

Hawthorn sat up to unbuckle his seat belt and felt incredibly woozy.

"Good thing too," Honey B continued, "She was getting so bad we were thinking of putting her in a home."

Faced with the sudden urge to puke, Hawthorn reached for the door and stuck his head out as far as he could, shooting hot apple vomit all over the driveway. It was mostly liquid and utterly awful; like a stomach cocktail of sour burning. He coughed and spit, taking a short break to catch his breath, and then resumed hurling. The ladies stood by.

"You hungry?" Honey B asked.

Once Hawthorn was finished, Honey B took them inside.

The front door led directly to a messy living room full of screaming kids and one tired man who was sitting on the couch. Usually Hawthorn reserved judgment upon entering a stranger's home but even he had to admit that it was a pigsty. Pieces of mail, beer cans and an assortment of children's toys were scattered everywhere, like a mailman had gotten into a drunken brawl with Santa Claus.

"Hey, babe," the strung-out man said in a daze. He was in his early forties, had an unkempt beard, pudgy body, and stringy long, black hair. Hunnie Combs recognized him as the burnout who bought them beer back in high school.

"Sup, dude?" said Honey Bunn to the man, "Primrose and her scientist friend are in town and need a place to crash."

"That's cool," he said lighting up a joint, "Me couch-o es su couch-o."

"You guys, come on in," Honey B waved them in, "Science man, why don't you take a seat."

Carefully, and with much effort, Hawthorn eased himself onto the couch, next to a shirtless baby sitting next to the man. The baby looked up at Hawthorn with wonder while the man simply nodded and took a hit.

"This is my husband, Buzz. He's an entrepreneur."

"Hello," said Hawthorn.

"I sell weed online," said Buzz with a puff of smoke.

Honey B went on to introduce the rambunctious kids who were running about; pointing them out one-by-one.

"And these, of course, are the screamin' demons; Harley and Gunner are his, Kiki and Pepper are mine, this is our little Baby Blue and we got another one on the way, we're thinking either Peaches, if it's a girl; Bandit, if it's a boy."

"Wait a sec," Hunnie Combs interjected, "You're pregnant?"

"Mother #@$%in' A!"

"You're just poppin' 'em out left and right."

"What can I say? I love the D and birth control ain't cheap!"

A little girl with dark-brown pigtails came up to Honey B and pulled on the hem of her shirt.

"Momma, we're hungry!"

"I'm sure you are, it's almost eight o'clock," throwing daggers at her husband before glancing back at Hunnie Combs, "Come on, Primmy, you can give me a hand in the kitchen, the only thing Buzz cooks around here is brownies."

The kitchen was equally messy with crusty dishes stacked in the sink and on every inch of countertop. Hunnie Combs recognized the brown refrigerator as the same one that had been in the house for as long as she had known the Bunn family. Except now it was completely covered in expired pizza coupons.

"So...." Hunnie Combs began, "you and Buzz, huh?"

"Yeah, and I know what you're thinking, so don't even say it," said Honey Bunn, opening up a succession of empty cabinets until she came across a box of Baloney Helper.

"Okay, I'm just surprised you guys ended up getting hitched."

"Well, we have a good time together and he *is* a good provider," Honey B went to the refrigerator and pulled out a package of sliced bologna, "Plus our kids all get along, so I decided it was time to settle down."

"As long as you're happy."

"I don't need to be happy. I'm a mother. The joy that comes from raising kids is a well that can't run dry and a keg that will never be empty."

To open up counter space, Honey B took a stack of dirty dishes and set them on the floor. Setting her ingredients on the counter, she proceeded to cut up the slices of bologna.

"So what about you?" she continued, "When are you and that slab of man-meat going to start makin' babies?"

"We literally just met the other day!"

"Dude, he's a scientist, a *handsome* scientist! You gotta jump on that pogo-stick and #@$% him 'til you get some super-cute super-smart kids!"

"Starting a family's really not at the top of my to-do list right now."

"Why not? Because you're a big shot superstar?"

"No, because I'm a little preoccupied not being killed by bees."

"Yeah, what's up with *that*, by the way?

In the living room, Hawthorn sat placidly on the couch watching television. Or, at least, trying to watch television. Even at full volume, it was a little hard to hear over the sound of Harley and Pepper sword fighting with steel fireplace tools, Gunner shooting bottle rockets up the chimney, Kiki standing in the middle of the room crying, and the baby babbling incomprehensive nonsense.

He felt like he should say something to the children. Something to bring order to chaos. Something like, "I highly doubt your parents would appreciate you hitting your brother in the head with a metal poker," but he didn't want to overstep his bounds as a stranger in their home.

Besides, their father clearly did not care. He was zoned out from the rest of the world, totally focused on his television program. So Hawthorn shrugged and went back to trying to make out what was happening on tv.

They were in the middle of watching The Littlest Medium on the Family Learning Channel. From what Hawthorn could gather, the "reality" show was about a man with dwarfism who claimed he could talk to the dead. The so-called medium stood before his client, a pretty young lady in a bright sundress, and held a stubby finger up to his temple.

With great concentration, he said, "....I'm sensing that your father was a very tall man, like he was much taller than me...."

"He WAS!" the woman happily exclaimed.

Hawthorn was aghast.

"When I was a boy the Family Learning Channel showed education programs, this is disgraceful."

Buzz shook his head and reassured him, "Naw, man, they still show that educational stuff, like, they got this one show that's all about Amish prostitutes!" The program he was referring to was called Amish Escorts and it aired on Mondays at 8:00, Wednesdays at 6:00 and Saturdays from 1:00 to 5:30 on the Family Learning Channel.

Hawthorn was about to ask how *that* program was supposed to be educational but was interrupted by the sound of young Gunner drilling holes through the floor with an electric drill.

"Aren't you concerned about that?"

"The way I see it, man, he'll either hurt himself or the battery will run out. In both cases, he'll stop AND learn an important life lesson in the process."

While Hawthorn's head was starting to clear, he wasn't up for questioning someone else's parenting style. Even if it was horrifying and wrong.

"What about you?" said Buzz, "You got kids?"

"No, I don't have children of my own."

"Why not? Something wrong with your dong or something?"

"Nothing like that, I simply haven't found a mate with the type of favorable traits that will provide our offspring with enough genetic variation."

"Oh... what about Prim? She's pretty hot."

Even though Hunnie Combs was quite fetching, Hawthorn felt the need to dissuade any feelings of attraction he had towards the charming young lady.

"I've only known Ms. Combs for a matter of days and our relationship is strictly professional."

"So?" said Buzz, disparagingly, "When I sold beer to high schoolers, I used to sleep with my clients all the time. I got paid and I got laid, you know what I'm saying?"

"I most certainly do not," Hawthorn protested.

"Listen, comprende, alls I'm sayin' is, chicks dig older guys and you gotta take advantage of that before you get *too* old."

"I can assure you that isn't going to happen."

"Well, if you two ever hook up, make sure you keep it casual."

"And why do you say that?"

"Hey, $#*%head," a voice from the kitchen yelled, "Your #@$%ing dinner's ready!"

"Trust me."

CHAPTER 15

It took a little while and a lot of effort for Honey Bunn and Buzz to wrangle the kids but eventually everyone was sitting at the dining room table. Hunnie Combs had set it herself, shoving the stacks of junk mail out of the way to make room for paper plates, plastic forks and an assortment of "collectable" glasses from gas stations and fast food restaurants.

"Pepper?" Honey B asked her two-year-old daughter, "Would you like to pray?"

With a toothy grin, Pepper nodded; short, black braids bobbing.

"Everybody shut the hell up, we're going to pray!" said Honey B.

In the momentary quiet that followed, the cute toddler clasped her hands together and began.

"Thank you for the food and the plates and the beer and the windows and the curtains, that we do not touch, and thank you for the chairs and the floor and the pictures and the lights and the....

"Okay, Hun, she's just telling us what she sees," Buzz said.

"Amen!" Honey B said, capping off the prayer, "Thank you, Pepper, that was very good!"

Hawthorn noticed the serving dish before him and shared a look with Hunnie Combs, who just shrugged.

"Everybody dig in, it's not getting any warmer."

The dinner guests started by helping themselves to a scoop of Baloney Helper and then passed the bundt cake pan to Buzz who began serving the kids. Unsure exactly what he was about to eat, Hawthorn took a sniff of his food before taking a reluctant bite.

"You guys pray before every meal?" Hunnie Combs asked.

Pouring out a box of something called "Fruitie Hoopies" for the baby, Honey B responded, "Buzz and I decided on raising our family in a Godly household."

"Since when did you start believing in God?"

Setting the cereal box aside, Honey B pontificated, "Things change once you start having children, you know? It's like, you get a whole new perspective on life. Your whole world changes, for the better of course; you don't go out as much, you party less, you learn how to take account of your life by taking care of one of these little miracles."

Hawthorn pointed towards her glass and said, "I don't think you should be drinking while pregnant."

"It's okay, it's light beer," Honey B said with a swig.

"That's not wh-"

"You know what's great about having kids?" she said, cutting him off, "They're cute. Like just the other day, I was giving KiKi a bath and she farted; she looks up at me and says, 'Mommy, my bottom is talking.' How #@$%ing precious is that?"

"Oh, yeah, that's really something," Hunnie Combs

said poking at her food.

"And you know what else is great about having kids? And science man, you'll appreciate this. The tax write off."

"Heh," Buzz laughed, "Like we pay taxes."

"Will you quit trying to convince me to have kids!" Hunnie Combs snapped, tossing her plastic fork on the table.

With as much innocence as she could muster, Honey B said, "What do you mean, Primmy?"

"Ever since I got here you've been going on and on about how I need to start a family and crap."

"We haven't seen each other in years, I'm just trying to share my life with you while you're still in town."

"Oh no, I know you too well, Hun, don't pretend you don't know what I'm talking about, I'm not one of your stupid kids."

For a moment, it looked as if Honey B would continue playing the innocent but then she realized how much work that would involve and gave up, "Okay, fine, you got me, big deal."

"Why do you want me to have children so bad?"

"Because we're best friends and we agreed on it back in high school, remember? We always talked about how we were going to have kids and then how they were going to grow up together and be best friends."

"So? We talked about a lot of crazy $#*% back then, we talked about having a threesome with Justin Bieber!"

"Which we can still do if you'd just introduce us!"

"Hey!" Buzz protested.

"Shut up, Buzz! We'd let you watch."

Hunnie Combs stood up and searched the cluttered table, "Where are your smokes? I need some air."

Finding half a pack resting in the napkin holder, she left the table, snatching a lighter from Harley who had been playing with it the entire time.

Hunnie Combs stood out on the front porch, which was little more than a concrete slab and a couple of steps. It was cold out. The temperature had dropped quite a bit since sundown. Despite the warm snap, it looked like the weather had come to its senses and decided that, yes, it is still winter.

Taking a draw on the cigarette, Hunnie was reminded of why she started smoking. And why she had quit. It was a relieving high that left her feeling gross afterwards. Much like hanging out with an old friend.

She exhaled the nasty puff of smoke and held the cigarette upright, next to her face.

Behind her, the front door opened and a rectangular light cast her shadow across the lawn. She watched the strapping silhouette of Hawthorn exit the house, pulling the door shut behind him.

"Why are you standing out in the dark?" he said, joining her.

"Porch light doesn't work; knowing Honey, it probably hasn't been changed in years," she replied, looking skyward, "Besides, it's nice to see the stars for a change."

"I can't imagine Los Angeles has much of an evening sky."

"Not like this."

Hawthorn tilted his head back and stared into the vast expanse of black. Among the countless sparkling stars, he only recognized a few simple constellations; the Big Dipper, the Little Dipper, Argo Navis. A pair of long, skinny clouds gradually crawled across the cold sky.

Cigarette smoke wafted into Hawthorn's face.

"I'm surprised to see you smoking," he said in a non-judgmental manner, "I'd figure you of all people would know of the harmful effects it can have on a singers voice."

"I know. I usually don't, in fact, this is the first time I've smoked since college," Hunnie thought back and chuckled, "it was actually the last time I hung out with Hun....Thanksgiving break, sophomore year."

"It's very nice of her to let us spend the night, I am sorry that this has been a stressful visit for you."

"Hey, what about this week hasn't been stressful?"

Hunnie flicked off some ash from her cigarette, shaking her head.

"I just wish she wasn't so hung up on me having a baby, you know? It's like, what business is it of hers?

Folding his arms, Hawthorn adjusted his stance and listened. She continued.

"I know she must think my life is incomplete because I don't have kids. But that's not me, not anymore. Getting married seems so pointless; it's either going to end in death or divorce."

Hunnie tossed her cigarette to the concrete, stamping it out. She resumed her thought.

"And if you have kids, there's no guarantee they're going to turn out the way you want. Even if you're a perfect parent, they can still grow up to be psychopaths. All I care about right now is my music; it's the only part of my life where I have total control and it can turn out exactly as I envision it."

With a deep breath, she looked at Hawthorn. She exhaled.

"Sorry, I've been kinda bottling that up."

"I can tell," Hawthorn nodded, he unfolded his arms and scratched the stubble on his face, "Believe it or not, I can actually relate."

"No $#*%?"

"Yes, my mother used to ask when I was going to find a nice young lady and start a family but between furthering my education and doing research at the college, I have been far too busy."

"Do you ever regret not getting married?"

"I have no regrets," he said, staring into the darkness, "I only mourn for what never could've been."

"How do you mean?"

Hawthorn thought for a moment about how detailed an explanation he wanted to give before deciding to go ahead and tell the whole, sad romance. Looking up to the stars wistfully, he began.

"When I was an undergrad, I dated a girl named Blossom Applegate, sociology major from Texas. She was an all-around beautiful person with a deep appreciation of nature. We used to do everything together; eat, sleep, have sex, even sit underneath the stars and talk about our dreams," Hawthorn motioned towards the sky above only to cast his gaze back down to earth, "But she was into astrology and eastern mysticism while I was a man of science.

"By the time we graduated our relationship had cooled and we both went our separate ways. Do I regret breaking up? No, we had fundamental differences that we couldn't resolve..... but I do grieve for the love that was lost."

In the three days that Hunnie had known him she hadn't seen this tender side of Hawthorn. First of all, she was surprised that he even *liked* girls, thinking he was either gay or asexual. But she was also surprised that he was capable of showing such emotion, most of the time he came off as such a stiff.

Hunnie felt sorry that things didn't work out between him and his college girlfriend.

"It's a shame, she's missing out on a great guy," she said, lightly touching his arm, "Does your mom still ask when you're going to give up on your dreams and settle down?"

"No, it would seem that she has all but given up on me."

"My mom died when I was a teenager so I never had to deal with any of that crap,"

Hunnie looked down at her hands and for the first time Hawthorn noticed a tattoo scrawled across the inside of her wrist. Written in black cursive was the name Melissa.

"Is that your mother?" he asked.

"Was."

"Forgive me it's too personal but how did she pass?"

Taken aback, Hunnie wrung her hands, fumbling for a response.

"It was…a farming accident."

It had been a long time since Hunnie had talked to anyone about her mother. She looked at Hawthorn, hoping that he wouldn't ask any follow-up questions but she could tell by his expression that his interest was piqued. She inhaled through her nose and began.

"Okay, it was my sweet sixteen and my mom had driven into town to pick up my birthday cake and on the way back she was playing a farming game on her phone. Well, she was in the middle of watering her rutabagas and wasn't watching the road and ended up crashing into a silo. She died on impact."

"I'm sorry for your loss."

"It's okay," she said wiping away tears from her eyes, "I had Honey to help me through it. What really sucked was watching my dad have his nervous breakdown. He didn't use to be the way he is, he used to be a radar operator until he started seeing UFOs and was forced into early retirement."

"I'm sure your mother would be very proud of your success."

"It's all luck," Hunnie said with a snort, "if it wasn't me, it would've been some other slutty girl with a catchy party anthem."

"I must confess that I have yet to listen to any of your work."

"I'm glad you haven't, it's embarrassing."

"Why?"

"I don't know," Hunnie shrugged, "I guess because I kinda care what you'd think."

"You have no need to worry, I know nothing of what separates good popular music from bad."

"Surprisingly little," she snickered, "My first music video wasn't even a serious attempt to be artistic or whatever. It was supposed to be a joke between me and my friends about drunk sorority girls. I didn't expect it to go viral."

"Are you happy with your success?"

Not used to other people being so blunt with her, Hunnie had to search her feelings.

"Let's just say it's lonely at the top," she said.

Hawthorn nodded, "It can be lonely no matter where you are."

"Ain't that the truth."

"I'm sure you must have many friends?"

Looking up at the stars, Hunnie briefly ran through a

mental list of friends she talked to on a regular basis. She came up with nothing.

"Once you get famous," she said, "it's hard to tell who's a friend and who's there to ride your coattails."

Out of the corner of her eye, Hunnie spotted a shooting star. In that moment, she silently wished for her dad to have a full recovery. Hawthorn, who also saw the splinter-like flash in the sky, didn't wish for anything because he didn't believe in such nonsense.

"You're a doctor," said Hunnie, "you think my dad's going to be okay?"

"I'm not that kind of doctor."

"Yeah, I know, I just needed some reassurance."

"Oh, um….I'm sure your father will be fine."

"I feel so helpless, I wish I could do something."

"Once your father gets out of the hospital, he's going to need you more than ever."

"That's true." she said, "Before this whole mess, Rosemary took care of dad and I supported them financially but now I'll have to fill both roles…. I guess it's what I deserve."

Thoughtfully, Hawthorn asked, "Why do you say that?"

"It's like, if I didn't become famous and move to Los Angeles I could've stayed here and helped my sister keep an eye on him and none of this would've happened," Hanna looked away, afraid that Hawthorn might see her ugly cry-face, "I just feel guilty."

"You shouldn't."

It may have been because she was cold and needed the extra body heat or it may have been that he was the first person she had opened up to in years but Hunnie Combs gave Hawthorn a good, long hug. Much to his surprise, he found himself hugging her back.

At the Daily Chronicle, Eddie Mallow sat alone in his office, which was little more than a closet under the stairs where they kept the servers. The editor-in-chief had asked Eddie to stay late and update the website.

"You know, add graphics or something, make it look *real* slick," were the only instructions given.

So, in the warm glow of his laptop, Eddie sat in the dark, burning the midnight oil. In this particular case, burning the midnight oil meant using the work computers for personal stuff because the internet at home was too slow.

The personal project he was working on was finding Hunnie Combs.

He had been paid a modest sum for the video he sent to the Falling Star Report, much more than what he was expecting. Even better than getting paid was getting the journalistic recognition from a nationally televised news organization. It didn't matter that it was tabloid news, it was exposure.

He had heard all about the mass murder at the motel and was able to sneak out on his lunch break and get some video of dead bikers being carted out. FSR paid him handsomely for the raw footage, even if it didn't feature Hunnie Combs. He had captured enough shots of the Cloud 7 Motel sign in the background that the producers could come up with a compelling narrative; *Hunnie Combz on murder spree, Hunnie Combz, bikers die in orgy, Hunnie Combz kidnapped by mysterious stranger, kills bikers in wake.*

It didn't matter to him, he had done his job. Now he just had to keep tabs on the pop star and get plenty of footage.

Eddie clicked around the many legitimate news sites that had covered the *Cloud 7 Motel Massacre* searching for clues as to the whereabouts of Ms. Primrose "Hunnie" Combs. Few had anything more than "singer Hunnie Combz had stayed in the hotel the night before" and "it is unknown if she was present for the attack."

In the background, he was listening to the county police scanner in case something came across the radio about Hunnie, but at the moment it was becoming more of a distraction. Something about an 11-41 and Code 30 at LPD, he didn't know. He turned it off.

Leaning back in his creaky desk chair, Eddie clasped his hands over his head and thought.

As far as he knew, he was the only paparazzi in the area. There was virtually no chance that any of the professionals would dare set foot this far from the coast. But there was still the possibility of other amateur photographers wanting a taste of Hunnie.

Eddie laughed at his own clever wordplay. Wishing he had someone to share the joke with.

He ran a search for 'Hunnie Combz' and came up with a bunch of the same celebrity garbage he was contributing to; tabloids, wikis and fan sites.

If he was going to stay ahead of the curve, he would have to dive deeper into her personal history. Going further back to before he knew her.

He typed out 'Primrose Combs' in the search bar and came up with a whole list of websites about bridal hair combs.

"Hmmmm," he mused. He hadn't even come across

people sharing the same name.

Undeterred, he narrowed it down further, searching for 'Primrose Combs Longville MO.'

Scrolling through the results, one particular link caught his eye.

"Here we go," he said with a grin.

CHAPTER 16

Hawthorn awoke to the smell of coffee and the sound of evangelical puppets singing.

He slowly opened his eyes to see two children sitting on the floor with their backs to him, looking up at the tv. Each child sat cross-legged, contently eating a bowl of cereal. They appeared to be watching some sort of religious children's program; there was a Jim Henson-inspired puppet that looked like a cross between Jesus and Bruce Springsteen holding a little electric guitar, it was singing an anti-abortion song to the tune of 'Born in the USA'.

"....Formed in my mother's womb, I was formed in my mother's womb...." the puppet sang.

Closing his eyes, Hawthorn rolled over on the air mattress and tried to fall back asleep. He felt a hard, rubber handle jam into his ribs and Hawthorn remembered that he wasn't sleeping on an air mattress but an inflatable pool float Buzz had dug out of the garage. Above his head, he heard the peaceful gasp of someone sleeping with her mouth open.

He knew it was a her because he let Hunnie Combs take

the couch while he offered to sleep on the floor.

Opening one eye, Hawthorn focused on Hunnie who was sprawled out on the sofa. Head tilted back. Mouth wide open. Half of her limbs hung off to the side. She looked like she was about to fall at any moment.

With a sigh, Hawthorn laid on his back and shut his eyes. He tried not to think but his mind wouldn't let that happen. He was already thinking of the challenges ahead; figuring out what to do about the dangerous swarm, getting in contact with the proper authorities, keeping Hunnie safe.

He glanced back at Hunnie on the couch. Why was the swarm after her? Hawthorn could think of no other explanation except that someone must have an outside influence on the swarm, dictating who they attack. He had once read about a man in England who had bred bees and trained them to sting specific people. But who wanted harm against Hunnie and how were they controlling the swarm?

Hawthorn was drowsy and couldn't think straight. He needed to wake up. He needed some coffee.

Quietly making his way in to the kitchen, he found Honey Bunn holding Baby Blue in one arm and a cup of coffee in the other. She must have been up a while, she was already fully dressed and made up. Same tight jeans as the night before, different low cut v-neck.

The baby, however, was only wearing a diaper and a thin layer of saliva.

"G'morning, sunshine," Honey B said, the shirtless baby turning to see who came in.

"Hello," said Hawthorn, looking down at his own clothes and realizing how shabby he must've looked.

Honey B took a drink from her Worlds Greatest MILF

mug and asked, "How'd you sleep?"

"Fine," he lied, "You?"

"I got a good four hours," she said, making the cheers motion with her mug, "Want some coffee?"

"Please."

"Here," Honey B handed off the baby to Hawthorn, "Hold this little guy for me."

Awkwardly, Hawthorn held the baby at arm's length as Honey B poured him a cup of coffee. Baby Blue gazed up at Hawthorn with his bright green eyes. Completely mesmerized. Hawthorn stared back at the pale, chubby baby and was reminded of the larva stage of a horse-fly.

Honey B asked, "So what's your game plan?"

"If possible I'd like to talk with a Ms. Carson Flowers; the sheriff said she's a local beekeeper and, frankly, I could use all the help I can get."

"Yeah, we buy honey from her from time to time," said Honey B, taking the baby off Hawthorn's hands and handing him a cup of coffee, "I can take you there after work, she lives just south of here."

"I would very much appreciate that, thank you," said Hawthorn, "But first I need to contact the proper authorities and let them know of our current situation."

"#@$% that noise!" she said with a look of revulsion, "I thought you trying to lay low? Now you want to draw attention to yourself."

"We need to let somebody know that we're safe, plus, I'm pretty sure the county police will want to know about the dead sheriff and deputy."

Honey B threw up her baby-free hand, "Contact the police if you want, hell, call the coast guard, marines and the FBI, but don't lead them here. Primrose is safe with us and you gotta promise me you're not gonna do anything to put her in harm's way."

Hawthorn hated making promises. There were too many unknown variables that could change the outcome. Especially when dealing with something as erratic and unreliable as a human being.

"Promise me," she said again, sternly.

Taking a breath through his nose, Hawthorn chose his words carefully, "I will figure out a way to keep her safe and hidden."

"Okay, then," Honey B said with a single nod, "I guess that will have to do."

It had only been five years since Eddie graduated from high school but it may as well have been a lifetime ago. Walking through the crowded halls of Longville R-I was like taking a step back in time. The entire school was a relic of the past; not at all like the up-to-date high school Eddie had attended but, rather, the kind of dilapidated institution he saw in old movies. The kind of school his parents went to.

He really should have been at work but as far as Eddie was concerned, the Daily Chronicle was a lost cause. Mismanaged, understaffed and overleveraged. It had already switched to being a biweekly publication and it would only be a matter of time before it was bought by the Grand Old Press, Corp.; a media conglomerate that was on its way to owning all the rural newspapers, radio channels and tv stations.

He had to think about his future.

Wearing a checkered zip-up hoodie and a #SoFleak t-shirt, Eddie was pretty sure he was fitting in. He only wished he had remembered to shave. But even with his wispy excuse for a mustache, he could easily pass as a high schooler. For all they knew, he was nothing more than the funky new kid from out of town.

Confidently strutting down the hall, Eddie tried his best to look like he knew where he was going.

All he had to do was find the library.

While he wasn't purposefully drawing attention to himself, he was getting looks from random students here-and-there. Perhaps trying to figure out who this new guy was. Several of the girls seemed intrigued; raising an eyebrow or giving a curious smirk. The guys, however, seemed threatened; staring him down the entire time. One tall dude with a tucked in flannel shirt and a Don't Tread on Me belt buckle looked particularly annoyed by his presence.

Eddie didn't care if some of the countryfried, good ol' boys glared at him, he knew he looked good. Why else were all these cute girls checking him out? He was too cool for school and he knew it.

He was also too old for school but nobody needed to know that.

Besides, Eddie thought to himself, girls like older guys. Especially the ones that put out.

Lost in the thought of dating high school girls, Eddie came across the library. He would have to think more about this later, when he was alone. There was another girl he was much more interested in.

Just as the eight o'clock bell rang, Eddie walked through the open double-doors of the library. Shoulder-high bookshelves aligned the walls of the room with short, square tables scattered throughout and a couple of rows of outdated computers in the center. To his immediate left, stood an old crone behind the information desk. The librarian gave Eddie a long, weary look before finally acknowledging him

"Yes?" she said in a most uninviting way.

"Hi," said Eddie, "You guys have any old yearbooks from like five to seven years ago?"

"We keep them up here behind the desk."

"Great, I'd like to check them out, please."

"Yearbooks aren't for checking out and must remain in the library," spat the woman.

"Oh, okay," stammered Eddie, put off by the librarians animosity, "Can I just take a look at them?"

"Why?"

"I'm with the school newspaper and we're doing a 'where are they now' type story on some of the graduates."

"Sounds like a depressing topic."

"Well...." said Eddie, lost for words, "I guess I won't know until after I've done my research."

Without breaking eye-contact, the librarian reached below and lifted up a stack of thin yearbooks from the past ten years. Each hardback book couldn't have been more than a hundred pages. She set the stack down and pushed it forward.

"Return them in the chronological order in which they were given," she said, "And absolutely no writing or drawing on any of the pages, do I make myself clear?"

"Okay....thanks," said Eddie, grabbing the stack and resisting the urge to tell her he hopes she dies a gruesome and untimely death.

Finding a table furthest away from the crabby librarian, Eddie sat down and got out his notes on Primrose "Hunnie" Combs. According to what he found online, Combs was on girls volleyball team in her senior year. He grabbed the appropriate yearbook and cracked it open. Flipping through page-after-page of awkward teenage faces, he got to the Sports section and found a group photo of the girls volleyball team.

Somebody had vandalized the page, drawing a red 'X' across the face of one of the players.

In the photo, there were nine cute girls on the team standing in two rows next to their homely-looking coach. They wore white jerseys and black short shorts. Front and center, happily holding a volleyball, was the young lady with an 'X' on her face. Eddie peered closely at the girl and recognized her. It was Hunnie Combs. Her hair was longer and it was a darker shade of blonde but it was unmistakably the future pop star.

Eddie found it odd that she was listed as Honey B. until he realized that he was looking at the names for the second row. Directly behind Primrose C. stood a tall, voluptuous woman with the body of a Norse fertility god and jersey number 69. She had almost the exact same short, platinum hair that Primrose would have when she became famous.

Thumbing through the Clubs and Activities section, Eddie landed on another picture of Primrose Combs. It also had a red 'X' scribbled across her face. She and the tall volleyball girl were singing in choir together.

On the next page was a featured photo of Primrose C. and Honey B. performing at the school talent show. Wireless mics in hand, they were both dressed in slutty outfits and were clearing having a good time. But like the rest of her photos, her face was crossed out in red ink.

He turned the page.

Underneath the title SUPERLATIVE WINNERS were

pictures of students voted Most Likely To, which included such categories as; Donate a Kidney, Die in a Car Crash, Embezzle a Million Dollars, and so on. Eddie was shocked to see that Combs wasn't voted Most Likely To Become Famous. Instead it was her friend Honey Bunn who won that category (along with Most Likely To Get an STD).

Pulling out his phone, Eddie decided to give Honey Bunn a look on social media.

It didn't take long for him to find exactly what he was hoping for.

At 7:20 P.M. last night, Honey Bunn had posted: SO HAPPY 2 B w/my BOO! #reunited #blessed. Underneath was a selfie of her and Combs outside of what looked like a bar. While Eddie didn't know where the picture was taken, he didn't have to look far to find out. Every other post Honey Bunn made was a selfie of her bartending at the Work Tavern.

Eddie chuckled to himself. It couldn't have been any easier. Lucky for him people could be so stupid with what they share online.

He gathered his things and made for the entrance, leaving the stack of yearbooks strewed across the table. Before the withered old bat could say a thing, he held up his hand and gave her the middle finger. Exiting the library.

Out in the hall, he could hear the librarian yell, "Principal Baldrian will hear about this!"

Eddie smiled. Knowing he had done the students a public service. He walked happily down the empty hallway until a muscular hand reached out from the boys restroom and pulled him in.

The hand belonged to the mean-looking country boy with the belt buckle. Lifting Eddie off the ground, he slammed him against the cream colored brick wall.

"Where's my math homework?" he snarled.

"I have no idea what you're talking about," Eddie said as calmly as he could muster.

"Don't play dumb with me," the country boy said, lifting him higher, "you said you'd get it to me first thing in the morning now where is it?"

"Dude, you got me confused with someone else," said Eddie, feeling a bit more desperate, "I don't even go here."

Pressing him against the wall tightly, the boy looked him in the eyes and said, "There's only one foreign kid in this school and you're it, Ping Pong!!"

"I'm not foreign!" exclaimed Eddie, trying to wriggle himself free, "I'm from St. Louis!"

With a sudden burst of anger, Eddie pushed his assailant back with his feet. Both falling to the ground.

The country boy pulled himself off the wet bathroom floor and said, "Alright, that's it!"

Enraged by Eddie's attempt to defend himself, the angry young man dragged him into the nearest stall, shoved his head in the toilet and gave him the swirly of a lifetime.

Fifteen minutes later, Eddie shambled out of the bathroom completely soaked from head to toe. He was dizzy and disoriented. After being dunked in every toilet and urinal, his black hair spiraled up at the top like a soft serve ice cream cone.

All Eddie wanted to do was get out of this hellhole and change into some dry clothes.

But a portly bald man with glasses stood in his way.

"Son, shouldn't you be in class right now?" he said, arms crossed, "Where's your hall pass?"

Eddie sidestepped the bald man, "Leave me alone."

"Hold on there, son," the man said, blocking his path, "Ms. Fingerkraut told me you flipped her off."

"I don't know any of you people," Eddie cried out, "I don't even go here!"

"Now, Ping Pong," the man calmly said, "I know you're not from around here but you are a guest in this country."

"Listen, dude, I don't know who you're mistaking me for but I'm pretty sure his name isn't Ping Pong."

"What has gotten into you? First you flip off our poor librarian and now you're talking back to authority," the man took out a pen and a small pink notepad and began writing, "Ping Pong, I don't like this new side of you. Not one bit!"

"I'm not #@$%ing Ping Pong!"

"And what's this I hear about you not completing Duke's homework?" he asked, looking up from his notepad, "He is our star horseshoe player and we're going to need him if we're ever going to go to regionals."

"Whatever, man!" Eddie said, throwing up his hands, "I'm out."

"You're not going anywhere, son," the man said, tearing off a pink slip of paper and handing it to Eddie, "You just bought yourself a detention."

After detention, Eddie went straight to the Work Tavern.

Entering the roadhouse, Eddie walked up to the bar and sat next to a lonely old timer. He nodded at the old man but he was too busy sucking on his beer to notice. Even if he did notice, the old timer was too drunk to care.

Eddie shifted in his seat and took in his surroundings.

The bar was everything he had hoped for. A total dive.

Cheap wood paneling, exposed wiring and signage from local businesses long since dead. He felt right at home.

The sound of classic rock cut through the smoky atmosphere and Eddie awkwardly bobbed his head to the beat. At the pool table, two men were playing a game of billiards. In the corner booth, a middle-aged couple enjoyed each others company by drinking and not talking to each other. And at the far end of the bar, two of the bartenders were chatting it up while one put glasses away. The one arranging glasses was a fifty-something year old woman who must've been quite the looker back in day. The other was Honey Bunn.

Eddie barely recognized her from her yearbook pictures.

She was just as tall as he was expecting but she had gained several more chins and her hourglass figure now looked more like a stopwatch. Feeling that someone was watching her, she looked in Eddie's direction and tapped her coworker on the shoulder. The middle-aged bartender walked up and greeted him.

"Whatdya have?" she asked.

"Mint Julep."

The barmaid looked at Eddie like he had two heads and exclaimed, "Huh?"

Eddie should have realized this podunk bar wasn't nearly as sophisticated as the cocktail lounges he and his friends would frequent. "Mint Julep," he began to explain, "It's Kentucky bourbon whisky, fresh mint leaves, sugar syrup, seltzer water and crushed ice," Eddie pointed at Honey Bunn who was playing with her phone, "and could you grab her for me?"

The bartender turned in Honey's direction.

"Hey, Hun," she yelled, "This guy wants to talk to you."

"Thanks," Eddie said meekly.

Giving Eddie a smug smile, the barmaid went about making his drink.

"Yeah? What dya want," Honey Bunn said, squeezing her body past her coworker, "I'm off the clock."

"I'd like to talk to you."

"Okay but if you're trying to get in my pants you should know that I'm a married woman."

Eddie shuddered at the thought.

"No, my name is Edward Mallow I'm a reporter with the Daily Chronicle."

"You sure don't look like a reporter," said Hunnie, eyeing up his disheveled hair, face and ridiculous hoodie, "you look like you got beat up at a rave....but not, like, a good one."

"Never mind that, I'm writing a human interest story and I'm looking for Hunnie."

"You found her," she said pointing both thumbs towards her chest.

"Combs."

"Sorry, we don't get many celebrities around here."

Raising an eyebrow, Eddie said, "Oh really?"

"Unless you count old man Curtis, here," Honey B reached over to the old timer sitting next to Eddie and patted him on the shoulder, "He's the king of karaoke in these parts, ain't that right, Curt?"

Excited to be acknowledged by the curvy young lady, the old timer blurted out, "I know every Elvis song there ever was!"

Honey B gave his shoulder an encouraging squeeze and said, "If you're looking for an interesting human, interview this guy."

"Actually," said Eddie, keeping his attention on Honey,

" I'd rather interview you."

Leaning back, Honey B folded her arms, "Oh yeah? And why's that?"

"You were friends with Hunnie Combs in high school, right?"

"Couldn't tell ya'," she shrugged, "I never met her."

"You went to Longville R-I?"

"Sure did."

"That's a pretty small school, you two didn't share any classes or anything?"

"Not that I know of."

"That's funny...." Eddie said taking out his cellphone and bringing up his notes, "....because I was going through some of your old yearbooks and it looks like you and her were in a number of clubs together; choir, volleyball, pole dance squad. But you have no memory of her?"

"I don't know what to tell you, dude," Honey B lashed out, "The chick probably had a crush on me, wouldn't be my first stalker."

Eddie had expected this kind of reaction but he was getting her right where he wanted.

"You know, she's back in town?" he said in a mock-conversational tone.

"Is that so?" said Honey B, mocking his douchey performance.

"Yeah, you haven't seen her, have you?"

"You're asking the wrong chicka."

"You sure?" Eddie asked, searching her eyes for any sign of misgivings.

Confidently staring right back, Honey B leaned forward and said, "Positive."

Eddie was about to call BS but his train of thought

was derailed as soon as his drink order arrived. The fifty-something barmaid tossed down a coaster and set Eddie's drink on top of it. From what Eddie could surmise, the bartender had merely made a whiskey and water on the rocks with two sticks of chewing gum sticking out of the glass. Eddie could only stare at his drink. Speechless.

"Now if you'll excuse me," said Honey B, " I've got to get going. Enjoy your Spearmint Jewel-Lip."

With his only lead about to walk out on him, Eddie panicked. Fumbled with his phone and stood up in his seat.

"Oh yeah?" he said raising his voice, "Well, if you haven't seen her then maybe you'd like to explain this."

On his phone was the picture Honey B had taken the other night. The whole bar stopped what it was doing to see what all hubbub was about. Curtis, the old timer, recognized the woman in the picture and got excited.

"Hey, I know her," he ejaculated, "I saw her here yesterday!"

Infuriated, Honey Bunn clenched her fists and gritted her teeth. Worse than being called a liar is being proven as one. Especially by a smug know-it-all.

"Listen bucko," she said, "I don't have to explain $#*% to you!"

"Maybe not to me," Eddie said coolly, "but I'm sure the county police will have a few questions about your friends whereabouts."

Honey B couldn't argue with that. Luckily she didn't have to. Two of her regulars took a break from their pool game and stood on either side of the gangly hipster.

"This little punk bothering you, Hun?" one of them said, pool cue in hand.

"As a matter of fact, he is," she said with a smirk,

"would you be a dear and show him out?"
"Gladly," said the other.

Eddie found himself in the dumpster outside.
On his back, facing skyward.
The overcast sky was painted in every shade of grey. A frigid wind from the northwest slowly pushed the solid wall of clouds above. In a couple of hours it would be dark.
Eddie rolled over in the lumpy heap of garbage bags and felt a loogie roll down his cheek. Still warm. A little souvenir from one of the men who threw him out. Wiping away the spit with his sleeve, Eddie reached up and grabbed the cold metal rim of the dumpster.
Pulling himself upright, he caught a glimpse of Honey Bunn leaving the bar. Pink camo purse slung over her shoulder. She entered her trashy, yellow Saturn, started it up the and drove off.
Frantically, Eddie fell out of the dumpster and scrambled for his tacky, plaid moped. He hopped on. Revved it up. And peeled out of the parking lot, tossing up loose gravel behind him.
In his haste, he didn't bother putting on a helmet. He was more concerned with keeping up with Honey.
Unaware that a large, swarming cloud was hovering directly overhead.

CHAPTER 17

" ....I'm someplace safe, that's all you need to know...."
Hawthorn took the empty tin can and nailed a hole through the side.

"....Say I'm in witness protection services or whatever....."

Pulling the nail out, he took the can and placed a screw over the newly made hole.

"....No, but they don't need to know that...."

Using a screwdriver, he went about attaching the tin can to the makeshift bellow; a triangular, wedge-shaped pump that was constructed out of two wooden planks, a door hinge, a couple of small springs, a plastic sack and a whole lot of duct tape. Sitting hunched over the coffee table, Hawthorn quietly worked while Hunnie Combs was on the phone with her manager.

"....We got it all figured out...." she said pacing the room, "...I'm staying here and my scientist friend is going to go to the authorities and help them with their investigation...."

Earlier that day, Hawthorn had a similar conversation with his supervisor at the college. Fortunately, the department head was willing to act as an intermediary between Hawthorn and the county police. Tomorrow morning Hawthorn would meet up with the police at the diner/bus depot and Hunnie Combs would be allowed to stay in her undisclosed location.

"....For however long it takes...."

He was taking no chances.

"....Felix, don't worry, I'll be fine..."

Not when her life was on the line.

"....we'll figure out the tour when I get back...."

From his place on the couch, Hawthorn looked out the window. Still cloudy and getting darker by the moment. If Honey B didn't get home soon, they wouldn't be able to visit the beekeeper before nightfall. Since Honey Bunn's husband was currently under house arrest, they had no other choice but to wait for her to get off work.

In the meantime, Hawthorn had decided to do something constructive. Something that might help them out of a tight situation. That's why he was building a homemade bee smoker out of trash.

Bee smokers were used to calm down a hive in the same way pot smoke would calm down Buzz. Of course, bee smokers didn't use marijuana and, as a result, the bees typically didn't get cravings for snack cakes and tacos at two in the morning. Nevertheless, it was a method beekeepers swore by for centuries.

Whether it would work on this particular swarm was another question entirely

"Hey, man," Buzz said holding up the bottom half of a smaller tin can, "how does this look?"

Setting his work aside, Hawthorn meticulously inspected the half-a-can. Along the side, three small legs had been cut out, making it look like a table from the world's crappiest dollhouse. On the bottom of the can, were a number of holes that had been punched through with a hammer and nail.

After gathering the supplies he needed, Buzz offered to help Hawthorn build a bee smoker. But despite Hawthorn's thorough instructions, the only thing Buzz was able to turn out was a makeshift bong, so he was put in charge of making the fire grate.

"This looks good, Buzz," said Hawthorn "can you make me another?"

Buzz turned towards the children, "Kids, we're gonna need another can!"

Out on the carpet, the kids were "helping" by opening up any cans Hawthorn needed and pouring its contents on the floor.

Next to Hawthorn on the couch, Buzz stared at the tools and materials that were laid out across the coffee table. Directing his attention to the half completed bee smoker, he asked, "What you gonna burn in these anyway?"

"In my experience, dry pine needles work best but anything natural that can smolder will do."

"If you want, I got some really good pot I been saving."

On the phone, Hunnie Combs was wrapping things up with her manager.

"Listen, I gotta go, but I'll be back in time for the tour, I promise," she said, "okay, bye."

Hunnie hung up with a sigh. Sitting on the armrest beside Hawthorn, she pointed at the bee smoker and asked, "How are these coming along?"

"As well as can be expected," said Hawthorn, placing the small, table-shaped fire grate inside the tin can.

"You think they'll actually work?"

"Doubtful. This swarm is unlike anything I've ever seen," he inserted one half-sized can on top of the other, "But it's better than nothing at all."

"You know what's really good at killin' bees?" Buzz said with excitement, "Fire. Put a homemade flamethrower on this bad boy and light 'em up!"

"Buzz, I really don't think Hun would appreciate you giving your son a flamethrower," Hunnie Combs said giving Gunner a side glance, "even if he has been a pain."

It was true. Hawthorn would have been done hours ago if not for Gunner; as soon as he finished one smoker, the little brat would find a way to steal it away and rip it to pieces. This pattern would have continued all afternoon if Buzz hadn't put his foot down and gave the boy something called night-night juice.

He was now sleeping comfortably on the floor.

When Honey B pulled in, Hawthorn was just putting the finishing touches on his bee smoker.

"Sup, dudes," Honey B said, sliding through the front door, "You guys ready or what?"

"About time," said Hunnie Combs, "I thought you said you were taking off early."

"I got held up at the office, some nerdy guy from the Chronicle was asking about you."

Both Hunnie Combs and Hawthorn stood at the same time.

"Don't worry about it," Honey B reassured them, "He tried following me home but I was able to lose him."

Just then, a man in a checkered hoodie drove up on a plaid moped.

"#@$% nuts," said Hunnie Combs under her breath.

"This does not bode well," Hawthorn added.

"Okay, relax," said Honey B confidently, "I got a plan."

Eddie Mallow dismounted his motorbike and put the kickstand down. The frigid wind from the drive had cut right through him, leaving his skin raw and his hair blown straight back in a comical fashion. Honey Bunn had done her best to lose him but it would take a lot more than a woman driver to dissuade him from getting his story.

Through the picture window of the brick house, he could plainly see Hunnie Combs and her male friend standing in the living room. Looking directly at him. The rotund figure of Honey Bunn stepped out in front. Holding up both hands, she aggressively criss-crossed her arms over her crotch while mouthing the words 'suck it.' And then proceeded to close the mini-blinds.

Eddie couldn't help but snicker.

He began to walk towards the house.

Pulling out his phone, he clicked on the camera app and selected video. Framing up the shot, he hit record. He was going to capture something good. Even if it killed him.

"That was your plan?!" Hunnie Combs cried, "Crotch chop and then shut the blinds?!"

Honey B shrugged.

"It worked, didn't it?"

"No!"

"Quiet," said Hawthorn, "I hear something."

The living room fell silent. Outside was the faint sound

of viscous buzzing. Getting closer. Getting louder. Even the playing children stopped what they were doing to listen.

Then, an excruciating scream came from the front porch.

Honey B and Buzz ran to the window, separated the blinds and peered out.

"Holy #@$%," Honey B exclaimed.

Rising from her seat, Hunnie Combs slowly joined the others. Hawthorn didn't need to see. He knew what to expect. Instead, he franticly went about preparing his bee smoker for action; stuffing cotton yarn into the fire chamber.

Through the gap in the blinds, Hunnie saw Eddie Mallow in hysterics. The swarm of bees all around him on the front lawn. Eddie running in circles, flapping his arms.

Not surprisingly, Hunnie Combs was terrified for her life. But she also felt something she had not expected; pity. Even if Eddie was a smug S.O.B., he didn't deserve to die. Not like this. If anything, he deserved a long, painful death after living a full life of annoying the crap out of people.

She still hated the guy but not enough to watch him die.

Making a dash for the door, Hunnie Combs snatched the bee smoker out of Hawthorn's hands. He had just lit the fire chamber and white smoke was beginning to bellow out of the hastily-made device.

"Hold on," Hawthorn protested, "Where are you going?"

"To help that idiot outside, come on!"

And before he could answer, she was outside.

The deafening buzz hit Hunnie's ears the moment she stepped on the porch. Eddie was sticking to his strategy of running in a large circle and screaming. The swarm right on top of him.

Hunnie wondered why he wasn't making a run for anywhere else. Then she caught a glimpse of why. His entire face, from forehead to chin, was covered with crawling, stinging bees. He couldn't see a thing.

Stretching out her arms as far as she could, Hunnie held up the tin-can smoker. Cautiously, she inched forward. Only getting close enough to release a puff of white smoke every time Eddie passed by.

Much to her disappointment, the bees didn't notice and continued chasing Eddie.

After several passes, Hunnie got frustrated and chucked the whole smoker at the swarm, accidentally hitting Eddie square in the head. She winced and watched as Eddie went down. Half the bees followed him to the ground.

The other half took notice of Hunnie and made their move.

Grabbing hold of her shoulders, Hawthorn pulled her back towards the house.

"Let's go back inside, shall we," he said.

In his haste, Hawthorn had left the front door wide open, which was good because the bees were baring down on them fast. Honey B stood in the doorway, watching in horror. But when she saw they were coming back to the house, she slammed the door shut.

Hawthorn and Hunnie Combs ran up to the porch and desperately tried to beat the door down.

"Honey, you lazy slob!" She screamed, "Open the #@$%ing door!"

"I'm sorry, Prim," said the muffled voice on the other side, "but I got to put my family first."

"I thought we were family!"

The swarm drifted slowly, deliberately forward and both Hawthorn and Hunnie found themselves backing up against the door.They were cornered. The buzzing intensified and the swarming appeared to get more violent the closer they got. Flattening themselves against the door, Hunnie clutched Hawthorn tightly and they huddled to the ground.

Hovering above, the swarm was on top of them now. They were close enough for Hawthorn to not only recognize individual species but feel their wings graze his cheek.

"YAARRRRGHHHHHHH!"

A blinding plume of yellow fire shot out across Hawthorn and Hunnie's face. If it had been any closer, the fireball would have scorched Hawthorn's five o'clock shadow.

Leaping out in front of the bees, with his long stringy hair wafting in the breeze, Buzz gave a boisterous battlecry and shot another stream of fire at the swarm. In one hand, a lighter. In the other, a can of "Dubbaya Dee Forty". And even though Hawthorn knew it not to be the manufacturer's intended use for their lubricant, he was glad to see how effective it was against the insects.

The tiny, blackened bodies of dead bugs came raining down on the concrete where they were left to smolder.

Buzz, like a man insane, warded off the bees further with a well-placed orb of fire.

"Now's your chance, homies," he called out, giving them a look over his shoulder, "Get on out of here!"

Clasping hold of Hunnie's hand, Hawthorn pulled her

up.

"Thank you, Buzz," Hunnie said before she and Hawthorn made their escape.

Running round the other side of the house, Hunnie and Hawthorn tore headlong into the woods. Weeds, bushes and branches slowed them down, but they kept their pace the best they could. Hawthorn had led them into the wooded area to give them some coverage but it was getting darker by the minute and if they weren't careful they would have to spend the night in the wilderness.

Initially, it seemed that they had gotten away from the swarm. But, over the sound of their own feet trudging through dead leaves, they heard the irate buzzing. Ever so faintly. Far away in the distance.

Hawthorn hoped he had taken them in the right direction. Once they reached Carson Flowers place, they could maybe hide out for a bit and catch their breath. But that was if they could find their way out of the forest.

The buzzing grew louder and more pronounced. It sounded as if it was way off until Hunnie made the mistake of looking back. The cloud of bees was streaming through the trees and it wouldn't be long before they were on top of them again.

Hunnie was exhausted. Both her legs and back ached. If not for Hawthorn holding her hand, she would have twisted her ankle on a dead raccoon a half mile back. The chilly air burned her lungs and it felt like it could rain any moment. She hated the decision to go into the woods but couldn't blame Hawthorn. They had to go somewhere. It may as well be the dark, scary forest.

The electronic buzzing continued to increase in

volume until it was roaring all around them.

Agitated bees began zipping wildly in front of their faces. Buzzing angrily in their ears. And, if they were anything like regular bees, releasing alarm pheromones right underneath their noses.

It was pointless to run, they had already been enveloped by the swarm. But they pressed on. Swatting at the bees madly.

Then Hawthorn tripped over a stick and fell. While trying to catch himself, Hawthorn accidentally ran into Hunnie and sent her toppling over. They both hit the ground rolling. The swarm at their heels. Hawthorn and Hunnie found themselves face down in the leaves, waiting for the inevitable.

Nothing happened.

Hawthorn opened his eyes first. He still heard vicious buzzing. Looking to see where the bees were, he was shocked to see that they were now just hovering. In place. Only feet away.

The swarm wasn't even swarming. Each and every individual bees was just floating there. Frozen in mid-air.

"Are we dead yet?" Hunnie asked, her head buried in leaves, "Or are they going to drag this thing out and make us suffer?"

Curiously, and with much vigilance, Hawthorn arose. Scrutinizing the swarm.

"I'm not sure what they're about to do," he said, softly, "but I think we should proceed with caution."

Hunnie glanced up. From her spot on the ground, the bees were lined up in such a way that they almost looked like they were behind an invisible piece of glass.

"What the hell?"

"Yes," said Hawthorn, helping her up. Both transfixed

by the suddenly serene swarm.

Hunnie looked back and forth between Hawthorn and the bees.

"Well, are they going to attack or what?"

A long, roll of thunder blasted across the darkened sky.

And then, the bees began to fly away, one-by-one in the opposite direction. Back into the gloomy forest.

"Now where are they going?" Hunnie asked.

The sound of water droplets hitting the forest floor gradually filled the air and soon it was pouring cold, sharp rain.

Hawthorn took Hunnie by the hand.

"Come along, let's find shelter."

CHAPTER 18

I n a rustic shack not far away, Ivan Crocus awoke to the soft pitter-patter of rain against the windowpane. Usually men in their early fifties didn't wake up on military-grade cots but Ivan was the kind of man who kept Army Surplus stores in business. Staring up at the plywood ceiling he wondered if today was the day? Was today the day when *they* would come for him?

He hoped so.

It was only a matter of time before he would have to fight, and possibly die, for his beliefs and he was prepared to do both. He was also prepared to take as many people down with him as he could.

In the meantime, however, Ivan got up and went about his daily routine. Gas up the generator. Check his email. Harass the survivors of Sandy Hook.

Once he had those chores out of the way, he would enjoy a bland breakfast of oatmeal and coffee cooked over a wood stove. It was a simple life but Ivan prided himself on his self-sufficiency.

Except for his internet connection, he lived completely off the grid. No phone, no plumbing, no other public utilities to tie him down. He was his own man and this was his own life.

Ivan put on his hiking boots and slipped into his camouflage poncho. He typically slept in the same clothes he wore during the day, jeans and a flannel shirt, in case he had to make a speedy escape in the middle of the night. One could never be too careful, especially with all the intel he knew. Vigilantly, Ivan stepped outside.

It was chilly and wet out but Ivan wore enough layers to keep him comfortable, if not a little on the cool side. A soft steady rain pelted the trees and forest floor. Aside from the sound of rain hitting the leaves, all was peaceful, all was calm. Ivan exhaled and walked out into the woods, checking the perimeter.

As far as he could tell, it had been another uneventful night. No one had fallen into one of the many trapping pits he had dug and none of the tripwires had been set. All he had left to check was the cave and it was unlikely anyone could've made it that far onto his property without him knowing.

From afar, the entrance to the cave looked untouched; the thick, metal door seemed to be securely in place. But, taking a step onto the gravel path, Ivan noticed a footprint sunken into the mud. It wasn't made by him and any guests of his, however infrequent, would've stayed on the pathway.

He hobbled towards the entrance and saw that, while the door had been shut, it hadn't been latched; which was something he made certain of whenever he pushed it closed.

Ivan drew his gun and readied his flashlight.

The heavy door creaked upon opening. All was dark and silent within. Ivan shined the his flashlight across the main chamber of the cave. The round spotlight glided across the main chamber; casting the craggily shadows of stalactites, stalagmites, and other formations across the crumpled, cavern walls.

He moved forward, careful to check behind any rock formations that would make a good hiding spot.

Ivan was about to move on to the next chamber when he shined his light behind a large boulder and found a man and woman huddled together, sleeping in each others arms.

"What the heck?" he said, the couple opening their eyes to the light. The man was stately and strongly-built but Ivan thought he could take him in a fight. The woman was small and athletic with a full set of curves. He recognized her from somewhere but couldn't quite place it.

"Who are you?" said Ivan, "What are you doing here?"

"We mean you no harm...." the man said, slowly raising to his feet, hands up in the air like he just didn't care for getting shot, "....My name is Hawthorn White and I must apologize for trespassing, on what I can assume is your property, but-"

Ivan held his gun, firmly pointed at the man while he searched the face of the young, blonde woman.

"Wait a second," he said in a wave of recognition, "aren't you Hunnie Combs?"

The man and woman exchanged glances. She nodded and rose from the ground.

"Yes," she replied, smoothing out the wrinkles in her clothes, "yes I am."

With a relaxed chuckle, Ivan lowered his firearm, "Well, no wonder you're hiding out here, you're trying to get away from those dang bees, aren't ya?"

Shocked, the young lady looked to her friend and then back at Ivan.

"You know about that?" she asked.

"Heck yeah!" said Ivan, holstering his weapon, "I've been following it on all the conspiracy forums, my condolences to your sister, by the way."

"Thanks?"

"Don't you worry though, I'm one of the good guys, in fact, I'm pretty sure I figured out what's causing it."

Hawthorn cut in, "Excuse me, mister....???"

"Crocus, Ivan Crocus?"

"Perhaps we can discuss your theory someplace that isn't a cave?"

"We can go up to my cabin, it's just a short walk."

"I suppose that would be fine."

"Great!" Ivan said, gesturing at Hunnie and Hawthorn, "Follow me."

Ivan led them back through the cave by flashlight. There was much to see; stalactites, stalagmites and enough bat guano to fill an above ground swimming pool. When Hawthorn and Hunnie had stumbled upon the cave, they only cared to find a safe place to stay out of the rain. But now, Hunnie could take a moment to appreciate their surroundings.

"So this is your cave?" she asked in a conversational tone.

"Yes, ma'am," said Ivan, "you're walking through the main chamber of Middling Caverns!"

"You get many visitors?"

"Absolutely! We had some a couple of months ago. This is our off season, of course."

"How long have you been in the, uh, caving business?"

Hawthorn asked.

"About five years now. I used to run my own business 'till the dang government infringed on my rights and shut down my puppy mill."

"What the #@$%!" exclaimed Hunnie, "That's awful!!"

"I know, that's why I always tell my Sunday school students to never trust big government. Anyway, since Uncle Sam took away my livelihood, I bought this plot of land and opened up the cave for to the public."

As they walked through the echo chamber, Ivan used his flashlight to point out several noteworthy rock formations.

"Those stalagmites to your left are called The Preacher and his Choir and those two big rocks over there are known as The Soapbox and The Heavy-Hand, you wanna see the video I play for tourists?"

Hawthorn shook his head.

"We really don't-"

"Great!" said Ivan, taking out a small remote from his pocket, "Here."

Ivan pressed a button on the remote and from the opposite side of the chamber, a projector whirled to life, throwing a rectangular light across the cave. Projected over the bare, sheet-like wall were the words 'Welcome to Middling Caverns!' in big, blocky, yellow letters. The yellow text dissolved away as a picture of the cave faded in. An unseen stereo system began to play The Star Spangled Banner. Music echoed off every wet surface.

Accompanying the video slideshow was a friendly, female voice, providing narration. The voice track, in its entirety, was as follows:

"Welcome to Middling Caverns, Missouri's Darkest

Cave! The history of these majestic caves go back almost 6,000 years, when God created the earth in about 24 hours. After the fall of man, caused by Adam and Eve's disobedience, these caverns were probably the home to a family of cavemen, resting after a long day of hunting dinosaurs. A few hundred years later, after the great flood, Indians most likely performed their pagan rituals where you're standing right now! Once the United States was discovered 1,776 years after the death of our lord and savior Jesus Christ, American outlaws such as Jesse James almost certainly used caves like this as a secret hideout. And that brings us to modern times, where visitors from across the county come to Middling Cavers to display the wonder and majesty of God's creation!"

The video presentation ended with a picture of the American flag and text from John 3:16.

"Well," said Ivan enthusiastically, "what'd you think?"

Bathed in the light of the projector, Hawthorn gave Hunnie a look before answering.

"Besides all of the scientific inaccuracies, I suppose it was fine."

"Now before you go attacking my faith, I'll have you know that I consulted with Dr. Leonard Bush about the accuracy of the video."

"I'm sorry, I don't know who that is."

"My pastor; he got a doctorate in bible-ology AND tithe-onomics."

"Well, Hawthorn here is an actual scientist...." said Hunnie, "....so he might know more about science and stuff."

"Yeah and I bet he's one of those orchestrators that says global warming exists."

"I can assure you, Mr. Crocus, it does," said Hawthorn calmly, "Pretty much every legitimate scientist across the globe is in agreement."

"First of all, contrary to popular belief, the earth isn't a globe, it's a disc, and second, each one of those so-called scientists are actors being paid off by the media to push their liberal agenda."

"Okay, I've heard enough," said Hunnie, storming off.

"Listen," Ivan called out, "if you need proof, I can email you the link."

"She's right," Hawthorn said, following her towards the mouth of the cave, "we really should keep moving,"

"Hey, wait a minute, I wanna argue some more!"

By the time Ivan caught up to the man and woman, they were all outside; speed walking down the gravel pathway that cut through the misty woods. He would have caught up sooner if not for the heel spurs that kept him out of the army.

"Don't you wanna know why the bees are acting the way they are?" he pleaded.

"Not if it's going to be something stupid!" Hunnie called back.

"It's not, believe me."

"We should at least listen to his theory," Hawthorn reasoned.

"Why?" asked Hunnie, "He's not a scientist, he doesn't know."

"Hey, you're the one with the killer bee problem," said Ivan, "if you don't want to hear my own independent observations, you can just go ahead and leave."

"We're trying!" Hunnie quickened her pace. They could see a small, wooden shack emerge from behind barren trees. Despite her lack of interest, Ivan began his theory.

"You see, all of that funny bee-havior is caused by those dang cellular phone companies."

"Here we go," said Hunnie dryly.

"Now, hear me out," Ivan proposed, "You see, the bees are becoming more aggressive and violent because of their rapid decrease in population...."

"That's not at all accurate," said Hawthorn.

Undaunted, Ivan continued, "....and the dramatic decline in the world's bee population is because of the constant barrage of harmful cellular signals from mobile phones....

"Also not true."

".... Since their little bee brains can't handle it, it messes with their navigation and stuff."

"Again, that's not accurate."

As if hearing Hawthorn for the first time, Ivan declared, "There have been over eighty-three experiments which have all yielded the same results. Eighty-three independent studies by actual scientists."

"Hold on," Hunnie objected, "you've been deriding science this entire time and now you're going to claim it proves your crazy conspiracy theory?"

"I don't see why not, scientists try to prove all kinds of crazy theories, ever hear of the *theory* of evolution? Only somebody with an anti-Christian agenda would try to disprove the Bible."

"Dude, it's taken generations of scientists to figure out evolution, if it wasn't true it would have been disproven by now."

"No it wouldn't," Ivan cried, "Stop attacking my faith!"

Hunnie stopped her march forward to look back at the little man.

"I'm NOT attacking your faith," she spouted, "I'm attacking your aggressive ignorance, you stupid #@$%!"

"Hey, you are a guest here!"

"Look man," Hunnie said, pulling back on her anger, "I know crap about science and even I can tell your crazy theories aren't true, right Hawthorn? Hawthorn?"

Hunnie turned to Hawthorn only to find him standing perfectly still. Gazing out into the forest. Listening.

Seeing the look of concern on his face, Hunnie fell silent and strained her ears. At first she heard nothing, but then a faint rippling sound could be heard above the trees. She didn't recognize the sound until it was right on top of them.

A helicopter whooshed overhead, flying so low the tree branches shook.

"Holy Mackerel!" Ivan shouted, "They've come for me!"

Hunnie grabbed hold of Hawthorn, who was watching the black helicopter circle above. He took her hand and gave it a comforting squeeze. He wasn't positive but he was pretty sure they were here for them.

The helicopter came back around and hovered directly over their location, blowing air into their faces and whipping up loose leaves all around.

Gun in hand, Ivan handed the weapon to Hawthorn.

"You know how to use one of these?" he yelled over the deafening chopper.

"More or less," he said.

Reaching under the cuff of his jeans, Ivan pulled out a spare pistol from his ankle holster.

"Here you go, little lady," he said giving the gun to Hunnie, "Shoot anything with an American flag on it!"

"What?!" she shouted, "Why?"

"They're probably here for the bombs I sent in the mail!"

"STAY WHERE YOU ARE AND PUT DOWN YOUR WEAPONS," a man's voice blared from the loudspeaker above.

"Great!" screamed Hunnie, "Now we're accomplices!"

"Don't worry," hollered Ivan, "Today we die patriots!"

Ivan then turned and ran for his shack.

"I'll be right back," he called out.

The moment Ivan disappeared into his home, two military Humvees came barreling down the gravel road. As the armored vehicles sped towards them, Hawthorn decided to place his gun on ground and hold up his hands. Hunnie wisely followed suit. The Humvees slid to a stop on either side of them and a combat-ready soldier jumped out of each vehicle. Seizing Hunnie and Hawthorn, the troops hustled them into the Humvees and sped off from where they came, the helicopter following in their wake.

The forest was as calm as dawn.

From his shack, Ivan rapidly tottered out, armed to the teeth. He looked like Rambo's dumpy, middle-aged cousin from Wisconsin. Weighed down by all sorts of weapons and ammo, Ivan made his way back to where he had left his friends.

Guns a-blazing, he cried out, "A bruised reed shall he not break, and smoking flax shall he not quench, till he send forth judgement unto VICTORY!!!!"

By the time he was done with his drawn-out battlecry, Ivan realized that they had all left him.

Once again he was alone in the woods

Defeated, Ivan lowered his rifles and slowly made the long walk back to his lonely shack.

CHAPTER 19

The military vehicles turned off the gravel road and onto the adjoining highway, leaving the woods behind. As they sped by open farmland, the black helicopter above eventually broke off from the convoy and disappeared over the tree line. The two Humvees raced on.

Inside the frontmost vehicle, Hawthorn sat next to the soldier who manhandled him into the back. Careful not to make any sudden movements, he glanced over his shoulder at the vehicle behind. It was close enough to see the dark silhouette of the driver but not much else. He wondered how Hunnie was faring in the other vehicle.

Turning to the infantryman beside him, Hawthorn broke the silence.

"May I presume that we have been detained because of our association with Mr. Crocus?"

Silence.

"Because before this morning we had no prior interaction with the man."

Silence.

"I don't suppose there's any use in me asking where

you're taking us."

No response.

"Thank you for your service, by the way," Hawthorn added. Since he was getting nothing from the military men, Hawthorn went back to staring out the window.

For the next twenty minutes, the two Humvees continued driving down the highway. Passing the occasional civilian vehicle every couple of miles. The only time the Humvee's slowed down was to turn off on an unmarked side road.

Despite paying close attention to their route, Hawthorn wasn't familiar enough with the area to know where they were going.

The worn and cracked pavement faded into a gravel road that cut through a field and went past a pile of rotten wood that was in the shape of a desolate barn. Leading through a cluster of trees, the road narrowed, sinking with the land. Low hanging tree limbs scratched the Humvees armored roof. Hawthorn wondered if there was even enough room for the military vehicle to make its way down the long, winding path.

They passed a sign; RESTRICTED AREA, it said in red and white. NO TRESPASSING, it continued below in thick black text, U.S. GOVERNMENT PROPERTY. There was also a portion of the sign written in Spanish but it had been blasted away by a shotgun.

At the bottom of the hill the road dipped, leading up to a steep incline. If not for the all-terrain vehicle, any other car would have had a dickens of a time making it up the hillside. Once they reached the top, the land plateaued and they reached a wide open field full of short, round trees.

It was an orchard.

The two vehicles drove through an open gate that was attached to a tall chain-link fence that was rusted beyond repair. Atop the nearest fence post sat a pair of security cameras. One pointed to the road behind them. The other was aimed at the orchard ahead. Gazing out the passenger side window, Hawthorn watched row after row of neatly planted trees roll by. All the branches were barren but he recognized them as apple trees. Hawthorn found himself less apprehensive and more puzzled.

Why had they been taken to an apple orchard out of season?

Up ahead, a one-story, ranch-style wood building came into view. On one side of the building, stood a radio tower. On the other, a small metal garage. The Humvees parked in front of the main building and Hawthorn was directed outside.

From the rear vehicle, Hunnie was pulled out but she jerked her shoulder free of the soldier's grip. Taking in their new surroundings, Hunnie took a couple of steps towards Hawthorn.

"Why did they have us take two cars?" she asked.

Before Hawthorn could shrug a response, they were being led indoors.

They walked through the single-door entrance into a wood-paneled reception area that looked like a relic from the cold war. Old pictures on the wall. Outdated office furniture. Even the old woman behind the desk looked like a relic from the sixties. On her heavy wooden desk sat a modern computer, phone and fax machine.

Following their military escort, they went down a narrow hallway. Black and white photos of military vehicles hung on either side. The frontmost soldier opened the third door to the right and gestured for

Hunnie and Hawthorn to go inside.

It was a square, white room with a heavy wood table and three aluminum chairs. On one side of the room was a large, wall sized mirror. Above their heads, an old-style fluorescent light hummed loudly.

The door behind them was pulled to a close and locked. It was now just the two of them.

"Where are we?" Hunnie asked, "What is this place?"

"I don't know," said Hawthorn, eyeing the mirror suspiciously, "Either a military outpost or a government owned farm."

"Did any of the army guys say anything to you?"

"Not a word."

"Me either."

"Did you say anything to them?"

"Yeah, I was trying to talk to 'em the entire time."

"You didn't say anything incriminating, did you?"

"Why? Are we in trouble?"

Outside the room, Hawthorn could hear the lock being unlatched.

"I think we're about to find out."

In walked in a middle-aged commanding officer with a magnificent mustache and a remarkable likeness to actor William Hurt. He had the no nonsense composure of someone who had been the military way too long. Under his arm was a manila folder.

"Dr. White, Ms. Combs," he said in a pleasant but professional manner.

"And how do *you* know our names?" Hunnie asked.

"I always do my homework before allowing people on my base, Ms. Combs," he said walking over to the opposite side of the table, "We've also been using your cellphone to keep you under surveillance."

"Great, so you saw me on the toilet."

"Yes, but I wouldn't worry about that," he sat down and outstretched his arm towards the two available chairs, "Please, take a seat."

Warily, Hunnie and Hawthorn seated themselves.

"Would you like anything to drink?"

Hunnie shook her head.

"Dr. White?"

"No, thank you," replied Hawthorn.

"Very well, let's get started. My name is Colonel Madder of the United States Army, I'm sure you're both wondering as to why we brought you here."

Hawthorn felt obligated to set the record straight.

"Well, if it has anything to do with our association with Ivan Crocus, I'm afraid I'm going to have to ask for a lawyer."

"No, nothing of that sort, Dr. White, we know you have nothing to do with him or his terrorist activity," said Colonel Madder, "As far as we're concerned, Mr. Crocus is the FBI's problem."

While it was nice to have their concerns of wrongdoing put to rest, Hawthorn still felt uneasy.

"If we're not here for that then why have you detained us in this manner? Why did you capture us, drive us to an undisclosed location and then put us in a-"

"Excuse me," the colonel interrupted, "why do you keep looking at the mirror?"

"I mean, it's a two-way mirror, right? There's someone on the other side watching us, taking notes?"

"No...no, we got a security camera right over there," Colonel Madder pointed to a ceiling mounted camera in the corner, "That's just a mirror," he said nodding at the wall.

"Oh."

"Now, as I'm sure you are both aware, the armed forces have a lot of secret projects in the works, some of which you will learn about today. So I must stress that anything you see or hear in this complex is strictly-"

"I'm sorry," Hunnie cut in with a derisive laugh, "I know you're about to tell us why we're here, and all, but this has been bugging me since you walked in," he turned to Hawthorn and pointed at the colonel, "You know who he looks like? William Hurt! Don't you think?"

Hawthorn gave Colonel Madder a look over and shrugged.

"From the Avengers movies?" Hunnie elaborated.

"I-I'm not William Hurt," said the colonel.

"Okay, sorry," Hunnie apologized with a bemused smirk, "Go ahead."

"As I was saying, anything you see or hear today is strictly confidential. Any classified information shared outside these walls will result with your immediate arrest and prosecution. Understand?"

"Yes," replied Hawthorn.

The colonel looked to Hunnie for a response.

"I won't tell anybody as long as you don't leak any pictures of me picking my nose."

Unsatisfied by her answer, Colonel Madder silently glared.

"Yeah, I understand," she said.

Folding his hands and setting on the table, Colonel Madder explained, "The reason why we brought you here is because of your connection with a series of bee attacks. These bee attacks came from an alleged killer swarm. This is the swarm that attacked your father, killed your sister and has been relentlessly pursuing you, killing everyone who gets in the way. Dr. White, you observed that these are no ordinary bees and you are obviously correct."

"Okay, so if it's not your normal, everyday killer bee what is it?" asked Hunnie.

"How familiar are you with colony collapse disorder?"

Hunnie shrugged, "I know bees are dying off and nobody knows why."

"Dr. White, care to elaborate?"

"Actually," Hawthorn began, "according to recent studies, CCD appears to be a result of Verona Mites and a combination of pesticides and poor nutrition; as a result, the bees are more vulnerable to viruses that have a devastating effect on the colony as a whole. But what does colony collapse disorder have to do with the killer swarm we've been dealing with?"

"In the early 2000s the department of agriculture noticed the rapid decline in bee population. Because bees are the lynchpin in pollinating crops, the U.S. government took action to save the bees. However, once it was found that global warming and pesticides were two possible culprits, the government decided to take a different course of action.

"Instead of "saving the bees" by fighting climate change and cutting back on harmful chemicals, we would simply make a better bee. One that would better suit our needs and maintain our gross national product."

"What do you mean by 'make a better bee?'" Hawthorn asked.

"The goal was to create a genetically modified bee that could peacefully coexist with humans without us having to change anything about our lifestyle. A superior bee that could survive harsh weather conditions, is immune to pesticides and disease, and one that isn't aggressive towards humans."

"Well, you guys #@$%ed that last one up real good," said Hunnie.

"No, not exactly, you see this genetic super-bee was never created."

"Why not?"

"With the United States in the middle of a War on Terror; we needed new methods to fight terrorism and this bee project captured the imagination of the top brass. They loved the idea of fine-tuning something as small and commonplace as an insect and using it for their own needs."

"And by 'their own needs' I presume you mean espionage and weaponization?" Hawthorn speculated.

"Affirmative."

"Wait," said Hunnie, "so you're trying to militarize bugs?"

"Animals have been trained for war for as long as there have been wars," said Hawthorn, "Horses, elephants, dolphins, I even read something about man-eating badgers being used by the British military. I guess insects aren't outside the realm of possibility."

Colonel Madder continued, "So Army Research, Development, and Engineering Command took over and secret project Mellona was started. But upon initial tests, we had one major problem…"

"It was a #@$%ing terrible idea."

"….the bees kept stinging people. There was no effective way to control a swarm one hundred percent of the time. It turned out that bees really don't care for taking orders; we'd give them a target and they would just fly off and collect pollen. We'd strap on tiny, little cameras and direct them to spy on someone and they'd either fly away or sting the person fastening the camera. They made really awful soldiers."

"As to be expected," Hawthorn remarked.

The colonel opened up the manila folder and pulled out some photographs and diagrams, he passed them across the table, saying, "In order to have total control over the bees, we went back to the drawing board with a completely different approach. Once we got approval, we started contracting the R & D to tech companies until we were presented with something we could work with."

Hawthorn picked up a technical drawing of a what looked like a bumblebee, he examined it and asked, "Colonel, what exactly am I looking at?"

"That is the blueprints for prototype BX-01."

Shuffling through the pictures, Hunnie asked, "What do you mean blueprints? I thought you said these were created genetically."

"Initially, yes, but when the biological specimens failed our tests, we took the project in a new direction that focused solely on microbotics."

Amazed by the technological implication, Hawthorn asked, "The swarm of bees is robotic?"

"Yes."

Hunnie, who was more alarmed than impressed, said, "You mean those things chasing us, killing people left and right, are tiny robots?"

"Miniature drones, yes."

"Incredible," said Hawthorn.

"You know what?" Hunnie said, setting her hands flat on the table, "I think I will take that drink."

Underneath his mustache, Colonel Madder smiled, "Of course."

"What kind of booze you got?"

CHAPTER 20

Drink in hand, Hunnie Combs followed the colonel down the drab hallway. Hawthorn, walking alongside, couldn't help but be impressed that the base was able to accommodate Hunnie's drink order. They not only had the ingredients for a Bahama Mama, but also sliced pineapple, a hurricane glass and tiny umbrella.

At the end of the hallway was an alcove with a single set of elevator doors. Next to the elevator, a 12-digit numerical keypad was attached the wall. Colonel Madder typed out 872178 and the elevator doors slid open with a pleasant ding.

"I'm going to take you down to the lab," he said, gesturing them onto the elevator, "the research team wants to talk to you."

Exactly ten seconds later, Hawthorn and Hunnie stepped out of the elevator and into a room that resembled an airport security checkpoint. Next to a metal detector, an armed guard stood by while a pair of technicians sat in front of an x-ray machine. Just past the checkpoint was a large, glass enclosure.

The armed guard gave Colonel Madder a salute, Madder saluted back.

"If you will, please?" said Madder stepping aside for his guests.

Hunnie stepped forward.

"Place your shoes and personal belongings in the plastic bin and make sure they are on the conveyor belt when you walk forward please."

Taking a moment to slip off her shoes, Hunnie placed her boots in the gray bin along with her phone and rainbow sprinkle ice cream cone lip balm. Sliding her possessions down the conveyor belt, she made for the metal detector but found herself stopped by the guard.

"No outside drinks of any kind are allowed."

Visibly hurt by the suggestion, Hunnie protested, "I just got this!"

"I'm sorry, Ms. Combs," said Colonel Madder, "But there are a lot of sensitive electronics past this point and we can't risk them getting damaged."

Disgusted, she exchanged glances between the colonel and the guard, who both stared right back.

"Fine," she said and spitefully downed her drink.

Handing the now empty glass to the guard, Hunnie stepped through the metal detector with no issue.

"Thank you, ma'am, and now, if you will, please remove all articles of clothing and prepare for decontamination."

"I beg your #@$%ing pardon?!"

Colonel Madder stepped in to reassure her, "Whole-body decontamination is another necessary measure we take to ensure that no foreign bodies damage our nano-technology."

"Seriously???"

Sternly, Colonel Madder nodded.

"Okay, #@$% it," Hunnie shook her head and began unbuttoning her shirt, "At this point, it's not like anyone hasn't seen me naked," she said referring to her performance on the VMAs.

As soon as she was undressed, one of the technicians took her clothes and placed them inside a large, rectangular machine Hawthorn recognized as an autoclave. The autoclave would use high pressure and intense heat to sterilize her clothes. While the one technician tended to the machine, the other directed Hunnie to the octagonal glass booth.

Feeling uncomfortable, Hawthorn promptly averted his eyes. He accidentally caught a glance of Hunnie's lower back tattoo; a Chinese character that was supposed to say hope but in actuality said noodles.

The booth technician closed the door behind Hunnie and said, "Stand in the center, feet shoulder-length apart, arms out to the side."

Stiffly, Hunnie obliged.

"Nice," remarked the technician, reaching for the control panel.

Disgusted by his comment, Hunnie shot the man daggers only to get blasted on all sides by streaming jets of hot water. Shutting her eyes and mouth tightly, Hunnie felt the shower wash away the dirt and grime she had accumulated in the forest. Soon, the water stopped and Hunnie found herself assaulted by a bright red light and hot roaring air. Besides all the dudes watching, it felt like being in a human car wash.

Once she was dry, the blowers and heat lamps powered down and Hunnie was escorted out. Being handed a neatly folded stack of her freshly decontaminated clothes. The whole ordeal leaving her a bit disoriented.

Colonel Madder looked to the technicians.

"If one of you could show Ms. Combs the powder room so she can compose herself."

Hunnie was promptly directed toward the nearest washroom.

"Dr. White, if you please."

Hawthorn took a step through the metal detector and had no issue.

"I guess you need me to undress as well?" he said, taking a look at the glass enclosure.

"Nah," the booth technician replied with a shrug, "You're probably fine."

Having cleared security, Colonel Madder walked Hawthorn and Hunnie through the labyrinth of underground corridors. Hunnie had put her clothes back on and put her hair up in a sporty ponytail. She wondered why the decontamination shower hadn't messed up Hawthorn's hair but found her thoughts interrupted by the colonel's tour of the facility.

"And over here we have our high-tech broom closet," he said, pointing out the door as they passed.

Besides having a yellow CAUTION, UTILITY ROOM sign, it didn't look different than any of the other metal doors. At least, not to Hunnie.

"Oh yeah?" said Hunnie, "What's so high-tech about it?"

"There's one of those Rumba-things inside," the colonel replied.

Hawthorn, who had been paying attention with acute

interest, asked, "Why is this portion of the base so much more advanced than up above?"

"During the Cold War this entire facility was a Launch Control Building, in case of a nuclear escalation with the Russians. After the fall of the iron curtain it was deactivated and, more or less abandoned. That was until about eight years ago when it was decided to be the location for Project Mellona.

"In order to remain inconspicuous to enemy satellites, minimal additions were made to the support facility above ground, while a state-of-the-art research lab and living quarters were built down here."

"And what about the orchard outside?" asked Hunnie, "Doesn't seem like the typical kind of thing you see on a secret military base?"

"As a way to test the flying capabilities of the bees and their ability to pollinate, an orchard was planted onsite."

Colonel Madder opened the door to their immediate right; inside was a small rectangular room, lit only by the glow of a dozen computer monitors mounted on the wall. Hunched in front of the screens, sat a strapping young man with a chiseled jawline. Madder entered the room, Hawthorn began to follow but stopped midway; noticing Hunnie hanging back near the door. A sullen look on her face.

"Originally this room was Missile Command," said the colonel, "now it's the Drone Control Station; before the bees went rogue, this is where we dictated where the drone swarm went and what tasks it carried out."

Approaching the youthful soldier, Madder placed a fatherly hand on the chair's headrest.

"Private Dogwood here is using satellite imaging in an attempt to locate our rogue swarm. What progress have we made today soldier?"

"Nothing new to report, sir."

"Ms. Combs, I believe you and Mr. Dogwood have already met."

"Unfortunately yes," Hunnie said sourly, "he was my brother-in-law....for a time."

Turning his attention away from the monitors, Private Dogwood looked to Hunnie and said, "It's good to see you."

He seemed genuinely pleased to see her but Hunnie was having none of it.

"Wish I could share the same sentiment," she said.

"I'm sorry about Rosemary."

"Yeah, I bet."

A painfully awkward silence fell between them and Hawthorne wanted desperately to leave.

Ignoring the mood of the room, Colonel Madder said, "Private, why don't you take a break from all this and join us in the command center."

A short walk later, Colonel Madder escorted them through a pair of double doors. The command center was little more than a modest-sized meeting room with a large monitor on the wall. Up on the Big Board was a strategic map of Missouri. In the center of the room was a white conference table. Seated around the egg-shaped table were two middle-aged men and one lady. All civilians.

"Gentleman," said Madder to the room, "may I present to you Dr. Hawthorn White and Ms. Hunnie Combs; they've been our unintentional test subjects these last couple of days. We all have much to discuss so if you'll both take a seat, we can get started."

Hawthorn and Hunnie sat themselves in front of the three civilians. To Hawthorn, the panel before them looked like a small but diverse group of seasoned professionals. To Hunnie, they looked like nerds.

Colonel Madder took his seat at the head of the table, where a wireless keyboard and mouse sat. He swiveled his chair towards Hawthorn.

"Unfortunately, our entomologist is currently AWOL but maybe, with your insight, you'll be able to help us."

"I don't know how much help I can be when I barely know what's going on myself."

"All in good time, doctor. You see, when Project Mellona was moved here, we reached out to specialists in a variety of fields and brought four on as independent consultants…."

Madder nodded at the stone-faced gentleman with thinning hair and excellent posture.

"….Dr. Daichi Sakura, our robotics specialist…."

Next, he looked to a cocky-looking guy in black rim glasses and a leather jacket.

"….Dr. Malcolm Critchlow, mathematician…. "

Finally, the colonel acknowledged the tie-dye clad woman with long, gray hair.

"….and local beekeeper Ms. Carson Flowers, whom I believe you were in the process of looking for when we picked you up."

"Namaste," the friendly woman said in a smooth and calming voice, "If you're interested in buying some local honey, I've got several jars in my bag here."

"No, thank you," Hawthorn replied.

Looking to the colonel, Hunnie said, "I get why you

might need the robot guy and hippy lady but why do you need a mathematician?"

Bemused by her observation, the gum chewing mathematician snickered, "I'm mostly here to be contrary and tell these guys they're wrong."

"You'll have to excuse Dr. Critchlow," said the colonel, "he's been contradicting us on everything."

"I'm going to go ahead and disagree with William Hunt here."

"I know, right?" Hunnie exclaimed, excited that someone else thought the same thing about the colonel.

The colonel was not as amused.

"Again, I am not William Hunt," he said upfront, "No matter how good looking or talented he may be."

"Colonel, please," said Hawthorn, wanting the group to get back on track, "Continue."

The colonel took a moment and collected his thoughts with as much dignity as he had left.

"As I was saying," he said, "we have been working with these individuals in perfecting the look and behavior of our miniature drones to match that of an actual swarm of bees. Our goal has always been to make them indistinguishable from the real thing. Thanks to their efforts, we've successfully made it to the testing phase and have even used one of the drones to gather reconnaissance on a possible terrorist cell of teenage girls. Unfortunately during one of these recon missions the drone swarm went rogue."

"What do you mean *went rogue*?"

Critchlow elaborated, "They lost control of the situation."

The colonel gave a heavy sigh and said, "Either through a programing glitch or human tampering, we have not been able to regain control our drones."

Critchlow laughed, grimly, "Which is an outcome I warned about the moment Dr. Sakura agreed to arm the little buggers with tiny syringes full of cyanide."

"Yes," Sakura spat, "and you have not shut up about it since!"

"Look, Sakura, I'm not saying you should get all the blame for this... just most of it, like maybe forty-three percent of the blame should be solely directed at you.

"You guys," Carson Flowers chimed in, "I'm sensing some really harsh vibes right now, maybe we can, like, take a moment and find our center over some herbal tea."

"Flowers, I know you're trying to compensate for selling out to the military but you're laying it on a little thick, okay?"

"Hey, man, like, this whole trip was supposed to be about, like, saving the bees and stuff, you know?"

"Of course you thought that."

Fuming at the head of the table, the colonel tried his best to once again take command of the meeting.

"Dr. Critchlow, if you're quite finished."

"I'll never be finished with this lame brain trust, but you go ahead."

Holding back his anger against the council of smug eggheads, the colonel picked up where he left off.

"Originally, we thought the drone system AI had become self-aware and had decided to rebel against humanity...."

"Sakura is the only one who thought that," Critchlow interrupted.

"You shut your damn mouth!" Sakura shot back.

Ignoring them both, the colonel proceeded, "....but we have since determined that the drones have been hijacked remotely and these individuals are using the swarm for their own nefarious purposes."

"That's the #@$%ing understatement of the year," said Hunnie, holding back her own frustrations.

"I assure you, Ms. Combs, there's nothing to worry about, more than likely, it's just some Russian hackers."

"If there's nothing to worry about, how come both my father and sister were attacked?"

"You must understand, our relationship with Russia is a bit....complicated, you haven't made any inflammatory remarks against Mother Russia or her President in the last couple of months, have you?"

"No, but I did make a post of me twerking on the Mother Teresa Monument," said Hunnie, referring to an incident that caused some mild controversy with the catholic church.

"Colonel," said Hawthorn, who had been quietly sitting, trying to make sense of it all, "someone is clearly targeting Hunnie but that doesn't explain why the swarm is killing indiscriminately. We've seen them attack whoever is nearby."

"That's right!" Hunnie blurted out, "Those suckers were after *us* and then they go and kill a room full of bikers and the Longville PD!"

"That would be the drones AutoKill function," Critchlow commented, "Right Dr. Sakura?"

"Drop dead!" Sakura said.

Turning a deaf ear to the squabble, Colonel Madder observed, "I still wouldn't put it past the Russians to use our own technology to spread general chaos."

"You're just saying that because you're scared of them," said Critchlow, snidely.

"I am not scared of the Russians!"

"Hey, it's not me you have to convince, it's whatever operatives are listening in this very moment," Critchlow picked up a wireless mouse and held it to his face, "Right, comrades?"

"Don't even joke about that, Critchlow!"

"Oh, wow, man, he's right!" said Flowers, "They've probably hacked every lamp and coffee pot in this place!"

Defeated, Colonel Madder rubbed his face and said, "This is why I hate working with civilians."

"Are you guys always this dysfunctional?" asked Hunnie.

"Only when Dr. Critchlow is present."

"If only *he* would go missing, instead of Dr. Bladdernut," said Sakura.

Critchlow chuckled, "But then there'd be nobody here to say I told you so."

"Hold on," said Hawthorn, sitting up in his chair, "Dr. Kenneth Bladdernut? Was he the entomologist on the team?"

Bladdernut was the foremost entomologist in the state, especially when it came to the study of bees. Hawthorn mainly knew him from various entomological events, in which he was usually a featured speaker. It was no wonder that the government would want his expertise when it came to their militarized bee project.

"That's correct," Madder said, "Dr. Bladdernut is a colleague of yours, yes?"

"I usually see him a couple times a year," admitted Hawthorn, "We're both members of the Entomological Society of America."

"And when was the last time you spoke?"

Hawthorn thought back to December. They were both at the same white elephant gift exchange; he had "stolen" a brand-new ant farm from Bladdernut and the poor guy got stuck with a second-hand baseball cap that said "Lice Lice Baby." Even though it was all in good fun, Hawthorn still felt a little guilty about it.

"I guess it was at the ESA Christmas party. Why? Where is he now?"

Worried looks were given around the table until Colonel Madder broke the uncomfortable silence.

"We were hoping you would know."

CHAPTER 21

"I haven't heard anything from him in months," said Hawthorn to the research team.

Unexpectedly, Hawthorn was being cross-examined about his relationship with Dr. Bladdernut but they were asking for personal details he simply didn't know.

"I thought he was a friend of yours?"

He only knew Bladdernut from academic events; lectures, symposiums, overpriced fundraiser banquets.

"Not exactly a friend, more of an acquaintance."

And now the colonel was expecting him to be an expert about the missing doctor.

"So you don't have any idea where he might be at this moment?"

Outside academia, he didn't know much about the man.

"No," said Hawthorn, "Outside academia, I don't know much about the man."

Dr. Critchlow sneered, "I told you he wouldn't know."

Tired of feeling out of the loop, Hunnie looked around the table and asked, "Why is it so important you find this guy?"

Barely masking his disdain for the pop singer, Madder answered, "We have a feeling his disappearance is connected to the drone swarm."

"Based on what?"

"Based on the fact that Bladdernut went missing two days after the drones were hacked."

"How do you know he didn't do it?" asked Hunnie.

"Excuse me?"

"How do you know he's not the one responsible for taking control of the swarm?"

Leaning forward, Critchlow answered, "Something you should understand about Dr. Bladdernut is that he isn't great with computers."

"It's true," said Hawthorn, "He was speaking at a conference in Cincinnati and instead of pulling up directions on his phone, he had to have someone at the hotel print them off and mail it to him."

The skeptical look on Hunnies face brought a smile to Critchlow's. He reassured her.

"If you saw him try to bring up his email, you would understand."

Looking to the colonel, Hawthorn asked, "How exactly did he go missing?"

Without a word, Madder maneuvered the mouse until a black and white security video was brought up on the front monitor. The video showed a little bald man with glasses scurrying out of the compound and getting into a gray Cadillac. He pulled the car out of the parking spot and sped off, driving past the security camera. Through the windshield, Hawthorn recognized the man as Dr. Bladdernut. The video played again on a loop.

Grimly, Colonel Madder said, "This is the last footage

we have of him."

"Where's he going in such a hurry?" asked Hunnie.

"He said he received a call from a work colleague and had to leave; since he was dividing up his time between here and the university, it wasn't uncommon for him to leave in the middle of the day, we assumed it was something on campus."

Hawthorn frowned, Bladdernut didn't seem like the type to just up and disappear. Then again, he didn't seem like the type to participate in a secret government project involving robotic bees. "I take it you already checked with the university?" he asked.

"They haven't seen him all week."

"Seems pretty suspicious to me," Hunnie remarked, "You sure he's not behind it."

Thoughtfully cleaning his glasses, Critchlow said, "Mathematically, it's highly unlikely and you're forgetting one important component in this whole Scooby Doo-level mystery. The motive."

"$#*%, I don't know, he hates my music and wants to get rid of me and my family."

Critchlow shook his head, "While I personally enjoyed the entire *Honeysuckle* album, I'm afraid Dr. Bladdernut only had a vague awareness of your work."

"Okay, well if you're looking for someone with a motive, you should probably talk to that guy over there," said Hunnie, pointing at Private Dogwood, who had been standing by the door the entire time.

Suddenly put on the spot, Dogwood shot a glance at the panel. Every muscle in his face, body and sphincter simultaneously tensed up at the accusation. A look of terror in his eye.

In a calming tone, the colonel stated, "I am familiar

with the rift between your family and Private Dogwood but I can assure you that he had no part in hijacking the swarm."

"You'll forgive me if I don't believe you, Colonel."

"At the time of the hack, Dogwood was in the middle of a mission where he was using a drone independent of the HIVE."

"Whatever that means."

Colonel Madder brought up another black and white security video, this one was taken from the Drone Control Station; like before, Dogwood was seated in front of the console, controlling a drone via joystick. Next to him, stood a fellow serviceman who was watching the screen intently. On the monitor, three high school kids were swatting at each other with pillows.

"This is video of Dogwood at the exact time of the alleged hack."

"Okay," said Hunnie cynically, "And....?"

"As you can see, he's gathering intel on a domestic terrorist threat."

"Looks more like teenage girls having a pillow fight to me."

"Two of those young ladies are Islamic extremists," said Madder, "It may not look like it but they're trying to recruit that all-american girl."

"The white one."

"Yes."

Hunnie rolled her eyes.

"What's that other man doing in the control room?" asked Hawthorn.

"He's....supervising."

"Is it common for your men to eat popcorn while on duty?"

"Only when something good is on," Critchlow interjected.

Figuratively, Madder shot Critchlow daggers but he would have preferred to have done it literally, perhaps with some kind of knife-gun or knife-crossbow.

"Hey," said Hunnie pointing to the security footage, "where's that guy going?"

Having seen something from the drone, the serviceman next to Dogwood rushed out of the control room. It was a little hard to make out what sent him running. From what Hawthorn could tell, the girls were just sitting on the bed talking.

Moments later, the serviceman returned with a whole bunch of other enlisted men.

"Where the #@$% did those guys come from?" Hunnie spouted.

Men continued to crowd into the small room until Dogwood and the monitor he was viewing were completely blocked from the security camera. Even when it looked as if there wasn't any more room, more men continued to cram themselves in. All spellbound by whatever Dogwood was watching.

Seemingly out of nowhere, the entire group of servicemen began cheering and giving each other high-fives.

While Hawthorn couldn't see what all the excitement was about, he could take a guess.

"Sir, this a serious invasion of privacy," he said.

"Read your Patriot Act, son," the colonel said, glibly.

"Why are you showing us this?"

With a few taps of the keyboard, Colonel Madder brought up an additional security video playing alongside the original. This footage was outside the building, looking down at the orchard from the front gate. It was dark out but the night vision exposed every detail of the orchard in creepy clarity.

The colonel pointed to the dual screens playing simultaneously, "Notice the timecode on both."

"They're the same," Hunnie noticed.

As the young men in the Drone Control Center continued their celebration, the security camera outside showed only peace and tranquility. If not for slightest of breezes wafting through the bare fruit trees, the video would have appeared frozen. Then Hawthorn saw it. At first he thought it to be a truck driving up the road but was way too small.

It was about the size of a go-kart with four, large wheels and a pair of headlights but there was no seat or handlebars. Instead there was only a trash can-sized metal dome

"What is that?" Hawthorn asked.

The go-kart bounced down the uneven road until it sped past the security camera and disappeared off-screen.

Pointing to the monitor, the colonel replied, "That is what we're looking for."

"Okay..." said Hunnie, slightly perturbed, "....but that still doesn't tell us squat."

On the monitor, Colonel Madder closed the security footage and brought up a 3D, wireframe technical schematic of the mysterious vehicle. Above the rotating model were the letters H.I.V.E..

"What you just saw is a mobile charging station and base that houses the entire drone swarm, we call it the HIVE...."

"Of course," remarked Hunnie from the corner of her mouth.

".... whoever hacked the swarm, first took control of it through this mobile unit and moved it to an, as of yet, unknown location."

Hunnie couldn't believe their carelessness; she didn't know anything about the military but she expected a little more precaution taken in a secret operation.

"For #@$%'s sake!" she exclaimed, "Haven't any of you heard of GPS?"

Feeling attacked, Dr. Sakura sat up in his seat and took the offense.

"It wasn't finished," he bellowed, "we were working out the bugs."

Critchlow eased his cohort back and smiled, "You'll have to excuse Sakura, he's taken this whole fiasco rather personally."

"He should," said Hunnie, "I mean, I've written some pretty bad songs but it's not like any of them have killed anybody."

"That you know of."

Sidetracked, Hawthorn found himself studying the HIVE schematic. Scrutinizing every inch of the 3D model as it slowly rotated on screen. From across the table, the colonel noticed the puzzlement on his face.

"Dr. White, you look confused."

"I'm having trouble understanding why you need an automated beehive on wheels."

"I'll take this one, chief," said Critchlow, "In addition to being recharged, the drone swarm has a very limited range and can only be so many miles away from a transmitter site. When the drones fly out of range, they no longer receive command signals and cease to function. That's where the HIVE comes into play; it was designed to be a mobile transmitter that can be moved anywhere on the battlefield. So as long as the drones don't go outside the coverage area, the sky's the limit."

Hawthorn asked, "What kind of coverage does the HIVE provide?"

Fielding the question, Critchlow continued, "The drones can receive a strong signal from approximately twenty-five miles away, any further and it gets kinda choppy."

"A total surface area of fifty miles? That's not very far."

"Yes..." said Sakura bitterly, "...the transmitting range was limited, that's why we were in the process of boosting the signal."

"How often do the drones have to be recharged?'

"Constantly," said Critchlow, "They can only be out for about an hour before having to go back to the HIVE"

"Only an hour?" Hunnie scoffed, "My smartphone can last almost twice that!"

With everyone in the room criticizing his creation, Sakura snapped.

"We are all quite aware of the HIVE's limitations!" he cried, "That's why it's a prototype, okay?"

Hunnie raised her hand but didn't wait for anyone to acknowledge her.

"So I got a question," she said, "what does HIVE stand for?"

The colonel rubbed his face and sighed,"You just had to ask."

"I mean, you came up with the cute little acronym, I assume it's short for something, right?

Critchlow cautiously replied, "It will....eventually."

"Eventually? You don't have a name for it now?"

"You see," he explained, "among the group, it's a bit of a sore spot."

Hunnie laughed, "Why?"

"Not that it matters to me but I thought HIVE should stand for High-Value Equipment.

Sakura, ready to pounce, exclaimed, "Then it wouldn't spell Hive, it would spell Hve!"

With a single finger-wag, Critchlow responded, "Not if you incorporated the 'i' in 'high'."

Carson Flowers, who was currently sitting in her chair cross-legged, calmly suggested, "Seeing as it's, like, a military weapon designed to bring harm, I think it should be called the Hyper Intelligent Violence Engine."

"That's preposterous!" said Sakura, "The acronym needs to be the Hexapod Integrated Vehicle Emitter!"

Critchlow shook his head, "Sakura, why don't you go out and perform seppuku."

"You bastard!"

Flowers, the peaceful voice of reason, said, "What if we all just calm down and see if we can reach a compromise?"

"Silence, woman!" Sakura snapped, "You bring absolutely nothing to the table."

"Oh, wow, I'm, like sensing some harsh vibes from you right now."

"You should listen to her, Sakura," Critchlow sarcastically suggested, "She's a self-proclaimed empath, she can tell when you're being a complete a-hole."

Their argument continued and Colonel Madder turned his attention to Hawthorn and Hunnie.

"Unfortunately, they'll be like this for awhile," he said. Taking a look at his watch, the colonel stood up and addressed the room, "Gentlemen, it's getting late and there's a pot roast waiting for me at home. I'll leave you to continue this discussion on your own."

"Hold on," said Hunnie over the chatter, "so are we free

to go or what?"

"Ms. Combs, this is not a prison, you are free to go whenever and wherever you like, however, the person who hijacked the drones is at large and you appear to be their primary target, I strongly suggest you and Dr. White stay under our protection until we decide a proper course of action…"

The colonel paused and gave a passing glance to the research team, who were carrying on with their bickering.

"….which will probably not be tonight," said Madder, "Now, if you'll excuse me, I must be going."

Walking towards the door, the colonel gave Private Dogwood a nod.

"Private, please show our guests to their quarters."

CHAPTER 22

Private Darren Dogwood took Hunnie and Hawthorn through the underground corridors. The shiny black floor reflected the fluorescent lighting in a way that made it look like a single, glowing tube of white light was leading the way. Hawthorn wondered how far the base extended.

Hunnie, however, had other thoughts on her mind.

"I guess this explains why you never paid your respects," she said sourly to Dogwood.

The young military man kept his eyes forward, maintaining his pace down the hall.

"Hunnie, you gotta understand that I'm just as sorry for Rosemary's death as anyone."

"Somehow I find that hard to believe."

"Just because we couldn't make it work doesn't mean I didn't stop loving her."

"If you really loved her you wouldn't have cheated on her in the first place."

"Look I'll admit that we had our fair share of marital issues."

"Marital issues?!" Hunnie exclaimed, "You slept with a

prostitute and had her dress up like me!"

"Now, in my defense, you are way hotter than Rosemary ever was, God rest her soul."

Hunnie could've slugged him right there. But didn't.

Turning a corner, Dogwood led them to the end of a hall with a pair of doors on either side, then grabbed a cardkey and unlocked one of the doors. He pushed open the door, inside was a small windowless room with a single twin-sized bed, desk and chair. It reminded Hawthorn of his old college dorm.

Dogwood went over to the door opposite and began to open it as well.

"Darren, be honest with me," said Hunnie, "Did you kill her?"

Closing his eyes, he held the door halfway open and sighed.

"No," he said solemnly, "I may not have been the perfect husband but I'm not a murderer.... Unless the Army tells me to be one but that's a whole 'nother thing and those don't count."

"Oh, that's comforting," remarked Hunnie.

"The point is, I want to find her killer just as much as you."

Dogwood open the door, revealing an additional dorm-sized room.

"These are your rooms," said Dogwood, "If you guys need anything just let one of us know."

After Private Dogwood left, Hawthorn took advantage of the adjacent bathroom. He washed his face and used a washcloth to scrub most of the dirt and grime off his body. Spending the night in the wilderness had left all sorts of muddy stains caked on his clothing, so he did his best to rub them out. With little-to-no success.

Hawthorn stepped out of the bathroom feeling somewhat refreshed and took a seat at the desk. Finding a pen and notepad, he began jotting down notes.

Since his arrival on base, so much had been revealed.

The history of Project Mellona. The names and specialties of everyone involved. Technical details of the drones and mobile transmitter. He didn't want to forget a thing.

Especially if they were expecting him to help find the swarm.

Suddenly, there was a knock on the door.

Before Hawthorn had the door halfway open, Hunnie Combs came barging in.

"I couldn't sleep, mind if I come in?"

Hawthorn could do little more than watch Hunnie whiz by.

"Please," he said.

Hunnie sat down on the bed, she looked like she had something on her mind. But Hawthorn found himself distracted by the curvature of her butt pressing down into the springs of his mattress.

"So what do you think of all this?" she asked.

Taken aback, Hawthorn said, "Uh... sorry?"

Gesturing at their surroundings, Hunnie replied, "The base? The secret project? The colonel? Take your pick."

Reflecting on how much time and resources it must have taken to dig out the underground facility and get the project started, Hawthorn said, "I think I might write my congressman and ask why so many of our tax dollars are going to such an unnecessary project."

"No, I mean, don't you feel like they're hiding something from us?"

"It's the military, they are most definitely hiding

something, we're extremely fortunate that they've told us anything at all."

"Do you think their theory about the Russians is true?"

"I highly doubt it," said Hawthorn, "they seem more interested in causing chaos through misinformation than targeting individual Americans."

"I don't understand who would do this to my family."

"You seemed quick to accuse your brother-in-law."

"EX brother-in-law...." Hunnie stressed, "....I don't think he did it, I just couldn't think of anyone else who could."

"The colonel was rather quick to dismiss your accusation and he appeared rather guilt-ridden when asked."

"Yeah.... But think about it; if you were working on something that inadvertently killed your ex-wife, you'd be feeling pretty guilty about it too."

"You said something earlier about upsetting the Catholic Church?"

It took Hunnie a second to figure out what he was talking about and then she remembered her recent trip to Milwaukee.

"Oh, that?" she said with a laugh, "I mean, they weren't exactly thrilled about what I did at the Mother Teresa Monument, but I doubt they would try and kill me over it."

"Maybe not the church but there are a lot of religious zealots without a sense of humor."

"I know, I'm still getting angry comments from them."

"All because you danced with a statue?"

"Well.... I did a little more than dance," Hunnie admitted, sheepishly looked down to her lap, "It was more of me grinding against it...."

Hawthorn felt a bit embarrassed but intrigued at the thought.

With a smile, Hunnie looked up and said, "I can show you if you would like?"

Before Hawthorn could reply, Private Dogwood appeared in the doorway.

"Hey, I got those maps you were wanting."

The private walked in and placed the rolled up maps onto the desk.

"Thank you," said Hawthorn, clearing space, "And the compass and protractor?"

"Right here," Dogwood set the drawing tools down.

"Great."

"What do you need all this for?" asked Hunnie.

Unrolling the maps one by one, Hawthorn said, "I have a theory of my own I want to work out,"

The maps ranged from topographic to road maps of Longville and the surrounding areas.

"Yeah? What kind of theory?"

Leaning over the desk, Hawthorn began to pour over the charts, "Remember last night, when we were being pursued in the woods?"

"How can I forget."

"Do you remember how close the swarm was from catching up to us?"

"They were feet away and then they just stopped and flew off."

"Precisely!" he said, holding up a pencil, "At first I assumed it had something to do with the rain but now, I'm convinced it's because of the technical limitations of the drones."

"They seemed pretty #@$%ing advanced to me."

"And they are, but even they have restrictions, right?"

Hawthorn turned to Dogwood, who was hanging about.

"Uh... yeah, yeah," he said, having been caught off guard, "We can't take 'em out for long before they need to be recharged."

Hunnie shook her head, "Those things could've killed us in less than a minute and had plenty of time to get back, why didn't they?"

"Because...." Hawthorn explained, "....the drones can only go as far as the HIVE's transmitter will allow; the total coverage area is fifty miles which means that they can only fly twenty-five miles away from the HIVE, correct?"

With a shrug, Dogwood said, "Sometimes it's a bit more, other times a bit less, depending on broadcast conditions."

"So the reason they didn't attack was because we had stepped out of range?" Hunnie asked.

"Yes..." said Hawthorn, "...and because of that we should be able to pinpoint the location of the HIVE."

"How are you going to do that?"

Rearranging the maps, Hawthorn pulled out the topographic map and set it on top of the others.

"This is Honey Bunn's house...." he said, making a mark on the map, "...This is Middling Caverns....." he made another mark on the map, "....The swarm pursued us south by southwest through the woods...." he hovered the pencil over the map and traced their estimated route, stopping just short of the cave, "...this is where I believe the swarm stopped pursuing us.... "

Taking the straight edge of the protractor, Hawthorn drew a line stretching from the swarm's end point to the Bunn house and beyond. Meticulously, he measured out an approximate distance of twenty five miles inward and marked a new point darker than the rest. Adjusting the compass appropriately, he used it to draw a perfect circle around the newest point on the map.

"This represents the total surface area the swarm has to fly, fifty miles, anything outside this circle is beyond its transmitting range, assuming the drones couldn't go past this point, the epicenter of this circle should be the location of the HIVE."

"Sure, as long as it's still there," said Hunnie, "The HIVE is a mobile unit, it could be anywhere by now."

"While that is a possibility, I have a feeling it hasn't been moved."

"What makes you say that?"

"The person or persons responsible are most likely trying to keep the HIVE hidden; Madder has been scouring the area in search of it, so it's most likely the HIVE isn't being moved needlessly lest they risk detection, which is why I hypothesize that the drone swarm and mobile transmitter are both located here."

Hunnie looked to Dogwood who shook his head in confirmation. It seemed like a logical argument. Deep within the pit of her stomach, Hunnie felt a sudden sense of urgency.

"Well, what are we waiting for?" she said, "Let's go check it out."

And just like that she was out the door.

"Just a moment!" said Hawthorn, springing from his chair and chasing after her.

In the hallway, Hunnie marched onward. Leaving Hawthorn and Dogwood striving to keep up.

"We don't have a moment," she said, "they could move the HIVE at any time."

Catching up to Hunnie, Hawthorn matched her speed.

"I'm a bit unclear about our course of action."

"It's very simple; the drones can't function without the HIVE, so all we gotta do is find the HIVE and destroy it."

They turned a corner and continued on the path Dogwood had led them down.

"How do you propose we do that?" asked Hawthorn.

"Get over there and smash it up with a baseball bat, I don't know."

"Assuming if we could, it's not like we could sneak off base."

"Darren," Hunnie gave Dogwood a passing glance over her shoulder, "Can you get us out of here?"

"Sure," he said in a slightly unsure manner, "But I got orders to keep an eye on you."

"And you will. You got a vehicle?"

"Yeah, but-"

"No buts," Hunnie stopped short and faced the young private, "Considering how you treated her when you were married, I'd say you owe it to Rosemary."

Pressing his lips together tightly, Dogwood took a deep breath and considered what his former sister-in-law had said. She was right; he had done Rosemary wrong in life and he couldn't help but feel partially responsible for her unfortunate death. Exhaling, he nodded.

Hawthorn hated to be the contrary one but he felt he should at least offer a less crazy idea.

"I can understand you wanting to get justice for your sister but don't you think it'd be best to inform the colonel first?"

"Hawthorn, did you ever stop and think that maybe you think too much?"

"No," said Hawthorn, trying to wrap his mind around the question, "That thought has never crossed my mind.."

"The colonel doesn't care about me or my family or anyone else who's been hurt by those drones, he just wants to find it so he can get back to perfecting the next death-weapon."

"That may be true but they have resources here that we don't."

"And yet, out of all their resources, you're the only one who's close to finding the swarm!"

"I'm just saying that the military might be better equipped to handle this."

"Oh, they're not," a voice said from behind a corner and out stepped Dr. Malcolm Critchlow. Smug as ever.

"I suggested an EMP generator but Sakura didn't want to risk damaging the drones, which isn't at all how EMPs work, by the way."

"Okay, you caught us," Hunnie confessed, "We don't need another speech about how you're so much smarter than the rest of us."

Critchlow smirked, "Caught you doing what? For all I know you're just looking for the vending machine."

Before saying a word, Hunnie looked to Hawthorn and Dogwood, who were just as surprised

"So you won't tell the colonel where we're going?" she asked.

"As long as you don't tell me, I have plausible deniability."

"Great, thank you!"

Hunnie rushed down the corridor with Dogwood close behind. Not entirely confident in their mission, Hawthorn hung back. If only for a moment. Critchlow raised an eyebrow.

"We could sure use some help," admitted Hawthorn, "If you'd like to join us?"

"No thanks, I don't feel like dying today."

CHAPTER 23

Hawthorn was surprised at how easily it was for them to sneak out of the secret military compound. All Private Dogwood had to do was tell the guards that Colonel Madder was through with his interrogation and he wanted them placed back into the hands of local law enforcement. Dogwood then secured a vehicle and drove them off base.

The Army Jeep sped down the gravel road, leaving the darkened orchard behind. Frigid air rushed past them in the open cab of the vehicle. Sitting in the back, Hunnie wanted nothing more than to cover her numb ears but, instead, had to hold on for dear life.

"Why the #@$% did we take something without a roof?" she yelled over the passing wind.

Keeping his eyes on the knobby road, Dogwood leaned back and shouted, "This is the vehicle I usually take to run errands in, I didn't want to raise suspicion."

"At least you could've gotten us something with seatbelts," Hawthorn added.

"Hey, man, this is a classic Willys MB, they don't even make these anymore."

"I wonder why," said Hunnie after a particularly rough bump.

"How long do we have until the colonel realizes we're gone?" asked Hawthorn.

"He won't be back until oh six hundred, so we got all night."

"I'd feel better about our mission if we had some military support."

"Don't worry," Dogwood said, "I know what I'm doing."

Hawthorn struggled with the map; doing his best to hold it steady and make out his notes by flashlight.

"How are we going to get close enough to the HIVE without being detected?" he asked.

"I'll park us three klicks southeast of our target, we'll walk the rest of the way, it's dark enough that we shouldn't have too much trouble. At the very least, we'll find where the drones are being held."

"Assuming they haven't been moved to a new location."

"Yeah..." said Hunnie, leaning forward, "...and assuming they don't kill us on sight."

Emerging from the woods, the military jeep turned on to the highway and headed north.

Twenty minutes later, Dogwood pulled onto a side road that cut through a field. A thick fog had settled on the countryside. Finding a secluded spot next to a small line of trees, he parked the vehicle. Its occupants, thoroughly frozen.

"W-well that w-was a #@$%ing miserable r-ride," Hunnie shivered.

Unconcerned, Dogwood looked about and said, "This ought to be close enough," he pointed out past the treeline, "our target is on the other side of that field."

From their angle, it was hard to tell what lay across the dark horizon.

Dogwood hopped out of the jeep, taking with him a pair of binoculars and an assault rifle. An M4 carbine if Hawthorn wasn't mistaken.

"Do you really think that's necessary?"

"Can never be too careful," he said giving the weapon a dramatic pump.

"Uhhh.... I don't think you can pump that kind of rifle," Hunnie remarked.

"Yeah, I know!" Dogwood said defensively, walking towards the brush.

Following his lead, Hunnie and Hawthorn hunkered down behind the trees and looked out across the farmland.

Dogwood looked through the binoculars, "There's a barn and farmhouse just ahead; I'd bet anything the swarm is in the barn."

"Of course it is," said Hawthorn "that's specifically the location that's marked on the map."

"So we go in there, take out the HIVE and capture the bastards behind it all," Hunnie recapped.

Dogwood smiled, "It's almost too easy."

"How many of these type of missions have you been on?" asked Hawthorn.

"This is actually my first," he said happily, "To be honest, I'm pretty psyched to finally see some action."

"Hold on, this is your first?!" Hunnie exclaimed.

"Semper Fi," whispered Dogwood, taking off into the field.

"That's the Marines, you jackass!"

Private Dogwood army crawled over the cold, hard ground; the crispy beige stalks of dead crops lay matted underneath. He glided over the frozen topsoil like an alligator on a skateboard. The starless night gave no hint of his shadowy silhouette.

Or, at least, that would've been case if Hunnie and Hawthorn weren't casually walking beside him.

"How much longer are you going to crawl like that?" Hunnie softly asked.

"Until we get to our target," he huffed

"Quiet," said Hawthorn, "Someone will hear you."

"Better....to be... heard... and.... not seen."

"Dude," stated Hunnie, "the barn is literally, like, right there."

The barn was only a couple of steps away.

He had crawled the entire time.

It wasn't that they didn't appreciate Dogwood's effort but it seemed a little pointless to crawl the whole length of the field. Especially when he was making twelve times more noise thrashing over the dead crops. As loudly as he was grunting, they would be lucky if no one had heard them at all.

Despite being a short walk from a well-maintained farmhouse, the barn looked long-since forgotten. Hunnie guessed that whoever owned the house must have leased the field out to a local farmer. That's what her parents had done in the past.

Most people who didn't use their barn let it slowly deteriorate over the decades. This barn was no exception. While it was still technically standing, it looked like it would collapse at the slightest breeze or if a dog barked at it.

The rickety barn was dark and ominous set against the evening fog.

Hawthorn wasn't even a superstitious man and this place gave him the willies.

As they approached the barn door, Dogwood jumped up and flattened himself against the wall. The entire structure shook.

Unphased, the private looked to the others and began giving hand signals. None of which were understood.

Exasperated, Hunnie asked, "What the #@$% are you doing?"

"You two... open... the door... I'll... go in... first!"

"Then why didn't you just say that?"

"Because I'm a highly-trained soldier," Dogwood replied, "Now stop your yappin' and let's get crackin'!"

Dogwood gave a nod to Hawthorn who pulled open the barn door.

No sooner had it been open, than Dogwood went rushing in.

"Hooah!"

From the black void, they heard him loudly trip and fall over something metallic.

"Ouch!" he cried.

"Uh..." said Hunnie, "...you okay?"

"Yeah.... I think I tripped over a bucket."

Hawthorn peered into the darkness, "Where's your flashlight?"

A couple of moments passed before Dogwood replied.

"I think I left it in the jeep."

"Unbelievable," said Hunnie.

"It's not my fault," Dogwood wined, "Doctor White's the one who used it last!"

Even in the dark of night, Hawthorn could see Hunnie

roll her eyes in frustration.

He asked Hunnie, "Do you still have that cigarette lighter on you?"

She reached in her pocket and pulled out the cigarette lighter she had snagged from Honey B's house. Handing it over to Hawthorn. He took the lighter and ignited it with a single flick.

Slowly walking to the door, Hunnie took Hawthorn by the arm and they entered the black void.

The flickering flame of the lighter danced, illuminating only a small portion of the barn. Mostly empty stables and bails of hay. They didn't find Dogwood until they were practically on top of him. He was strewn across the dirt floor, tending to his poor foot. Lying next to him was an old hurricane lantern.

"Some soldier you are," said Hunnie, helping Dogwood to his feet.

Hawthorn picked up the lantern and used his flame to light it. Miraculously, it still had enough fuel to catch fire. While it wasn't enough to light up the entire barn, it gave enough light for them to see their surroundings. To their left was a wooden ladder leading up to the hay loft. To their right, a broken down tractor and a can of gasoline. Directly in front of them was the HIVE.

"Oh, there it is."

The HIVE stood silently. Inactive. At a little over five feet tall, Hawthorn was surprised by how big the contraption was in person. The silver dome was large enough for a grown man to sit comfortably in, assuming that grown man wasn't claustrophobic and enjoyed being stung by thousands of robotic bees.

"Looks like it's been off road," said Hawthorn, pointing to the HIVE's mud-caked tires

Dogwood pulled stray strands of hay out his rifle and took aim.

"Well it won't be going anywhere else, that's for sure!"

While not the most elegant of solutions, destroying the machine was the most urgent. Hawthorn prepared himself to witness an onslaught of bullets rain down upon the death-dealing device. So it came as a shock to see Hunnie, of all people, put a stop to it.

"Hold on, I hear something."

Both men stood very still and listened.

At first they didn't hear anything but then they did. A muffled voice. Mumbling in the dark.

Holding up the lantern, Hawthorn looked about. The voice sounded like it was coming from somewhere close to the ground.

"I think it's coming from over here," said Hunnie, motioning to the shadowy space behind the HIVE.

They carefully moved past the idle machine and Hawthorn shined his light to the rearmost wall. There, bound and gagged to a block of straw set upright, was a little bald man in glasses.

"Doctor Bladdernut!"

Hawthorn set down the lantern and pulled the oily rag out of his colleague's mouth.

"Are you alright?" Hawthorn asked.

The man seemed dazed and abused; there was a nasty looking bump on the top of his head. Upon recognizing Hawthorn, Dr. Bladdernut regained some life in his eyes.

"Doctor White! Is that you?"

"You had better take it easy."

Bladdernut weakly tried to wiggle out of his ropes, "Can you... untie me?"

Stepping in with his rifle, Dogwood took aim.

"Leave that to me, Doc!"

"Will you put that away!" Hunnie barked.

Dogwood obediently set his gun aside while Hunnie helped Hawthorn with the ropes. Whoever tied Bladdernut up had done a crappy job because they had him free in no time. Delicately, they lifted him to his feet

"Are you alright?" Hawthorn asked.

"I'll be better once I get out of this blasted place; all of this straw is murder on my allergies!"

"How did this happen?"

"I received a call from one of my associates at the university; he lives around here and said he saw a funny looking swarm in the area, thought I'd look into it myself."

"Who did this to you?"

"I... I don't know," he said, holding his head, "The last thing I recall is seeing the barn and thinking it would be an excellent hiding spot for the swarm..." he paused, struggling to remember, "....I opened the door, went inside, and then something.... something hit me.... When I awoke I was bound to this hay bail."

"We're going to get you out of here," said Hunnie, holding the frail man in her arms, "Do you think you can walk?"

"Oh, in my weakened condition, I don't know if I should, perhaps you can carry me?"

Hunnie wasn't crazy about the idea so she looked to Hawthorn who said, "Of course."

"Yeah, okay," she shrugged, "as long as you don't mind waiting in the- DARREN! WHAT THE #@$%, MAN?"

In the short time since they had untied the poor doctor, Private Dogwood had grabbed a gas can and was in the process of dousing the HIVE with gasoline. Stopping only when confronted by Hunnie.

"What?" he asked, innocently.

"Could you at least wait until we're outside?"

"Why?" Dogwood haphazardly tossed the gas can aside, "We light the fire and run out the front door. Easy."

Suddenly, from the other side of the barn, the front door slammed shut!

"You were saying."

CHAPTER 24

Dr. Bladdernut bolted across the barn and began pounding on the door. Screaming.

Under normal circumstances, Hunnie would've called him out for over-dramatizing his injury. But nothing about their current situation was normal. Instead, she and Private Dogwood ran for the door with Hawthorn picking up the lantern and joining them.

Hunnie and Dogwood hit the double-doors with all their might. The entire building shook. Dust fell from the rafters. Hawthorn, afraid they might bring the barn down on top of them, gently pushed his weight against the door. Meanwhile, Dr. Bladdernut sunk to the ground and wept.

The barn doors shimmied and shook but they didn't open.

Dogwood took a break to gather his thoughts.

"I think it's locked...." he said, placing his hands on hips, "....from the outside."

"Oh, you think?"

"I'm just assessing our situation."

"How about assessing a way for us to get the #@$% out

of here!"

Squatting to the ground, Hawthorn set the lantern aside and scooped up a bit of dirt.

"Perhaps we could dig a hole just big enough for us to squeeze through."

"Then what are we waiting for?" said Hunnie, crouching next to Hawthorn.

Shoveling handfuls of dirt, she glanced up at Dogwood, "Don't just stand there, give us a hand!"

Private Dogwood got down and followed their lead.

"This would be a lot easier with my gun."

"Just shut up and dig, army boy."

"Seriously, if I grab my rifle I could tear through this door like it was nothing!"

"We don't need you drawing any more attention to us!"

"Someone already knows we're here and what if they're waiting for us on the other side?"

"He has a point," Hawthorn admitted.

"Okay, fine, where's the gun?"

"I think he left it back...." Hawthorn stopped mid-sentence. The HIVE, which had stood as a silent hunk of metal, now had a small red, light blinking at its top.

"Uh oh," said Dogwood.

Dr. Bladdernut, who had been rocking back and forth next to the comforting light of the lantern, suddenly jumped up and went back to banging on the barn doors. Screaming like a baby.

"Someone want to clue us in about what's going on?" said Hunnie, trying to remain calm.

The little red light continued to blink as a thin, metal rod extended from the top of the HIVE like a car antenna. Once fully extended, the blinking red light switched to solid green. Within the device, servos whirled to life and a set of four motorized entry tunnels folded out from each side.

Hawthorn was both terrified and fascinated. His heart was racing almost as fast as his mind; trying to think of a way out. Then, he felt Hunnie grab hold of his hand. He gave it a supportive squeeze.

Tiny robot bees came rushing out every side of the HIVE. Simultaneously rising into a buzzing cloud of doom.

"Now I *really* wish I had my gun," said Dogwood.

Unfortunately, he had set the gun right next to the HIVE.

"If only we had some kind of diversion," Hawthorn reasoned.

The swarm drifted towards them, almost in slow-motion. Hearing the all too familiar sound of electronic death, Bladdernut turned and faced the swirling mass.

"DRONE SWARM! ARGHHHHHHHH!!!!!!!"

In that instant, Dogwood grabbed hold of Bladdernut and pushed him into the center of the swarm. Knocking over the lantern in the process. Immediately, the bee's auto kill function kicked in.

"There," said Dogwood over the helpless screams of the poor doctor, "That should buy us some time."

Horrified, Hunnie could only watch as the bees turned all their attention to Bladdernut. Making him into a human pincushion. A pincushion that screams, bleeds and wets itself.

"What the #@$% kind of diversion is that!" Hunnie screeched.

Hawthorn turned away from his colleague's gruesome death. Sickened. Then he noticed the fire that had spread from the broken lantern. He began stomping it out but felt a tug at his shirt.

"Leave it," yelled Hunnie, "Come on!"

Over excruciating screams, the group left the fire behind and ducked in an empty stable. Gaining a momentary refuge. Private Dogwood scoured his bag and pulled out a grenade.

Hunnie didn't like where this was going.

"What are you going to do with that?"

"What do you think?" he said, getting ready to lob it at the HIVE.

"Don't," she said holding his arm back, "There's a man still out there!"

Huddled together on the ground, the three of them sat. Awkwardly listening to Dr. Bladdernut's final moments. Which mostly consisted of screaming.

After only a few seconds, Hunnie turned to Hawthorn and said, "I'm sorry for your friend."

"We…. we weren't really close."

The tortured screams continued.

"Still," he added, "a terrible way to go."

More screaming.

"In a way," Hunnie ruminated, "he's giving his life so the rest of us can live."

Hawthorn nodded, "Let's hope so."

The screaming seemed to be getting weaker. Hunnie sighed. Hawthorn glanced at his watch. And Dogwood innocently played with the grenade.

Suddenly, the private perked up.

"I heard it's supposed to snow tomorrow!"

The others agreed that they had heard the same thing.

And then, with a life ending gargle, the screaming stopped altogether. The only sound left was the roaring buzz of bees and the sharp crackle of a quickly spreading fire. For all intents and purposes, Bladdernut was dead.

The young Private looked to Hunnie for approval, who gave a single nod.

"Hey, bees!" he called out, "Pollinate this!"

Dogwood lobbed the grenade at the HIVE and the three of them hit the ground, covering their heads.

Lying next to her ex-brother-in-law, Hunnie turned her head and asked, "Did you just think of that?"

"Actually it was in the jeep," he admitted.

Seemingly out of nowhere, the swarm gathered directly overhead in a tightly knit mass. Having retrieved the hand grenade, they were poised to drop it at any moment!

"Uh oh."

There was a scramble to get out of the animal stall but only Hawthorn and Hunnie jumped out in time.

They hit the ground just as the grenade exploded. The barn shook. Bits of shrapnel whizzed by. To Hawthorn's surprise, when he looked back, the private was not only alive but on his feet.

And completely engulfed in flames!

Horrified and confused, Hawthorn choked out, "That's....that's not how grenades work."

Much of the barn was already on fire and now, the human torch formally known as Private Darren Dogwood, was speeding up that process. Spreading fire with every step.

Having locked on to their target, the swarm followed. If the fire didn't finish him off the drones certainly would.

Seeing their chance, Hunnie pulled at Hawthorn's shirt, "We should probably go."

Hawthorn nodded and the two of them crawled away from the carnage. The only good thing about the fire was that it was much easier to find their way around the barn. Everything else about it was bad. Really bad.

They followed a dirt path to the entrance but now the doors were not only locked but on fire.

Searing heat radiated off the rising flames.

There was no way out. They were trapped like rats in a forced conversation about politics with their racist boss.

"Sorry, I didn't really think this through," Hunnie sighed.

"It's not your fault."

"Yeah, no, it kinda is," she sat up and rubbed her temples, "We shouldn't have come here on our own, you were right."

Their situation had gone from dire to worse. Hawthorn's mind raced for a solution. Unfortunately they had run out of options. For Hunnie's sake he decided to keep a more positive outlook.

"If it makes you feel any better, we'll probably die from smoke inhalation before the fire gets us."

It didn't.

But it also didn't matter. They had something more pressing than the fire to deal with.

"You're forgetting one thing," she said with a glance.

Hawthorn followed her gaze.

Behind them, the motionless body of Dogwood lay on the ground, surrounded by fire. Silhouetted against bright orange flames were a thousand swirling, black drones. Slowly advancing in their direction.

They would have backed up against the wall if it wasn't on fire. Instead they stopped when the heat became too intense to move any further. Hunnie looked for an escape but saw only searing fire. They were cornered.

"Any last minute ideas?" she asked.

"None."

"Yeah, me either."

The drones closed in around them. Close enough to feel the buzz of each individual, mechanized wing. Hunnie never thought it would end this way. Killed by a swarm of robotic bees. It all seemed so unlikely.

At least she wouldn't die alone.

"Well," she said holding out her hand, "It was nice knowing you."

Seeing this was his final moments in life, Hawthorn took the young woman's hand and pulled her in for one last hug, "I wish it were under more pleasant circumstances."

"Me too," Hunnie clung to him tightly, "I guess I'll see you on the other side."

"I don't believe in an afterlife but, at this point, I wouldn't be opposed to it."

"Hey, Hawthorn?"

"Yeah?"

"Why aren't they attacking us?"

It was valid question. As close as the swarm was, they weren't attacking. Cautiously, Hawthorn opened his eyes.

They were in the center of the swarm but the bees were frozen in midair. Hovering. If Hawthorn or Hunnie made any slight movement, they would bump in to one of the hundreds of tiny drones.

Then, from the center of the barn, sparks began spewing out of the HIVE. The kerosene that Dogwood had recklessly poured over the HIVE had caught on fire and now the silver dome was covered in flames. Small explosions periodically popped out of the machine like popcorn.

All around them, bees started dropping like flies.

Individual drones bounced off them as they fell harmlessly to the ground.

Breathing a sigh of relief, Hunnie relaxed her body and rested her head against Hawthorn's shoulder. He tenderly patted her head.

"I hate to ruin this moment," said Hawthorn, "But we need to find a way out of here."

Fire raged on all sides. Smoke burned their eyes as it filled their lungs. Hawthorn felt as if he had done a nasal rinse with liquid smoke.

Squinting through the haze, Hunnie noticed the ladder that led up to the hay loft. She took Hawthorn by the hand.

"Follow me," she said, steering them through the labyrinth of fire and smoke.

They had almost reached the ladder when the HIVE unexpectedly sprung to life! Tires spinning, the burning buggy lurched forward, nearly hitting them. It stopped abruptly and shot backwards until it hit the busted-up tractor. Immediately, it thrusted forward like a broken toy gone mad.

Hunnie ran for the ladder, dragging Hawthorn along.

"This way!"

They scurried up the ladder, reaching the loft just in time. The moment Hawthorn took his foot off the last rung, the ladder was taken out by the malfunctioning HIVE. He fell to the splintered, loft floor.

"What....what now?" Hawthorn coughed. While there was less fire in the loft, the smoke was even thicker. It was nearly impossible to see. Each breath burned more than the last. Hunnie pointed to the front of the barn, where thick plumes of smoke were being drawn out of a small rectangular window.

"If we can make it to the loft door, we can jump out."

"Okay," Hawthorn nodded.

Together, they walked cautiously across the loft. Smoke streamed through the cracks in the floor. The brittle planks flexed under their weight, revealing an intense orange glow beneath. Even as the fire roared, they took their time. But one wrong step was all it took for the floor give way!

Hunnie fell. Her insides jolted. Wood, smoke and fire rushed past her face. Blindly, desperately, she reached out for anything to grab hold of. Her left hand happen to catch a support beam.

She swung from the hole in the ceiling, hanging above the blazing fire. The out-of-control HIVE spinning on the ground below. Looking up through the hole, she saw Hawthorn standing above her. A worried look on his face.

"A little help," she said.

Laying facedown, Hawthorn reached down and grabbed Hunnie's sweaty hand. Hawthorn strained to hold on. He tightened his grip and pulled. The shattered floorboards scrapped their skin but Hawthorn was able to hoist Hunnie up through the hole.

Hunnie and Hawthorn were out of breath and getting extremely lightheaded. They lifted each other up and slogged their way through the thick cloud of smoke. And then they reached hayloft door.

They pushed the small rectangular door open and leaned out.

It was literally a breath of fresh air!

Hawthorn steadied himself against the doorframe and looked down to the ground below. They were a little over ten feet off the ground; not high enough to kill themselves but just the right height to twist an ankle or break a leg if they wanted.

"I take it we're going to jump?" said Hawthorn.

"That's the idea."

Briefly, Hawthorn thought of throwing down some hay to soften their landing. But there wasn't time. The smoke was getting thicker. The heat, unbearable. The lighting, good but not great.

At any moment it could all come crashing down with them in it.

"You ready?" he asked.

#@$% no, but let's do it anyway."

Taking each other by the hand they both jumped out into the open air. For the briefest of moments, they were soaring like eagles before gravity took hold and sent them falling like turkeys. They hit the ground just as gracefully, rolling to a stop. The patch of dirt they landed on was soft and moist, almost like clay.

Sprawled out on the ground, Hawthorn took a moment to access the damage; his knees hurt the most, followed by the left side of his shoulder and face. Nothing felt broken but there was no feeling in the arm laying across his chest. Then he realized it belonged to Hunnie.

Groaning, she tried to move but gave up halfway.

"Hunnie?" he said, placing his hand on top of hers, "Are you hurt?"

"Nothing that a Vicodin and a fifth of whiskey can't cure," she winced.

Painfully, she rolled on her side and noticed a man standing over them.

He was wearing a bathrobe, slippers and a pair of blue army service pajamas.

"What in blazes is going on here?" Colonel Madder asked.

CHAPTER 25

Hawthorn slowly rose to his feet.

"Colonel Madder?" he said, "Why are you here?"

"I live here, what in the hell did you do to my barn?"

Behind them was a real barn burner. The once gloomy structure was now glowing orange; emitting flames from every orifice, like a frat boy after too many hot wings.

"We didn't know it was yours," Hawthorn responded, giving Hunnie a helping hand, "We didn't even know this was your house."

Dusting herself off, Hunnie cut in, "Hawthorn figured out that someone was hiding the HIVE in there."

"Here?" sneered the colonel, "Impossible."

From the broadside of the barn, the mobile HIVE unit burst through the wall like the corporate mascot of a popular drink mix. Covered in flames, the mobile unit ran amuck until it slammed into a nearby tree. Coming to a perpetual stop.

"Okay," said the colonel, "Apparently I stand corrected."

An attractive woman in her forties walked up to

Madder. She was also in a bathrobe.

"Honey," she said, "who are these people? What's going on?"

"I'll tell you what's going on, lady," Hunnie intervened, "Your husband's been using military drones to try and kill me, my family and anyone else who happens to be around me at the time!"

Hawthorn cleared his throat, loudly.

"Oh," said Hunnie, "And him too!"

A look of concern washed across the wife's face, she turned to her husband.

"Honey, is this true?"

"I wouldn't have #@$%ing said it if it wasn't!"

"She was asking me," uttered the colonel, who then addressed his wife, "You see dear, a couple of days ago someone hacked our drones and it seems that they've been using our barn to hide them right under our noses."

"That doesn't make sense!" she exclaimed, "Why our barn? I haven't seen any drones. Why are they using them to attack this lovely.... Wait, are you Hunnie Combs?"

Feeling a little perturbed, Hunnie gave a shrug and nodded.

"Oh my gosh, I love your music! Bee Seen, Not Herd is my own personal anthem! And our son has the biggest schoolboy crush on you, isn't that right, George?.... George?"

Colonel Madder had a faraway look on his face, the flaming barn reflected in his eyes.

"Where is Jeremy?" he asked.

His wife seemed surprised by the question.

"In bed as far as I know."

Even as the barn collapsed before them, the colonel looked in the opposite direction. At the house.

"Ms. Combs, Dr. White, if you'll follow me, I think I know who hacked the swarm."

◆ ◆ ◆

Colonel Madder lead them through his home; a well-maintained, two-story farmhouse. Climbing up the solid, wood stairs, Hawthorn felt like he was in a rural bed and breakfast. Quaint, country themed wallpaper adorned the walls and every space was decorated with some kind of antiquated farm equipment; a butter churn here, a milk can there, a pair of castration pliers on an end table. That kind of thing.

Finally, they came to a stop in front of a locked door at the end of the hall. A thin strand of light shown underneath.

"Open this door, young man," the colonel thundered, "This instant!"

No answer.

"Jeremy!" the colonel pounded on the door.

No answer.

"I know you can hear me!"

A muffled voice spoke up.

"You don't know that."

The colonel's wife approached the door and gave it a shot.

"Jeremy, listen to your father!"

"He's not my real father!"

"Then listen to me…. Now!"

There was a long moment of silence, then the door was unlocked.

Colonel Madder barged in with the others in tow. Inside the room was an immaculately organized office.

An open laptop computer sat on the desk. On the computer screen was a cluster of dialogue boxes and prompts. Hawthorn caught a glimpse of one that said: Operation failed. System error. Please contact your system administrator.

Beside the door, a short and scrawny teenager stood with a sour look on his face.

"You know you're not allowed in here," said the colonel.

The boy rolled his eyes. Not saying a word. Hunnie searched his greasy, little face. There was something about the kid that looked familiar. The colonel continued.

"How many times have I told you that my work computer is not a toy?"

Behind the boy's eyes was a seething anger, the kind that leads alienated young men to do terrible things; like post hateful comments online or go on a murder spree. But there was also an aura of pathetic desperation that had him on the edge of tears. This was what Hunnie was trying to place.

"Been using my work computer for your own personal use? Is that right?"

The only response given was a hate-filled stare.

"Thought you'd help your country out by giving the drones a little test flight?"

Flaring his nostrils, the boy kept his mouth shut.

"Colonel," said Hawthorn, "Am I to understand that your son-"

"Stepson."

"-is the one responsible for hacking the swarm and using it terrorize and kill?"

"Well, Jeremy?" the colonel said, looking to the boy, "Is that what happened?"

There was a long pause. The solemn teenager cast his eyes to the hardwood floor and bitterly said, "Yes, sir."

It was at that moment that Hunnie remembered where she knew him from.

"Wait... I know you, you're that kid who made the video asking me out to homecoming!"

The anger that was brimming just under the surface suddenly came out of the boy in full force.

"Yeah and you stood me up you dirty skank!"

"Jeremy!" his mother exclaimed.

Hawthorn pulled Hunnie aside.

"You were supposed to go to a high school dance with this boy?"

"Yeah, it was one of those things where he posted a cute video asking me out and Felix thought it would be great publicity, so I thought, you know, why not?"

"And, I take it, something else came up that night?"

"Tom Green invited me to the premier of *Freddy Got Toed*, I couldn't say no to that."

Jeremy looked to his parents and whined, "Do you know how embarrassing that night was for me? I was a nobody until she agreed to go out with me!"

"Dude, I'm sorry it didn't work out but I don't owe you a thing!"

Clenching his fists, the teen stepped up to Hunnie. Hawthorn placed himself in between. If he was willing to use secret government technology to enact revenge then hitting a woman probably wasn't beneath him.

Instead, Jeremy spoke to his obsession face-to-face.

"Everyone at school loves you, when you said that you'd go out with me, people started treating me with respect, like I mattered, and then, to stand me up in front of the whole school, even after you promised to be there, that was the most humiliating moment of my life."

"That's still no excuse for your behavior, young man," said the mother, "I think you owe Ms. Combs an apology."

"He murdered my sister," Hunnie reminded the room.

Jeremy threw up his hands, "Okay, I'm sorry, geez!"

"First of all, I don't really think you are and second, are we going to get the authorities involved or what?"

Shaking his head, the colonel took the office phone and placed a call to headquarters.

"I hate to do this, stepson, but you've left me no choice," Holding the handset to his ear, he waited for a response, "Maybe some time in a military prison will set you right."

"Aw, man!"

Someone on the other end answered and the colonel was taken aback.

"Hello... Dogwood?...."

"Uh," said Hawthorn, raising a hand as if he was getting a waiter's attention, "He's dead."

"Oh.... well, this is Madder, send two MP's to my house at once, we've apprehended the hacker...."

Ten minutes later, the cavalry arrived and the Madder residence was swarming with military vehicles and men. A helicopter hovered overhead, casting a spotlight on the ground. The clean-up crew tended to the burning remains of the barn. From the house, a line of Military Police Officers came out; one had confiscated the laptop as evidence while the other two led his stepson away in cuffs.

The colonel and his wife were close behind, a worried

look on her face.

"Honey, where are they taking our boy?"

"I'm sorry, dear, but that's classified."

Witnessing this all happen before their eyes, Hawthorn and Hunnie stood out in the yard, next to a decorative wishing well. They were close enough to see but far enough out of anyone's way. Hunnie was wrapped in a blanket.

"Where did you get that blanket?" asked Hawthorn.

"I found it inside, aren't you cold?"

"A little."

As they watched the responsible party being taken away, Hawthorn shook his head in disbelief.

"I can't believe that it was just a seventeen year old kid."

"I can't believe it was one of my fans."

"Did he make any threats to you before?"

"Well, yeah, but I never thought he'd follow through with any of them."

Hawthorn wanted to ask why she didn't see that as a red flag but held his tongue.

Feeling his stare, Hunnie explained, "I'm a female celebrity, do you know how many times men threaten me online *on a daily basis?* It's insane!"

The colonel watched his stepson be placed into a Humvee and driven off. He then noticed Hawthorn and Hunnie were watching him. With as much dignity as a man in bathrobe can muster, he stomped across the yard and acknowledged them.

"Is that my wife's wool blanket?"

"Yeah, I found it in the living room."

"Keep it, I never liked it anyway," without so much as a transition, Colonel Madder switched subjects, "I take it the medic has examined you?"

"Yes," replied Hawthorn, "She said other than a few scrapes and bruises, we're fine."

The colonel nodded with indifferent approval, he then said, "Ms. Combs, as I understand it, your father is doing much better, if you like I can have one of my men drop you off at the hospital."

"Sure, whatever, just as long as you get me there."

"I have much to attend to myself, so I will be going back to the base. But I must stress the importance of not disclosing what has transpired here; rest assure that this probably won't happen again."

Hawthorn didn't like the sound of that.

"What do you mean probably?" he asked.

The colonel pretended not to hear the question and moved on, "Ms. Combs, because of the personal toll it took on your family, you'll be pleased to know that you will be well-compensated for your cooperation. Dr. White, you will also be reimbursed for your role in apprehending the suspect."

"Whoopty-#@$%ing-doo," said Hunnie.

"Your government thanks you for your service and apologizes for any inconvenience or death this incident may have caused you. Good night."

With that, Colonel Madder turned and walked away.

"Okay, well, tell the Avengers I said 'hi'!" Hunnie called out.

Without breaking his stride, the colonel marched into the house.

To their right, the fire had finally been taken care of and the clean-up crew had started digging through the embers. From the smoldering wood pile, two blackened bodies were pulled out, stuffed into plastic body bags and placed on gurneys.

As they were being wheeled away, a man in a black leather jacket snuck up next to Hawthorn.

"Now I'm really glad that I didn't go with you earlier."

"Dr. Critchlow," said Hawthorn.

"I hate to say I told you so…."

"I highly doubt that," Hunnie commented.

"….but, once again, I was right."

"How long have you been here?" Hawthorn asked.

"Not very, I came with those guys," Critchlow pointed at two people tending to the HIVE. Kneeling next to the burnt and broken machine was Dr. Sakura, who was weeping uncontrollably, and Carson Flowers, who was quietly counseling the grieving doctor.

"Poor guy will have to start from square one."

"It's sad none of you feel the same about your colleague," Hunnie grimly observed.

"Losing Bladdernut is as much a tragedy as it is a setback but, I believe, we have the perfect replacement."

"And who might that be?" asked Hawthorn.

"We were hoping for you, Dr. White."

Hawthorn found himself horrified by the mere thought of helping the military prefect their newest weapon.

He looked Critchlow dead in the eye and said, "You can find someone else because I'm not interested."

"Sure you don't want to discuss it?"

"I want nothing more to do with this abysmal use of science and technology."

"Well, I can't say that I blame you, it's a shame, though, our team could've used someone with an actual brain."

"I prefer to use my expertise to move mankind forward, not set it back."

284

"That's very cliche, doctor, but commendable."

Hawthorn felt Hunnie's soft hand on his forearm, gently pulling forward.

"If that'll be all, we really must be going," she said, leading them away from Critchlow, "My father's still in the hospital and I'm sure Dr. White would rather be there with me than here with you."

With a smile and a shrug, Hawthorn said, "She's right."

Together they walked towards the nearest officer, in hopes of arranging a ride into town. But Critchlow quickly caught up to them. In his hand, he held a folded up piece of paper.

"Ms. Combs, before you go," he said unfolding the paper, "My daughter is quite the fan of yours…."

He handed it to her and she saw a picture of herself. It was one of the headshots she had professionally taken in Hollywood. He had printed it off the internet.

"….Could I get an autograph?"

EPILOGUE: I'LL BEE MISSING YOU

J ust north of Longville was the extinct town of Carbon. In its heyday it was a mining town with a mineral rich quarry. Now the only remnant was a big hole in the ground.

The abandoned quarry was eventually filled with water, where it became the favorite swimming hole for generations of local children.

Primrose "Hunnie" Combs was among those who spent all summer swimming in its murky, black waters.

In those days, she and her sister would stand at the cliffs edge and argue over who would jump first. It always ended with them jumping out together. Laughing on the way down.

But those days were no more.

Forlorn, Hunnie stood on the edge of the cliff overlooking Carbon Quarry. Her sister confined to a small vase. A copper urn holding her ashes.

On one side stood her father: head wrapped in bandages, arm in a sling. He used his free hand to play a tribute on the harmonica. Which would have been lovely if he knew how to play.

On the other side was Hawthorn. Looking dapper as usual.

Solemnly, he listened to Mr. Combs squeak and squawk through *Amazing Grace*, taking in their surroundings. Everything around them was cold and grey. Every nearby tree was as lifeless and still as the stagnant water below. Yet, there was a stark beauty of a midwestern winter.

Especially when snow was in the air.

As Mr. Combs brought his musical tribute to a close, the final notes echoed off the quarry walls, lingering for miles. The sound of softly falling snow filled the void. Hunnie began:

"Rosemary, I can't help but feel a little responsible for your death. If it wasn't for my fame and the actions of one deranged fan, you'd still be alive today. While I was in college and out in Hollywood, you were here, taking care of dad. You put our family first because you cared the most. You were the best of us. We may have had our differences but I never stopped loving you. And I know you never stopped loving me. Although death has taken you away, you'll always be my sister."

Tears swelling, Hunnie found herself cradling her sisters urn. She blinked away the tears and cleared her throat. Pushing her shoulders back, she continued.

"You were taken from us too soon and I'm gonna miss you. I'm gonna miss your smile, your laugh, and the way your face turned red when talking about boys you liked. And if you're not flirting up a storm up in heaven, I swear, I'll start murdering eligible bachelors down here for you!"

Hawthorn understood the sentiment but still felt a little worried.

"I love you, sis."

Hunnie paused for one last moment with her sister. Patting the top of the urn, she warily handed it to her father. Mr. Combs stepped up to the very edge of the cliff and gazed off into the distance.

"Webster's defines funeral as: of, relating to, or constituting a funeral. I don't know what that means but I know that you're my daughter and your sister says you're never coming back. So we put you in this little pot and then we took you to your favorite spot."

He glanced back at Hunnie, smiling.

"I remember one summer, I took you girls here to go swimming and every time I said it was time to go, you and your sister would look at me and say, "But daddy, just five more minutes, please?" and you kids were so cute and you were having such a fun time, I thought, okay, five more minutes. Seven hours later, you girls were still at it, even though it was late and the sun was going down, all you wanted to do was swim, and I'll never forget what I said to you, I said, "GAWD DAMMIT, IF YOU DON'T GET OUT OF THAT #@$%ING WATER I'M GONNA DRAG YOU OUTTA THERE MYSELF, NOW GET IN THE GAWD DAMN CAR!"

Usually, emotional outbursts made Hawthorn uncomfortable. And this was no exception. Switching back to his more pleasant self, Mr. Combs proceeded to finish things up.

"Anyway, I guess what I'm trying to say is, you're free to swim as long as you want. Have fun."

Bowing his head, Mr. Combs gave the urn a single, tender kiss. He lifted up the vase of ashes, holding it out over the water, and let go of his youngest daughter, urn and all.

Hawthorn found it strange that he didn't simply pour Rosemary's ashes out. Then again, he wasn't surprised by it either. Hunnie was even less surprised by her father's actions. Just disappointed.

"You weren't supposed to toss the....you know what, it's fine."

Unceremoniously, Mr. Combs turned and walked away like he had just thrown away an old toaster. Hunnie leaned forward, watching the urn slowly sink below the lake's dark surface. At least it was over.

Her sister was at peace.

Hawthorn took a few timid steps towards her, awkwardly placing his hand on her shoulder.

"That was a....lovely tribute."

Looking out over the water, Hunnie shook her head and snickered.

"I know it was a $#*%show but, these days, that's kinda my life in a nutshell."

"Any idea on what you going to do with your father?"

"Actually, I was thinking of taking him on tour with me," she said without an ounce of irony, "Obviously I can't leave him here on his own but it'll give him a chance to get out of the house, spend some time together. It'll be good for him. Good for us."

Hawthorn gave her shoulder a squeeze, "I'm sure it will."

"What are you going to do now that you don't have to follow me around everywhere?"

"I suppose go back to the college, continue my work."

"Sure you can't stay an extra night?" she said, hopefully, her eyes sparkling in the falling snow, "You know you're more than welcome."

He wanted to but felt obligated to politely decline, "I appreciate the offer but I should probably get going."

Smirking, Hunnie nodded. Not fully convinced

"Well if you change your mind, let me know."

"Thank you," he said with a warm laugh.

The snow fell. Heavier than before. But just as peaceful.

"It's really starting to come down," said Hunnie, "We should get you to the bus station."

She turned to walk back to the truck but stopped halfway.

"Unless you want to stick around?"

"I mean..." Hawthorn began, trying to figure out what he meant, "...it's not supposed to be *that* heavy of a snow and I can always take a later bus."

"Then we have all afternoon if you want to do something?" said Hunnie, raising an eyebrow, "Maybe grab a bite?"

Hawthorn wasn't in any hurry to get back. Even if the weather got bad, he had plenty of personal time saved up at work. With all they had been through he could use an extra day off, but he would only use it if necessary.

"Alright," he said cheerfully, "What are you in the mood for?"

She looked at him and smiled and he figured he could stay one more night.

APPENDIX A

Artist: Hunnie Combz
Album: Honeysuckle

Track   Song
1. Thirsty Thursday (club remix)
2. Queen B
3. Hunnie Do
4. Gimmie a Buzz (U up?)
5. Time 2 Pollen 8
6. I Want UR Honey Dripper
7. Flight or Fight
8. Walk of Same
9. Love Stings
10. G'bye, Hun
11. Bee Scene, Not Herd

Bonus Track
Thirsty Thursday (acoustic)

APPENDIX B

Hunnie Combz
Honeysuckle Tour
North America - Spring

MAR. 25	Alamosa, CO
MAR. 26	Albany, GA
MAR. 27	Amarillo, TX
MAR. 28	Baltimore, MD
MAR. 29	Belle Glade, FL
MAR. 30	Brooklyn, IL
APR. 01	Camden, NJ
APR. 02	Clearlake, CA
APR. 03	Cleveland, OH
APR. 04	Council Bluffs, IA
APR. 05	Detroit, MI
APR. 06	Gary, IN
APR. 08	Hartford, CT
APR. 09	Kansas City, MO
APR. 10	Kenai, AK
APR. 11	Lawton, OK
APR. 12	Lubbock, TX
APR. 13	Memphis, TN
APR. 15	Newark, DE
APR. 16	New Orleans, LA
APR. 17	North Battleford, SK
APR. 18	Portsmouth, OH

APR. 19   Reno, NV
APR. 20   Rockford, IL
APR. 22   St. Louis, MO
APR. 23   Tacoma, WA
APR. 24   Trenton, NJ
APR. 25   Wall, SD
APR. 26   Williams Lake, BC
APR. 27   Wilmington, DE

ACKNOWLEDGEMENTS

There are several people who should share the blame in the writing of this book, mostly by encouraging me to do it. First and foremost is my ever-loving wife Allison who has listened to me drone on endlessly about my book over last few years. Somehow, at no point, did she ever say "that's a really dumb idea" which allowed me to actually finish the damn thing. Unfortunately, I feel like her reading that first, unaltered draft left her somewhat traumatized. We're all hoping for a speedy recovery.

Second is a group of friends who are also writers themselves; Nigel Church, Brian Katcher, and Valerie Puri. They have each offered advice and answered every little question I've had about writing and self-publishing. Also, they are quite talented authors and you should totally check them out.

Third is a coworker of mine, Zack Dooley. I was talking with Zack about the book (the character of Hawthorn, in particular) when he recommended me the name of renowned beekeeper Jerry Hayes. While it may seem like I didn't do any research for this book, the work of Jerry Hayes provided some real-life inspiration and offered some actual scientific merit.

And finally, I would like to thank another coworker of mine, Ellen MacPherson for being more than willing to take some impromptu photos for my Author Bio. Happy to say we got it on the first shot!

Oh, yeah, I should also probably thank you, the reader, for putting up with all this nonsense. And kudos for taking the time to read the acknowledgements! I'm sure I lost most people at the appendices (if not way before) so thanks for taking a chance on a brand new author!

I can't tell you how much I appreciate your readership and I look forward to seeing you again!

ABOUT THE AUTHOR

Once described by a friend as "a patchwork quilt of comedy", Jonathan Yeakey is a humorist of all trades and master of none. He's tried his hand at improv, stand-up and sketch comedy. As someone with a short attention span, he's always looking for new creative outlets for his manic sense of humor. Unfortunately for the literary world, he's finally finished his first novel *Drone Swarm*.

Follow Yeakey on the World Wide Web

Website
www.jonathanyeakey.com

Facebook
www.facebook.com/yeakeydoodle

Twitter
https://twitter.com/yeakeydoodle